PRAISE FOR CRAIG LANCASTER

Edward Adrift (2013)

"Edward Stanton is one of the more distinct and interesting characters you'll encounter in contemporary fiction, and it's never dull accompanying him. *Edward Adrift*, like *600 Hours* before it, is such a well-written, big-hearted book that its pages fly by and will leave its readers no doubt hoping for a trilogy."

—*Billings (Mont.) Gazette*

"It's hard to know who I adore more: Craig Lancaster's character Edward Stanton or Lancaster himself for creating him."

—Jessica Park, bestselling author of
Flat-Out Love and *Left Drowning*

600 Hours of Edward (2012)

Montana Honor Book and High Plains Book Award winner

"It's a spare, elegantly crafted whizz-bang of a book that, on its surface, is as quiet and orderly as Edward Stanton, but underneath, also like Edward, a cauldron of barely repressed rage and desire seeking escape."

—*Missoula Independent*

"This is a wonderful book. Mr. Lancaster's journey . . . into the imaginative pages of fiction was one well taken, for himself, for readers and certainly for the lovingly created Edward Stanton."

—*Montana Quarterly*

Quantum Physics and the Art of Departure (2011)

Independent Publisher Book Award gold medalist;
High Plains Book Award finalist

"Have you ever felt in your pocket and found a twenty you didn't know you had; how 'bout a hundred dollar bill, or a Montecristo cigar or a 24-karat diamond? That's what reading Craig Lancaster's *Quantum Physics and the Art of Departure* is like—close and discovered treasures."

—Craig Johnson, author of the Walt Longmire novels

"It's a real delight to inhabit Lancaster's lonely, darkly majestic Montana locations and desperate characters."

—*Chicago Center for Literature and Photography*

The Summer Son (2011)

Utah Book Award finalist

"A classic western tale of rough lives and gruff, dangerous men, of innocence betrayed and long, stumbling journeys to love."

—*Booklist*

THE
FALLOW
SEASON
OF
HUGO
HUNTER

Also by Craig Lancaster

The Summer Son
Quantum Physics and the Art of Departure
600 Hours of Edward
Edward Adrift

THE
FALLOW
SEASON
OF
HUGO
HUNTER

Craig Lancaster

LAKE UNION
PUBLISHING

Published by Lake Union Publishing, Seattle

www.apub.com

Amazon, the Amazon logo, and Lake Union Publishing are trademarks of Amazon.com, Inc., or its affiliates.

ISBN-13: 9781477825440
ISBN-10: 1477825444

Cover design by Jason Ramirez

Library of Congress Control Number: 2014938754

Printed in the United States of America

For my stepfather, Charles Clines, who gave me the great gift of boxing when I was a scared nine-year-old. It settled my fears and focused my aspirations—namely, that I didn't want a second season of it. You've been a role model and an uncommonly good friend.

1

The last time I saw Hugo Hunter in the boxing ring was on a miserable Tuesday that pissed down freezing rain in Billings, Montana. I stood in the shadows of the Babcock Theatre, past its prime just like Hugo, the stale stench of a century's cigarettes climbing down from the rafters. I stood just out of the reach of the houselights but not nearly far enough away from what I was seeing—Hugo, on his hands and knees, a gloved hand pawing blindly for a mouthpiece that sat four feet behind him, drops of blood from his ripped brow dotting the canvas.

The kid who'd knocked him out, Cody Schronert, had already left the ring, he and his buddies making a jubilant procession of it. Biggest night of that guy's life, beating Hugo Hunter. It was something he'd tell his kids about if any woman made the mistake of letting him father some. Schronert was a punk clear back to the days I covered him as a running back for Billings Senior High School. He'd crow about this, his newfound currency as the triumphant conqueror of the great Hugo Hunter. That would be his right, I suppose, but it would be a right asserted in opposition to a moral truth. The man he left crumpled under the Babcock lights bore about as much resemblance to the Hugo Hunter I once knew as Schronert, the blond-haired frat-boy son of Billings's most vicious personal-injury attorney, bore to Mike Tyson.

Hugo at last gathered in the mouthpiece, and the crab hand formed by the leather glove slipped it into place, as if he had work yet to do. He pressed the gloves against the mat and pushed himself up, his chest rising, a fleshy roll tumbling over the belt line of his red satin trunks. A tucked right leg gave him a measure of stability, and he clambered to his feet, unsteady as a newborn colt.

The place had gone dead silent, largely emptied out. I'd watched as the people walked by, limp arms carrying spent bags of cartoon-yellow popcorn. They didn't exhibit the cackling electricity I'd seen in most fight crowds, that pent-up aggression turned loose by overstimulation. This was sorrow on parade. They knew what they'd seen, and most of them looked as though they hadn't contemplated what it all meant until just now. A scant few paying customers lingered, and most of them had the good manners to turn away as Hugo crept through the ropes and down the ringside stairs.

Not me. I stepped a few feet closer. I always watched, even when I didn't want to. It's what I did, my role on this temporal stage. I was the fly on the wall, the little birdie, the man who knows, the guy in the scene but not of it.

It made me sick sometimes.

2

I'd come to the Babcock that night hoping I wouldn't see what I saw, and knowing that hope doesn't stand a chance against the unraveling of an old fighter. Hugo, out of the game for three years and a certifiable failure at every working-stiff job he'd tried in that time, had launched his hometown comeback a few months prior amid about as much hoopla as you're going to see in a rag like the *Billings Herald-Gleaner*. He and one of his old trainers, Trevor "Squeaky" Feeney, held a press conference at the Crowne Plaza to announce a winter series of Tuesday night fights, a little sanctioned violence to soothe the weather-weary souls of Billings. At the newspaper, we gave it the big treatment: centerpiece on the front page, big photos, a timeline of Hugo's rust-caked ring career.

Squeaky tossed it off as something local and fun, and Hugo went to great lengths to say the fights would be more like exhibitions for him, one more chance for everybody to see this town's biggest star. And sure enough, every two weeks he'd be at the Babcock, taking on some local boy who thought the haymakers that cracked jaws in the parking lot of the Wild West Saloon might somehow work in the ring. Hugo liked to talk it up as if he were doing a civic favor, lending his fame to a small-time operation meant to entertain the restless locals, but it was plain to see that he was grabbing those $300 checks a little too eagerly and coming back for more a little too often.

I went to the first few fights, which was my duty, I suppose. God knows I'd long since made a name off being the guy who knew everything about Hugo Hunter. It hadn't gotten me anything other than perhaps a cushy gig in the newsroom and a few appearances on ESPN back when Hugo's fame was still untarnished, but it was more than I'd have had otherwise. Where Hugo went, I went. Barcelona. Las Vegas. London. And, much later, the Babcock Theatre, a two-block walk from the newspaper office downtown.

Hugo, at thirty-seven years old and far outside his prime, won those early matches, as he well should have, but something wasn't right. The damage he incurred was glancing but obvious. You could see that Hugo wasn't training. He was soft around the middle, dimpled with cellulite. A straight punch, which Hugo could surely throw, was enough to finish off the brawlers who were climbing in against him, but he was taking punishment he'd never absorbed before. Black eyes, a lumpy forehead, split lips, headaches that would level him, reducing him to talking to me through the front door of his house. "Not feeling so hot," he'd say, the pent-up mustiness of his grandmother's home slipping out and bumping into me. "We'll talk tomorrow, OK? Keep your chin tucked, buddy." Back when times were good, the ESPN guys called Hugo "the Minister of Defense." You wouldn't have believed that was possible if you saw what I saw those nights at the Babcock.

I knew what was coming, and I told Trimear, my boss at the *Herald-Gleaner*, that I'd just as soon move over to high school basketball and that Olden could take the Hunter beat, that it'd probably be good for the kid to cover a true star, or at least as close to one as we had in Billings.

Sometimes I wonder if I chickened out, bailing on Hugo because I could see the bad ending coming. I wasn't brave enough to stand in there and take it, the way Hugo did, and that bothered me. The truth is, I did something you're not supposed to do in the newspaper game. I got too close. Somewhere in between watching Hugo captivate the world as a seventeen-year-old and seeing him laid out on the canvas twenty years later, I came to care about him as the boy and man he was, not merely as a subject of the stories I wrote. I crossed a line and gave him my heart. That kind of proximity provides insight and access, but it's dangerous. You become part of the picture, and then you're in a position to change the trajectory of the story you're trying to tell. Then, I couldn't let that happen. Later, I realized that trying to change the story was the only thing that made sense.

———

Two weeks before that last fight, Olden came scurrying into the office, his cheeks red, his eyes alight. I knew the look. That's a guy with a big story on his hook.

"He lost."

Trimear stopped assaulting the keyboard with his meaty hands and walked over. "For real? To who?"

Olden grinned and swept a hand across his face, as if he could wring out the callowness. "Second-round TKO. Couldn't defend himself. The guy, man, he was just all over him. Ref had to dive in there and save him."

"What guy?" Trimear torqued his neck. Rising irritation. Olden, a fresh graduate and new to us, wouldn't know that Trimear wanted everything right now, no suspense. He'd learn, though. Same as we all did.

Olden looked at his notes, and Trimear's tic went into overdrive. "Seth Prosinski."

"Who the hell is that?" Trimear asked.

"Just some dude. Came over from Watford City. Bakken roughneck. A nobody."

Trimear moved in, almost on top of Olden's desk now. "Was Larry there? Do we have art?"

"Oh, yeah," Olden said. "He said he got a great picture of the ref hugging Hugo, holding him up. He's tearing up. Maybe sweat. I don't know. Larry says it's great."

Trimear practically did cartwheels across the newsroom. "McDonough," he barked to the layout man, "pull up that weak-ass centerpiece. We've got something better."

I slipped down into my chair, trying to see the words of a half-written high school game story that would probably be relegated to an inside page somewhere. I couldn't find my way back in.

Olden came over. "Mark?"

"Yeah?"

He leaned in, talking low so Hop Raymont couldn't hear him. "I don't know how to write this, Mark."

I tried a smile that about half worked, for Olden and for me. He shuffled his feet, and I bit down on the urge to commandeer his beat again. I could write the story, sure as anything. But it wasn't my gig anymore. "Sure you do, kid," I said. "They taught you how to write a lede at U of M, didn't they?"

"Yeah." He balled up a fist and flushed a shade of anger, a show of the spunk I liked so much the first time he set foot in the office.

"It's nerves, is all," I said. "Start with how it ended and work your way through it."

Olden frowned. "Yeah. I guess." He started to turn to his desk, and so help me, I had to ask.

"Bobby? Did Hugo go down?"

Olden shook his head. "Technical knockout. He wasn't fighting back, but he didn't drop."

"What'd he say?"

The kid pulled his notebook to his face, and I stifled a laugh. When you're a rookie, you're so busy making sure you write down the answers that you never actually hear them. He ran his index finger under the lines as he read them in staccato.

"He said, 'It was a fluke. All credit to that kid, but he got lucky. I'll get 'em next time.'"

"Trevor going to let him fight again?"

"I think so. Didn't seem real happy, though." Olden's tone kind of rocketed up there at the end. He must have seen my surprise—or my anger. "I mean, I asked. He didn't say anything except that we'd do it again in a couple of weeks."

"Goddamnit."

"What?"

"Never mind, kid. Deadline's ten thirty. You better get to work."

———

That pretty much clinched it. Hugo's descent into cliché and Squeaky Feeney's neglect made it a sure bet that Hugo would return to the Babcock in a fortnight. Between editions, Trimear and I shivered under the *Herald-Gleaner* awning and worked through a couple of Camels each. I told him I'd like to take a day off.

"You gonna take that kid's beat back from him now that your boy's a loser?" Trimear choked out a nicotine laugh, and I set my hand against my lower back and leaned into the sandstone so I didn't punch his fat face.

"Naw, I'm gonna take a night I usually have to work and go to the fights like a regular paying customer. Maybe have me a steak at Jake's beforehand. Do it up right."

A chuckle rasped out of him. "He's done, you know."

"No shit, Gene. Why do you think I'm asking for this time?"

"Big night. We got West-Senior. First place on the line. Not sure I can spare you."

"You ever think about maybe trying to cover a game?"

"I gotta work the desk."

I ditched my cigarette and smothered my other hand behind me. Trimear had a way of challenging my pacifist tendencies.

"You know, Raymont's been your assistant for sixteen years," I said. "You might try letting him run the show a night or two. He might surprise you. Or send him to the game."

Trimear mashed out his cigarette on the building. "You're a funny guy. Take the night, then. But when I have you working back-to-backs come tournament time, I don't want to hear any bitching."

I held my arms out, palms to the sky, a martyr to my cause of taking an irregular day off. "Well, jeez, Gene, you know me. As long as the queen doesn't need me, I'm at your disposal."

That sandpaper laugh again and then Trimear swiped his key card to head inside. A second or two later, he stepped back out.

"Forget your charm?" I asked.

Trimear didn't laugh. He just looked at me, through me, to the street.

"I was just thinking," he said. "You did the Hugo Hunter beat for a long time. Twenty years, right?"

"Yeah. So?"

"Nothing. I was just thinking."

I stared back at him. There was nothing to say to that. Trimear's way was inscrutability or jackhammer obviousness. He didn't dabble in the in-between.

"It's been a good run—better for you than for him, I figure," he said. "You've got your health, at least. What does he have?"

The speed with which Trimear got his useless sack of skin back inside suggested that he didn't expect an answer, which was just as well. I didn't have one.

3

So there I was, at the Babcock, two weeks later. I hustled back to the warm-up area ahead of Hugo, dashing headlong into a noxious gumbo of sweat, urine, and vomit. I gave a terse wave to Olden just inside the curtain. He was pinned against the wall, taking in an earful of Cody Schronert's soliloquy on the greatness of himself. I guess you couldn't account for that night without talking to the little thug, but I was irritated just the same. The only story worth telling was trailing thirty feet down the ramp, blood flowing into his eyes from a brow split wide. He was the biggest sports star this town had ever seen. I'd like to say Hugo deserved better than this, but he had landed here mostly by way of his own bad choices. Whatever the case, though, he sure as hell deserved better than Cody Schronert as a dispatcher.

Squeaky Feeney, the self-styled Tuesday night boxing impresario, stood waiting for Hugo, a set of surgical scissors in hand. We nodded at each other and went through our usual routine—"Westerly" from him, "Squeaky" from me because I know he hates that nickname—and then I faded back to the wall and leaned against it.

Hugo shuffled up the ramp. I checked the whiteboard across the room. Hugo had fought at 193 pounds—up five pounds from where he was four weeks earlier when I'd last seen him and almost fifty beyond the welterweight days of his prime. I could see where those pounds had gone. Straight to his vast middle and his ass, the two places an aging boxer can't afford to carry extra baggage.

Hugo kept his head down as he approached, without even a nod to Schronert, and for that I gave him credit. He stopped in front of Squeaky and held his gloved hands out, wrists up. Feeney, himself a former welterweight and now even heavier than Hugo, shook his engorged head and set in with the scissors, snipping away the tape to shake loose the Everlasts, then cutting at the gauze around Hugo's hands.

"That's it, you know," Squeaky said, the shrill words in double time and his head bobbing from the effort of spitting them out. "Never again."

Hugo kept his eyes cast down. "Kid got lucky."

Squeaky pulled at the unraveling gauze, a simple act performed violently. "Seems like everybody's getting lucky against you these days, huh?"

I stepped forward, then thought better of it and settled back into the wall. The movement caught Hugo's eye, and he looked up and gave me a grin marbled with mouthpiece.

"Hey, Mark," he said, the words turned to mush. "You keepin' your chin tucked, buddy?"

I smiled back. With Hugo, I couldn't help it. "I might ask you the same thing." I regretted it the moment the words spilled, their tenor too harsh by half. But Hugo, he just grinned at me again.

"Kid got lucky."

Squeaky loosed the last of the gauze and threw it in a heap against the far wall.

"Horseshit," he said. "Go over to the sink. Let's get that cut fixed up."

Squeaky's harangue continued through the washing of the cut, the tamping it dry, the splash of alcohol, and the sterilized needle and thread to stitch it up.

"How's it feel to be getting old, Hugo? That kid tonight, he's nineteen, twenty years old, right? He busted you up but good. It's an embarrassment, what he did to you." The words had an upward lilt to them, Trevor's voice getting higher with each one. He may well hate being called Squeaky, but he puts that saddle on himself.

I kept waiting for Hugo to snap—hell, I'd already left the room once so I didn't hit Squeaky in the mouth, an act of aggression I wasn't sure I could back up. But Hugo just sat there, almost serene, while Squeaky stitched together something that looked like railroad tracks laid down by a couple of drunks.

"It's a fluke," Hugo said. "I'll do better in a couple of weeks."

Squeaky clipped off the last bit of surgical thread. "There ain't gonna be a couple of weeks for you, I already told you. You were out, Hugo, and that's a minimum of four weeks downtime. But this ain't the minimum. You're done."

The anger I'd been waiting for at last rose up in Hugo. He pushed off the towel Squeaky had wrapped around his neck, moving away. "I wasn't out."

"The hell you weren't."

"The hell I was."

I moved in and set a hand on Hugo's clammy left shoulder. "Listen—"

He shucked me off. "I wasn't out."

I tried again. "I'm just saying, Hugo, maybe—"

He moved in on me, and his face became a blend of the kid I first knew and the man I now pitied. The hair jet-black, same as it was in the winter of '92 when you couldn't pick up a box of breakfast cereal without Hugo staring back at you. The crinkles at the corners of his eyes that followed a family pattern. I could have closed my own right there and sweetly conjured up the visage of the woman Hugo knew as Grammy and seen the same design.

Hugo leaned in. "You don't think I can do it, do you? You think I'm done."

"Kid, we're way past the point of believing in you having a damned thing to do with it. You're pushing forty years old. Everybody's done at some point, and most of them well before now."

"I know you can't do it," Squeaky said. "I know you're not gonna do it."

It was the damnedest thing. I was ready to make a run for it when Squeaky poured on the gas like that, but the torment simply squeezed out of Hugo's face, as if someone had pulled a drain plug from it.

"Whatever, man," he said. "Where's my money?"

———

I lingered behind Squeaky as he folded up chairs and swept away the leavings of athletic tape, congealed nachos, and stale popcorn.

"I don't think he was out, Squeaky."

He dumped a dustpan load into a basket. "Shut up."

"Good counterpoint."

"I said shut up."

I was prepared to follow this circular route for a while longer, just as an intellectual exercise, but Squeaky dropped the dustpan and turned to me.

"Look, man," he said, fetching a box from his shirt pocket and shaking loose a cigarette. He held the box out to me, and I declined. I'd rather suck Squeaky's face than smoke a menthol. "I don't give a good goddamn whether he was out. He was down for ten seconds. That's enough for me."

"OK, yeah, but you know he's gonna see it different than that. Down isn't the same as out."

"As long as he's done, I don't care how he sees it."

I whipped my hand in the air, dispersing Squeaky's smoke. "I'm just saying, it's a pride thing. A dignity thing. Let him have that. All the shit he's been through—"

"Not just him."

"—and all the shit you and your old man have been through, and not once did anybody ever shut off the lights on him. You gotta let him have that, at least."

Squeaky blew another cloud toward me. "I don't get you, man. Surely you don't want him back in—"

"Of course not."

"—because that would be stupid, if you did."

I cleared the air again. "Oh, I'm plenty stupid. But not on this. And I'm not cruel. Don't let him fight again. Hell, you shouldn't have let him fight tonight. I'm all for that. But it's not going to kill you to let him go with the knowledge that nobody ever knocked him out cold. Besides, it isn't me you have to convince anyway." Squeaky ran the gym, ran the Tuesday night fights, but his daddy, Frank, was the boss. He knew this sure as I did.

Squeaky mashed the cigarette butt under the toe of his boot and pulled a cell phone from his back pocket. "Yeah, yeah. I'm on it."

Squeaky turned from me and walked into the darkened heart of the emptied-out theater, the phone pressed against his ear. I zipped out the side door, into a frozen night that fused my nose hairs, crossed over to Broadway, and jogged north, toward the *Herald-Gleaner.* I swore I wouldn't do it, that I wouldn't interfere, but I couldn't shake the feeling that Olden was going to pound out entirely the wrong story.

4

Frank Feeney's pub sits squat on a corner of lower Montana Avenue, shoved in among the haughtier places that took root twenty years ago when the Billings city fathers decided to sweep out the hookers and the hustlers and bring a better grade of people downtown. If you like your talk straight and your sandwich on white bread and you wouldn't dream of putting a slice of fruit in your beer, Feeney's is the place for you. I prefer a nice rib eye from Jake's, but that's neither here nor there.

"He's already gone." Frank stood behind the bar, shaking a rag at me as he spoke. The night's clientele was down to a single old coot at the end of the bar, his sleeping head next to a bowl of lentil soup.

I slipped inside and took the stool nearest Frank. He looked like a twenty-years-older version of Trevor—the same angry mustache, the same horseshoe of mowed-down hair wrapped around a bowling ball of a head. The difference is that Frank stood about four inches taller than Squeaky and had a good seventy pounds on his boy, which would put him at least in the zip code of three hundred pounds. In nearly thirty years of the newspaper game, I hadn't seen much point in being intimidated by the people I covered, but I'd always made an exception for Frank. Even when we were on the best of terms, which was most of the time, I knew he was smart enough to keep up with me and mean enough to bring the hurt if I got on the wrong side of him.

"I was hoping to talk to you," I said.

"Yeah?" He wiped down the bar in front of me. "You want something?"

"To eat or—"

"Hugo took my last sandwich. You could have Carl's soup." He gestured down the bar to our drowsy colleague. "He ain't eating it."

"A beer, I guess. Whatever's handy."

He tilted a glass under the tap and drew in a perfect pour—a brew the color of my leather lace-ups.

"Give this a whirl," he said, pushing the glass across to me. "Got it from that new microbrewery down the street. Slumpbuster, they call it. A working man's beer, but I'll give you a pass on that."

I took a sip. "Smooth. Like your head."

"Not flat, like yours?" The words came out mirthful enough, but trouble still crossed his face. "Or flat like the kid?"

I set the mug down. "He told you?"

"Trevor told me before he did, but yeah."

"What'd you tell him?"

"Same thing Trevor did: that he's finished. I can't take it anymore."

Frank had been on this ride longer than anybody, clear back to when Hugo's grandmother, Aurelia, pulled a scared little eleven-year-old into Feeney's South Side gym and told Frank to give the boy some courage to deal with the neighborhood kids who taunted and beat him over his heritage and his bastard parentage. For nearly thirty years, Frank had gotten more than he ever bargained for in Hugo Hunter—heady days and heartbreak in unequal measures. Had Hugo reached his potential, Frank might never have crawled behind a bar and left the fight game behind.

"Hugo can't take it anymore, either," I reminded Frank gently. "What'd he say?"

Frank counted bills from the register, stacking them by denomination and tucking them into a blue bank bag. "Well, it didn't end well." He chuckled. "The kid gets his back up. I get mine up. He swore he'd be fine, that he'd be back in form next time, same as he said a couple of weeks ago. I told him when he started out, this thing—the fight game—it doesn't last long. He didn't listen. It's like he can't look in the mirror and see that those days are gone. So I told him, look, Trevor says you was out—"

"He wasn't out."

"Right, yeah, whatever. The point being, if he was out, he's gotta sit out four weeks minimum. We're done for the season in two." He shrugged his shoulders. Problem solved and all that.

"And he accepted that?"

"Ah, hell no. Bunch of bitching after that." Frank lowered his voice to a mimicry of Hugo's basso profundo that's so jarring the first time you speak to him. "'Come on, Frank, I never went out. You gotta believe me. Ask anybody who was there.' So I say, OK, smartass, I tell you what: you go down to the Billings Clinic and you get one of those head doctors to look you over, and if he says you can fight in two weeks, you can fight again, because it's none of my goddamned business if you want to get your brains knocked in."

"Probably a good idea, even with the risk that he'll be cleared, huh?" I said. "Maybe a doctor can put a little fear or wisdom into him."

Frank let out a sigh. He looked spent. "Maybe. I told him, look at what they're finding out from all these football players. Their heads are so messed up they're killing themselves and talking in tongues and stuff. You don't want to mess with that. He didn't care. He just saw the opening—get a doctor to say it's OK, and it's OK. So he's happy. He bounces out of here with a sandwich and a growler of my good beer—didn't pay for either one—and an agreement that I'll even pay the goddamned hospital bill. It was the same old thing, Mark. He jabs at you and jabs at you and makes you so friggin' crazy, and then, on a dime, he's the happiest guy in the world and you're doing exactly what he wants."

I fished out a fiver and pushed it across the bar as payment for the beer that I hadn't touched since that first swallow. Frank waved me off.

"I'll go see him tomorrow," I said. "See what he's thinking."

"All right, Mark. You know I love the kid, right?"

"Yeah, of course."

"I just want him to disappear for a while, that's all."

It was the kind of thing a father—even a father who's drafted into the duty, like Frank was—says in exasperation. I know that. In my head, I can still see my old man, God rest him, looking at me after some bit of juvenile malfeasance and telling me to go play in traffic for a while, meaning nothing at all by it except frustration. It's a tossed-off release of the bile that will otherwise consume you. I know my dad didn't mean it, and there was no way he could know how that phrase would come to haunt me long after he was gone. I know it. I know I didn't mean some of the things I've said, and I imagine Frank has his regrets, too.

Fact is, if Frank had it to say again, I'm certain he'd choose his words differently. We all would.

5

When I got home that night, I had a powerful compulsion toward nostalgia that rattled me a little bit. To see Hugo at seventeen again meant I would have to find the VHS tape of the fight that made him famous, and that meant I'd have to remember where I stashed all the stuff that had Marlene's handwriting on it. And if I found the tape, I'd also have to find the VCR. I'm 60 percent Luddite, but even I eventually succumbed to the clarion call of DVDs, and sometime in the next decade or so, if the breaks are right, I might warm up to this streaming thing. Stranger things have happened.

As serendipity would have it, I found everything in the same place—the VCR in the attic because I had a memory of seeing it there when I hauled up the Christmas junk a couple of months earlier, and the tape because, in a rare bit of logic, I'd put it with the VCR.

Marlene's cursive across the yellowing adhesive on the spine was precise and overly informative, just as she tended to be: "Lightweight final, 1992 Barcelona Games, Hugo Hunter vs. Juan Domingo Ascencion." Seeing her handwriting again brought on the old pangs, the ache that is perpetually inside and never fully lets up. Some days, you get clear through to the afternoon before you think about it. Some days, it's waiting for you at breakfast. You never know, and you don't get to choose.

Marlene was six months plump with our child when I left for Barcelona, a trip I never expected to make given the *Herald-Gleaner*'s tight-with-a-buck ways. Two weeks before the Olympics began, Trimear dredged the budget for enough dough to get me there and back, and Frank Feeney wrangled me a coach's credential and promised me a spot on his hotel room floor. And so it was that in late summer 1992, I knelt before my wife and kissed her stomach and said, "Be sure to tape Hugo's fights. I'd like to see them again when I get back."

She held up her end of the bargain. The stroke of her pen is the only thing I have left of her, and it's a reminder that I didn't hold up mine.

———

Once the tape started rolling, the memories weren't of being there, ten feet from the ring when Hugo was flat-out robbed—an event that, strangely enough, made him a bigger sensation than he would have been otherwise. Even though I could see myself on the long TV shots of the ring, I was thinking about another viewing of this footage, right here in Billings, three days after the fight.

We'd settled into Aurelia's house after the crazy scenes at the airport and downtown as Billings welcomed its son home. Frank was the one who insisted that we all take another look, as if we didn't know what had gone down. Hugo had protested, saying he just wanted to get some sleep.

"Where you're going from here, Hugo, there's likely to be disappointment along the way," Frank told him. "You gotta learn to take from it what you can."

And so we all watched the fight with Juan Domingo Ascencion, the Spaniard, the hometown boy. An Olympic gold medalist for all time, that guy. I still can't quite believe it.

In the first round, both fighters shook out the nerves. Hugo, at his best, was all about timing and precision. He was a counter-puncher, the best I've ever seen. He'd make the other guy commit to a course of attack, then he'd slip the incoming punches and exploit the openings. But against Juan Domingo—on my screen two decades later, in Aurelia's living room that fine August day, in my memories forever—his timing was all off. The Spaniard came into the ring on trembling legs, a fact that Frank had smugly pointed out to me at ringside, saying, "He's all ours." In the first round, he was throwing punches that fell far short of Hugo, but every time the kid would try to step inside Juan Domingo, he'd miss. With about a minute to go in the first round, Ascencion dangled a left jab out there, and Hugo came hard with an overhand right that had a bit too much on it, and Hugo damn near tumbled through the ropes. It's an embarrassing moment—if you watch the clip, you can hear the catcalls from the partisan Spanish crowd—but Hugo had learned something important.

"There it is," Hugo said in Aurelia's front room. "See how he lets his right drop below his chin as he throws that left? I saw that. And I knew he'd do it again."

At the commercial break, Frank turned to him and said, "Do you remember what I was saying to you?"

"Huh?"

"It's between the first and second round. Do you remember what I said?"

"Yeah . . . I . . . something about slowing down."

"That's it. Slow down and take him. That's what I said. He was all ours. You can see that. He was right there for the taking."

They looked at each other, and then they looked at me, and I could see that this was how our shared experience would be. We were identical images of stomach sickness. It's unseemly, perhaps, to complain about your lot when you're an Olympic silver medalist, but Frank and Hugo knew something, and as the chronicler of their deeds, I was privy to it. The things the kid had done to get ready for that moment—the solitary miles and the time on the bag and the gut-busters and all the rest. A loss under any circumstance is unsatisfying. To lose the way Hugo did that day in Barcelona . . . it's now been nearly half my life, and I don't think I've ever found the words.

At the start of the second round, Hugo was off the stool and across the ring before Juan Domingo left his corner. The Ugandan ref pushed him back, and the Barcelonans again grumbled their discontent. It was no matter. Hugo had gone into the zone, that place where, as he described it to me later, the noise stops and the clarity begins and every target—Juan Domingo's nose and forehead and chin and liver and gut—looks three times bigger than it is. Hugo had him lined up for the fall, and as we watched Juan Domingo's eyes on Aurelia's ancient Zenith, we could see it. As I watched in my living room, alone, all these years later, I could see it.

Juan Domingo threw a left hand—a little sharper than before, but nothing Hugo didn't see coming. Hugo gave a little deke left and dug a short hook into the Spaniard's rib cage. It's the punch I've always considered the most crucial, aside from the infamous one. Juan Domingo's spittle flew halfway across the mat. That's the moment he knew he couldn't win, I think.

Next came the hunt. Juan Domingo got on his bicycle and started moving—back, back, back, left, left, left. Hugo came forward, a shark. It was all pressure now, all closing the distance and figuring out the trajectories. Hugo's right hand batted down another weak left from Juan Domingo, while the kid's left popped Ascencion in the nose. Off-balance, Juan Domingo threw an awkward right hand that whiffed, and Hugo brought two quick hooks—one to the ribs and one that glanced off the top of the head. An inch or two down, on the temple, and it would have been over.

When Juan Domingo danced away from that danger, Hugo committed his one truly stupid error of the entire tournament, a fact he lamented to me off and on in the years that followed. He got anxious, because he knew he'd taken Ascencion's will. "It's something you can feel," Hugo told me once. "When another fighter doesn't want to be in the ring anymore, you know it sure as you know anything." Hugo lunged with a right that Aurelia could have seen coming. Juan Domingo bailed out of there, but as he did, he caught Hugo dead-on in the face with a right hand that was maybe at 70 percent of his power.

Frank, in Aurelia's house, said, "That was dumb."

"I'm in no danger, but I'm stung," Hugo conceded. "But look at me—I'm pissed." I remember being amused at how clinically he broke it down. We were barely seventy-two hours clear of his life's biggest disappointment, and still he could talk about himself as if he stood outside his own experience. He was seventeen years old. Invincible.

This one sign of life from Juan Domingo set the crowd off, and he moved in and started unloading wild shots, the vast majority of which hit Hugo's gloves and arms. Hugo grabbed the Spaniard's arms and put his head in his chest, forcing the referee to come in and extricate them.

Next came the fateful moment, as the NBC guy repeatedly said during the interminable replays and mounting dismay of the aftermath. I've seen this play out three times: on the scene, with certainty, until all hope was lost that Hugo was taking the gold; on Aurelia's couch three days later, the injustice of it all leaving us steeped in anger; and in my own house, a generation later, holding on to the fantasy that somehow the outcome will change, that if we can alter this one little thing, everything else will be spun out different and better, too.

After separating Hugo and Juan Domingo, the ref did his little karate chop to the air to tell them to get back at it. Hugo waded in, watching that languid right hand as it drifted down, down, down just as Juan Domingo started unrolling his lazy left. Hugo's shoulders dipped, the launching pad for the prettiest left hook he ever threw. It was bang-bang-bang: Hugo's gloved fist, flush against Juan Domingo's jaw, the buzzer to end the round, and Juan Domingo's body crumpling to the canvas.

It was over for Juan Domingo. He was out, eyes closed, for a full fifteen seconds. His trainer leapt into the ring, screaming in frantic Spanish, rushing here and there. Frank was in there, too, his arms around Hugo. The ringside doctor was at Juan Domingo's side, and I remember the black dread of that moment. Until I saw the Spaniard's eyes flicker open, I was sick with worry that he might be badly hurt. Flashbulbs went off at 360 degrees, leaving traces of burned-out air.

Then came the chaos. The referee told the judges that Hugo hit Juan Domingo after the buzzer and it was a disqualification. It took a while for this message to come to us, given the necessary translations, and when it did, Frank just about lost it. He went at the Ugandan ref, face red and neck veins bulging, and was held back by a cadre of Olympic officials. On the tape, Hugo wanders around, his gloves already cut off, holding out his gauze-wrapped hands with a searching look, as if he wanted someone to sit him down and explain what just happened.

No one ever did. Not really. The audio on the replays was conclusive, remains conclusive. First came the pure tonal bliss of leather against skin, then the buzzer, then Juan Domingo's imitation of a potato sack. Bang-bang-bang. The NBC guy frothed on the telecast, and Juan Domingo's hand was raised even as he sat on a bench, unable to stand on his own. Frank and the US delegation put in the inevitable protest, which was summarily dismissed, the TV evidence no match for glad-handing between the International Olympic Committee and the host city, and Hugo ended up on the medal stand with Juan Domingo and the German guy, Dorfschmedder, whom he'd beaten in the semis. Frank talked for a while about staying away from the ceremony out of protest, like the '72 US basketball team that got jobbed, but in the end nobody—not even Frank—saw poor sportsmanship as a satisfying response to flagrantly bad judgment.

To this day, it's surreal, remembering that scene from the medal stand, with Juan Domingo inexplicably standing on the tallest riser. I recall Hugo leaning over and saying something to Ascencion, and back home in Billings, as the smell of *chile verde* wafted in from his grandmother's kitchen, I asked him what he'd uttered.

"I told him, '*La próxima vez, te llevaré a cabo rápida,*'" he said.

"Which means?"

"Next time, I'll take you out quick."

"What did he say?"

"He didn't say anything. He couldn't even look at me."

"Wow."

"Yeah," Hugo said. "It was pretty rad. Those two years of Spanish are turning out to be worthwhile after all."

6

The newspaper thumped against the screen door just after four a.m. I stood in front of the bathroom mirror in a T-shirt and sweatpants, brushing my teeth in preparation for sleep that wasn't likely to take hold. It's always been this way for me—not insomnia, exactly, but nothing more than a flirtation with REM sleep. Marlene used to tell me that I lived too far inside my own head and couldn't shut off my thoughts long enough to sleep. There might be something to that. The career I chose certainly did me no favors in that regard. The cityside reporters all go home at five o'clock, but for me, most nights, dusk is when I'm just getting started, my life aligned to the schedule of nighttime sports. That used to piss Marlene off something fierce, that I'd rarely be able to find my way home for the dinners she eventually gave up making, and I'd end up coming through the door after midnight with a sack of tacos, the leavings of which she'd find in the garbage the next morning. We expended so much energy fighting about things like that; it seems particularly cruel that it was all nearly ten years in the rearview and still I spend an inordinate amount of time cataloging my regrets.

I fetched the paper from the stoop and brought it into the house, spreading the four sections across the kitchen table like an oversize deck of playing cards.

Hugo's fight dominated the front-page skybox, running six columns across where, in any other Wednesday paper, we might promote some local story about the latest schoolkid to build a dancing robot and some outdoors piece about a yutz who backpacked naked through the Beartooths. The teaser headline—"End of the Line?"—wasn't especially original, but it brought the most salient question to the fore. That day in the newsroom, I'd collared Larry Grubbs, our chief photographer, and told him that he couldn't send David Mayer to the Babcock unless he wanted to see only a single, out-of-focus shot of Hugo in the paper the next morning. Larry didn't have to chew on that long to know I was right, and he penciled out Mayer and put himself down for the duty. I was happy to see he got the right image for the skybox, a head-and-shoulders shot of Hugo from behind, cast in a half-light, as he walked up the ramp alone, beaten.

Over on the front of the sports section, I noted with a tinge of melancholy that we weren't even entertaining questions anymore. The six-column horizontal photo of Hugo on his hands and knees, sweat beading on a face that had been pounded into hamburger, rode over the top of a headline that was flatly declarative: "Over and Out." I sent up a silent wish that Hugo wouldn't see it and fixate on that last word, lest he come after me and force me into a tedious explanation of the difference between a newspaper reporter and a headline writer.

Then I saw the byline, and I resolved to piss in Gene Trimear's coffee mug. I hadn't asked for a credit line when I'd scooted back to the office to help Bobby Olden with his story, didn't want one, didn't want any part of this sad denouement, and yet there I was, first billing in the morning paper.

By MARK WESTERLY and ROBERT OLDEN
Herald-Gleaner Staff

He's been on magazine covers and cereal boxes, TV talk shows and pay-per-view megafights. But Tuesday night, Billings boxing star Hugo Hunter was on his back on the Babcock Theatre canvas, knocked out in the second round by Cody Schronert, and there's considerable doubt that his once-sterling career can or should continue.

It's a good lede, and I'm glad Bobby kept it after I pecked it onto his computer screen while he was in the can taking a squirt. He'd started with Schronert and his "shocking" victory—it was the who-what-when-where-why thing that is mandatory equipment when you're in J-school but has little currency in a story that requires nuance and institutional knowledge.

If this is indeed the end, it came at 2:14 of the second round, compliments of a right hand by Schronert, a former Billings Senior football standout, that put the former Olympian down for the count.

Nobody's a former Olympian. An Olympian is an Olympian is an Olympian. It's like being a lawyer or an alcoholic; once the tag is affixed, it's there to stay. Dumb mistake for Olden to have made. Dumber still that Trimear didn't catch it.

Afterward, Hunter repeatedly said "the kid got lucky," suggesting that he would be back in the ring when the Tuesday night fight series returns for its final installment of the season in two weeks. But Trevor Feeney, the promoter and organizer of the series, suggested that wouldn't happen.

"Our rules stipulate that any knocked-out fighter spend a minimum of a month out of action," he said. "It's a sad end to a wonderful career, but we should be grateful to have had so many memorable years of watching Hugo Hunter in action."

With your more inarticulate sources, you sometimes have to help them say what they mean. Squeaky, when I called him from the office to get an official comment, didn't say precisely what I put into the story. The actual squeak was something more like this: "Goddamnit, Westerly, I just fucking told you an hour and a half ago that it's over, he was out, he's done. I'm not being goddamn arbitrary here. It's in the frappin' rule book, you thickheaded bastard. I know you just love Hugo and think he's the queen's tits, but it's over, OK?"

After Bizarro Trevor Feeney's quote, I mostly skimmed the remainder of the article. I'd dumped all the background stuff into an e-mail for Olden, the dates and the places and the people branded into me like computer memory, and just as accessible. Once we all came back from Barcelona in '92, my life changed. I was on the Hugo Hunter beat, and I saw it all, the good, the banal, and the horrifying. That night, after I'd left Feeney's, I spilled the distillation of all that into a message and sent it off to Olden. After I went home, I tried to make sense of it all, everything, twenty-some years of Hugo Hunter. I've had better nights.

7

I showed up at Hugo's at ten a.m. with a cup of coffee and a sausage-and-egg bagel, all the better to wrangle an invitation inside if he balked. I never really knew with him.

Outside, among people in town, Hugo had a thirst for attention I'd never seen from other people with notoriety, who tended to shy away from it or even greet it with hostility. Long after Hugo had surely met everyone who wanted to meet him, and certainly after his greatest wave of fame, he yearned to be recognized, to be praised, to be approached. I used to think it was a manifestation of the way Aurelia and Hugo's mother, Helene—when she was still alive—had fawned over him, and the absence of a known father. Later, I discounted that. It's not a role that Frank necessarily wanted, but he became the de facto daddy the day Hugo was put in his charge. Hugo had a funny way of making you family, and your own desires weren't much of a determinant. My standing on his doorstep with a food offering proved that. I'd long since concluded that Hugo believed he had only one contribution, one thing he could do that no one else could match, and no amount of attention could slake his desire for recognition.

At home, however, he turned inward. We saw it that day we came off the plane from Barcelona, the way he receded into the haven Aurelia maintained for him. After the four dozen fights that followed, home always pulled him back in, safe from a world that wanted a piece of him, Aurelia's love at the ready to patch his wounds and fill his cup again. He might have been OK if Aurelia could have lived forever, but that's not happening, not for any of us. I looked over at the spot where Hugo had found his grandmother four years earlier, slumped forward into the soil that held her perennials. Like Aurelia, they were gone.

"Hey, Mark." The muffled voice came from the other side of the door.

"Hugo. You up?"

"Never went down for good. Been upstairs. Dark up there."

I stepped back and looked up at his bedroom window. A sun-bleached blanket blotted out the light.

"Can I come in?"

"Maybe some other time. I'm a mess."

I held the bag up to the peephole. "I brought breakfast."

A few pregnant seconds passed before the dead bolt withdrew and the door fell open. I let myself in and followed Hugo into the living room.

I hadn't been in the place since the potluck on the day we put Aurelia into the ground. Save for a robust layer of dust, nothing much had changed.

Hugo lowered himself into a recliner. His robe, open to the navel, sprang a flabby leak, and he looked back at me through sunglasses. Squeaky's half-assed stitching job had come partly undone, and a trail of dried blood slipped off Hugo's brow and made switchbacks down his temple.

I stepped over and handed him the coffee and the sandwich, and Hugo motioned for me to take the adjacent couch.

"Thanks for this," he said.

"Not a problem. Wanted to see how you were feeling."

He chased his first bite with a swig of Colombian. "Been better. I think that kid had silver bars in his glove." He cupped his jaw in his right hand and slid it back and forth, Tin Man–style.

I sat forward and ground my palms together. I hadn't given much thought to how I'd open things with Hugo, and I found that I was stuck. I decided to let him eat.

"I dreamed last night," he said at last.

"Most people do."

"Yeah, but this was different. It was like I saw things as they actually were. It wasn't all bits and pieces of random stuff that doesn't make sense when you wake up. When I had my problem, I used to dream about talking frogs and flying cakes and stuff like that—just way out there kind of stuff. It wasn't like that, either. I recognized this."

"You want to tell me about it?"

Hugo folded the foil around the uneaten half of his sandwich and set it aside. Off came the sunglasses. He greeted the scant light in the room with a scowl, and I took grim inventory of the rotting-meat array of purples and greens around his pummeled eye.

"It was a long time ago," he said. "I ever tell you about the first match I fought?"

He hadn't, but Frank had talked about it one night after lights-out in Barcelona. He didn't linger over details—except in the context of a fight plan, Frank Feeney wasn't a fine print kind of man—but I got the gist of it as he whispered into the space between his comfortable bed and my sleeping bag on the hotel room floor. About the last person he expected to bring him there to Barcefreakinglona was the little black-haired boy Hugo's grandma had dragged into the gym six years earlier.

"No," I said. "Tell me."

Hugo nestled back into the chair and closed his eyes. "It was against Trevor," he said.

I hadn't heard this before. I sat there, a little dumbstruck by the idea that after all this time there was something more to learn about Hugo.

"I think Frank had told him to go easy on me. I was scared—so, so scared. Frank didn't even work his own kid's corner. He stayed with me, made sure the headgear was on me good and tight, and told me to use the punches he'd shown me. I knew a jab and a right cross. That's it. My left hook, it still looked like something you'd build with one of those toy cranes.

"The thing is, telling Trevor to take it easy was about the worst thing he could have done, because that wasn't Trevor's way. He came across the ring and hit me directly in the eye, and I started crying. I just dropped my hands and bawled, and Frank was in the ring lickety-split and hugged me and told me I didn't have to fight."

Hugo dropped his head, and his shoulders heaved. I looked at my hands.

"Grammy, she was so worried that night that something was going to happen to me, and I was so ashamed of what I'd done—or what I hadn't done. She'd told me that I was his boy now, that what Frank Feeney said was the law as far as I was concerned, and I was afraid that I'd let him down and that he wouldn't let me fight any-more. On the drive home, Frank's talking to me, he's telling me that I'll be measured as a man by whether I get in that ring the next time and fight. I'm in the backseat, I've got this bologna sandwich next to me that I can't bring myself to eat, it's gone all soggy, and I'm try-ing to listen to him, and Trevor is mocking me and laughing at me because he's given me a black eye." Hugo pointed a finger at the same eye, mangled this time by Cody Schronert, and I wondered what he must have thought of Squeaky Feeney's proximity to both of those indignities.

"It was snowing that night," he said. "Frank pulled up in the slush next to the house and he let me out. He says to me, 'Next time, you'll get back in the ring, Hugo. You'll get back in there, and you'll fight, and nobody will care about tonight. You hear me?' And I'm all, 'Yes, sir,' because Grammy told me to be sure to call him sir all the time.

"They were just about to leave, and I tapped on Trevor's window. He rolls it down, and I point at my eye and say, 'It doesn't hurt.' I did it to impress Frank, not to agitate Trevor. But you know what? I think he's hated me ever since. Which is cool. If I was him, I'd probably hate me, too."

At last, I looked up at him.

"So that was your dream?"

Hugo smiled. "Mostly. I've been thinking about it all morning. It woke me up about five, and I couldn't get back to sleep. It must mean something, right?"

"You mean beyond the fact that it all actually happened that way?"

Hugo motored on through my answer. "I think it's about loyalty. You know, I was scared of Frank from the beginning, scared and respectful. But that night, I knew—I knew he cared about me. And from then on, I cared about him. That's how it worked. He was for me, I was for him."

I nodded. "You've been lucky, Hugo."

Hugo pushed himself out of the recliner and pigeon-toed into the kitchen to toss the rest of his sandwich and the paper cup. I held my spot. When he came back in, he hung his hands atop the doorjamb.

"I've been reading Grammy's old ladies' magazines when I'm on the shitter," he said. "You know what self-awareness is, Mark?"

"I'm aware of it."

Hugo smiled at the slight wordplay. "I've been working on it, trying to understand it, because I took the little quiz in the magazine, and it said I'm not very self-aware. You want to know what I've decided?"

I chuckled. "Sure." I was still trying to sort out the hilarity of Hugo Hunter reading *Cosmopolitan* with his drawers around his feet.

"I didn't ask for any of this to happen. I didn't. I was good at it, and they kept putting better and better people in front of me, and it just happened. Every time you put my name in the paper, it either has words before it, or it has a comma after it and then some phrase. That phrase is the definition of me, at least according to your article." He reached for an end table, fetched the morning's sports section, and read aloud. "'Billings boxing star Hugo Hunter . . . the former Olympian . . .' Today, according to you, that's who I am."

I looked again at the floor. Swear to God, I'd never thought of things this way before, and I picked up what he was saying with such clarity that guilt and shame crowded in on me.

Hugo's voice grew faint. "I don't want to be that anymore. I just want to be Hugo. How do I do that, Mark?"

8

No matter what the kid chose to do with his life, he was never going to be just Hugo. When he was born, in 1975, the five most popular boys' names were Michael, Jason, Christopher, James, and David—a whole passel of biblical hosannas right there. The neighborhood where he ran in subsequent years was thick with Jeffreys and Kevins and Richards and Jeremys, and on the South Side of Billings a fair number of Juans and Joses and Estebans, too. You couldn't have turned up another Hugo in Yellowstone County. Maybe not even in all of Montana.

I'd have liked to ask his mother why she didn't think twice about hanging such a mouthful of a name on her son, but I never knew Helene. I do know, however, that Hugo didn't see it as an albatross. He told me as much the first time I met him, in the spring of 1991 when he brought home a national Golden Gloves title and forced us—I'm speaking here of the *Herald-Gleaner*—to acknowledge him.

We sat on the ring apron at Feeney's gym and talked. Tried to, more like it. Most of Hugo's answers were monotone and as briefly worded as he could manage. Back then, we had little inkling of the media darling he would become. He couldn't tell me how he beat opponents, just that he did it. He had little to say about school or girls or growing up. He was close to being of age for a driver's license, a milestone to which he was oblivious.

But when I asked about his name, he prattled on like an old man about the weather.

"You know anything about poetry?" he asked me.

"There once was a man from Great Falls—"

"Real poetry."

"It's not really my thing, no."

"My mom was a poet. She named me after her favorite poet of all time, a guy named Richard Hugo."

"Wait," I said. "I know that name. Montana guy, right? Wrote about small-town bars and stuff."

"Washington guy," Hugo said. "But, yeah, he taught at the University of Montana. My mom, she was one of his student aides."

"No kidding?" I might have feigned wonder then, just to keep the kid talking to me. That I knew anything of Richard Hugo could only be attributed to the fact that I lived in Montana and read a newspaper once in a while. Years later, though, Hugo Hunter would give me a book of the original Hugo's poems on a flight to London, and I'd break into tears right there in business class at the beauty of the gesture and the words on the page.

I think that's something we—me, Frank, Squeaky—lost sight of in the later years, when Hugo was less this enthralling kid and more a slouching-toward-middle-age man on a dubious streak of fuckups. He had a remarkable blend of attributes—the shy bookworm with the tactical mind and a willingness, even an eagerness, to put a man on the ground and keep him there. Helene and certainly Aurelia gave him the sensitivity, and Frank gave him the gravitas.

After the interview, I hung back to chat with Frank. Hugo shook my hand and called me "Mr. Westerly," a nicety I short-circuited on the spot, pointing out that I was only thirteen years older than he was.

"So what'd you think of the kid?" Frank asked.

"What's not to like?"

"His patience, or lack of it. Kid presses too much, too hard sometimes."

"That's your department, coach."

Frank wasn't a laugher. About the most you'd get from him was a little double-clutch chuckle. I felt honored to elicit it.

"You know, Mark, you should hang around here more often."

"You need someone to mop up the spit?" No chuckle. Damn my overreach.

"I'm serious. Hugo's going to be a big story."

"How big?" I thought of Gene Trimear and his blind spot to sports that weren't played with a scoreboard or some sort of flung projectile.

Frank grinned like he'd eaten a flock of canaries. "Big like this: Next June, we're going to Phoenix for the boxing trials. Hugo's beaten every other lightweight on the list. That means we're going from there to Barcelona."

"You sound certain."

Frank nodded, his face mugged by a smile. "I am. He's going to be a star, Westerly. Huge."

9

Hugo called me Friday morning to ask if I could take him to Billings Clinic at nine thirty.

"You're lucky I don't have a life," I told him.

"I was counting on it," he said.

Smart-ass.

———

We drove along Broadway, Hugo staring peaceably at the unfolding road and me stealing glances at him as we went. The stitched-up eyebrow looked better, moderately.

"Where's your car?" I asked him.

"In somebody else's driveway."

"Huh?"

"Sold it."

"Who you seeing at the clinic?"

"You know. Frank told you."

"I'm confused," I said. "I thought you said you didn't want to do this anymore."

"Look, man," Hugo said. "You can just drop me off at the corner, OK?"

"No, I'll take you."

"Enough with the questions."

"OK, OK."

I turned into the tangle of lots around the hospital and clinic and found a parking spot. "You want me to wait here?" I asked.

Hugo sat still, hands squeezing his knees.

"Hugo?"

Softly now, he said, "You can come in." And then: "Hey, Mark?"

"Yeah?"

"This isn't going to hurt, is it?"

———

I sat in the waiting room for the balance of the morning and beyond—long enough to skim every back issue of *Sports Illustrated*, and even most of an *Us Weekly*, which let me know at last what a Kardashian is, a bit of knowledge I'd just as soon give back.

I'd spotted the woman at the reception desk on our way in. It took a lot to ring my bell—for a long time after Marlene, I couldn't really bring myself to contemplate being with a woman, and even after I grew tired of my own touch and tossed off my vow of celibacy, I tended to keep some distant boundaries. I told Trimear once during a smoke break—the only time I could stand to be around the haughty prick—that my ideal woman lived four blocks away and had something better to do six days out of seven. He laughed and told me not to worry, that my balls would drop someday.

I never really had a type when it came to women. Marlene turned out to be everything I'd never choose, exacting on things that didn't require precision, a talker far beyond the necessities of conversation, demanding of grace while stingy with it when others transgressed. That last part may be unfair. I was a chronic transgressor, forgetting social engagements—or worse, remembering and just not wanting to go—and far more absorbed in my own world than in hers. I know it must have been lonely for her to live with the likes of me, even before the end came. I'd been living with myself since she left. I knew.

My point is, we fell in love before we recognized that we weren't right for each other and never would be. By then, my pioneer urge to outlast my troubles had kicked in, and we were really doomed.

There was nothing about the woman at the desk that demanded my attention. She was pretty enough, a little plump, looked eight or ten years younger than I was, give or take. Nothing about her was remarkable, except for the fact that I just couldn't take my eyes off her, couldn't stop thinking about her gentle, genial way with Hugo when he checked in. So I stepped out of my usual character.

Two hours into a wait that ended up being three, after enough surreptitious glances to ensure she didn't have a ring on her finger, I ambled up to the desk during a lull in patients. "If I have a complaint about the magazines, do I talk to you?" I asked.

Her smile was like melting butter. Smooth and warm. Honest to God, I'd have handed her my wallet if she'd asked.

"Sure," she said. "I can't do anything about them, but I'm happy to hear you out."

I held up the *Sports Illustrated* I'd been reading. "It's just that you have two kinds of magazines here, and they're like polar opposites. This one"—I shook the magazine to make sure she saw it—"is all testosterone and beer ads. The other ones are all estrogen and feminine hygiene products. What about people who aren't manly men or girly girls?"

During my spiel, which I made up on the fly, she twinkled. I'm serious. She was like a gem, and I was smitten in a way that demanded I follow my faux outrage as far as it would take me.

"You mean, what about magazines for someone like you?" she said.

"No, I'm a manly man."

"Then what's your complaint?"

"I'm arguing on behalf of the people. Not necessarily for me."

"There's nobody here but you."

"Theoretically, I mean."

"I see."

"You're not buying this, are you?" I said.

"Not especially, no."

I lobbed the magazine into the nearest chair. "OK, then, I'm going to have to hope that you at least think I'm cute, or sufficiently interesting to make cute not a make-or-break proposition." I puffed out my hollow chest.

"I'd say you're safe."

Those four words—OK, six if you count the contractions— brought my pecker into the proceedings. First time in the better part of a year without pharmaceuticals. Who's the lucky boy?

"What would you say if I asked you what's going on with my friend back there?" I said.

"I'd say that he'll be up here soon enough and can tell you him-self, if he wants to."

"Privacy stuff, huh?"

"Something like that."

"Would a safer question be what are you doing tomorrow night?" I tried to put on my best apple-polisher smile, which elicited a grin in return.

"Maybe."

"How do we turn that into a yes?"

She pulled a brochure from the reception desk and wrote her name—Lainie—and phone number. She handed it to me.

"You call me this evening and ask me properly," she said. "Now please sit down. Your friend will be out shortly."

I jaunted back to my chair, impressed with myself. Maybe bra-vado suited me after all.

———

The exam hurt Hugo, just not where you could see it.

He walked past me without a look. Lainie had to chase him down with a slip of paper containing details of his next appointment. He took it, stared at the words as if they were written in a lost language, then continued on. I jogged to catch up to him.

"What'd he say?" I asked.

Hugo shuffled onward, not looking at me.

"Come on, man. It can't be that bad."

"Can't fight," he said.

"In two weeks? Ever? What?"

"Can't fight."

"Hugo, what did the man say?"

He offered no acknowledgment of me. We walked a line through the foyer to the street, Hugo in a dazed march while I tagged after him, hectoring, like a needy child.

In the parking lot, Hugo stopped. He turned a circle, staring into the distance.

"Where's your car?"

I pointed down the row we stood in. "Right there."

"I have to talk to Frank."

"Sure."

"I'd walk, but I'm tired. I need to talk to him."

"Yeah, sure, Hugo. Of course."

"If it's any trouble—"

"Hugo, get in the car."

I pointed out the direction again, and as we covered the thirty or so yards between us and my old Malibu, I set a hand on Hugo's shoulder. I don't know when I let him in, when I relaxed the pose as objective journalist long enough to let myself love him, but whenever it was, it couldn't be undone, even if I'd wanted that. Some days I felt like an older brother. Others, like this one, when Hugo's vulnerabilities seemed to overwhelm him, my role was almost that of a father. I tried to stay on the safe side of almost. It was a dangerous piece of hubris, the idea that I could light the way for Hugo.

Because, really, who the hell was I?

10

At Feeney's pub, everything Hugo wouldn't or couldn't tell me came tumbling out.

The CT scan and the written acuity test would clarify the diagnostics soon enough. Hugo said that once the doctor knew the particulars—that he'd been unable to protect himself and was pounded into human hamburger in consecutive fights—there was no way he was signing consent on another beating.

"That's it, then," Frank said.

"Frank," Hugo pleaded, "he never said I couldn't fight. He just said that he preferred I didn't, that's all."

There's a term for that line of argument. Desperate, yes, but brass balls is more like it. And yet, it was in character for Hugo, who could be as adept at parsing words as he once was at taking away an opponent's offense. I watched Hugo and Frank go at it from a table a safe distance away, my role as observer coming to the fore, and my mind flashed on a happier time, at the training camp before Hugo's first title shot. In the evening, after Hugo's ring work was done, we'd sit around the cabin on Flathead Lake that Hugo used as a training base and we'd rip on each other—just ball-busting guy stuff, since the camp was all testosterone, the sparring partners, Hugo, Frank, Squeaky, and me. I'd long since adapted to Frank's habit of on-the-fly portmanteau words, the most prominent of which, when it came to Hugo, was "flustrated," but Hugo had heard enough.

"It's two words, Frank," he said that night, as the rest of us roared and Frank fought gamely against the grin pulling at the corners of his mouth. "Flustered and frustrated. One means you're out of sorts. The other means you're out of patience."

"Oh, yeah, smart-ass?" Frank said. "If I hear any more out of you, I'm going to kick your motherfunking ass." God, how we howled at that.

Frank slapped the bar with a towel, pulling me out of my memories. "He sure as shit didn't say you could fight, Hugo. That was the deal, remember? Written approval. You had a nice run, kid, but it's over now. Go home, make peace with it, get on with your life."

"Frank—"

"Not another word. It's over. It's done. I don't want to hear about it anymore."

Hugo looked to me, searching. I averted my gaze.

"I've got nothing without it, Frank," he said.

Were it me, I'd have come from behind the bar and hugged Hugo, some small suggestion that it would all be OK, even if I had my doubts. Maybe I was too softhearted, or maybe I'd gotten too close, but I had sympathy for Hugo. The one thing Hugo did better than almost anyone else, the one constant for much of his life, was being taken away in a most ignominious way. It deserved some ceremony, some deference. At least I thought so.

Frank, though, stayed rooted to his side of the barrier.

"You're going to be alive tomorrow," Frank said, soft as he was capable of being in that moment. "That's good enough for me. Damnit, Hugo, it ought to be good enough for you, too."

11

Frank knocked on my door just after three a.m. I watched him through the peephole as he listed like a grade-schooler in a carnival funhouse. I opened the door, and he belched forth a gaseous cloud of his own product.

"I knew you'd be up," he said.

I motioned him in. "I'm predictable that way." Another evening of watching teenage boys and girls play basketball, followed by a breathless account for the next morning's paper, was behind me. I was making a hell of an impression with my life's work.

I brought Frank into the living room and poured a pot of coffee into him. That seemed to level him out a bit. What began as a mal-formed lamentation—"That kid's driving me crazy," over and over, the words changing here and there but the sentiment straight and true—became a more coherent thought.

"I put the kibosh on him," Frank said.

"Oh?"

"Called the sporting authority in the Dakotas, Wyoming, Colorado, Utah, what's that state above Utah?"

"Idaho?"

"Idaho! And Washington. Called them all. Told them about Hugo and said not to sanction him for a fight. I figure that's as far as he can get on a bus. He ain't got a car anymore. I don't know. Maybe he can get to Nebraska. If he can get to Nebraska"—Frank held up his coffee cup in a toast—"more power to him, let him fight. Screw Nebraska."

"So that's it, then?"

"That's it." Frank gave the thumbs down, a *pffffffbbbbbbtttt* for emphasis.

"Have some more coffee," I said. "You did the right thing."

———

While Frank recounted the back-and-forth in his bar, as if I hadn't been there and seen the whole thing, I tried to noodle out how to tip Olden off to a story we'd have to do. The end of Hugo's fighting career, even in this advanced state of erosion, was capital-*N* news, but I didn't want to open Hugo to the indignity of how it ended and how Frank had necessarily sandbagged him.

"I wish Aurelia was here," Frank said, the first thing to penetrate my own foggy thoughts. "She'd straighten him out."

"She was something special," I said.

"Dignity and grace." I looked over at Frank as he spoke. He lay on his back across my couch, his eyes lost in the maze of the ceiling pattern. "I never met anybody like her. First time she brought him to me, she laid it all out. 'He's being beat up and made fun of. He's scared. Your job is to make sure he can defend himself and that he isn't scared anymore.' Just like that. It wasn't a request, just an order. You think I was going to tell her no?"

"And look what you ended up with," I said. "Did you have any idea?"

Frank scoffed. "Shit, no. Pure athletic ability, sure. I saw that almost immediately, but in boxing, that's not near enough. I had to find out if he was hard enough to do what needed to be done. You remember watching Roberto Duran?"

"Sort of," I said. "I saw the two Leonard fights when I was in high school. You know, *no más* and all that."

Frank whistled, a long, baleful blast, and he flopped onto his side. "Oh, man, you should have seen Duran as a lightweight. That's when he was a killer. *Manos de piedra*, hands of stone. He used to convince himself before fights that the other guy had killed his mom. He'd come in there with a rage. I mean, he hated those guys he fought. It was scary. And then it'd be done, and he could flip it off and be a regular guy." He looked me over. "Anybody can learn the punches. The willingness to hurt another man for no reason at all, and for every reason there is—that's the part you can't teach."

"That's the part I never got," I said. "Hugo's not cold-blooded. Far from it."

"No, he's not. But he's hungry—or he was. Think about all the things he didn't have—no dad, no mom after he was ten years old, no respect in his neighborhood, him and Aurelia living hand to mouth in that house. You give me a kid who doesn't want, and I can't do anything with him. You give me a kid who's nothing but desire, and now you're talking. When I saw what Hugo had inside"—he thumped a fist against his chest—"I told Aurelia that she didn't have to pay a dime for him to work out with me. As if she could, anyway."

I sat quietly. I wasn't sure how to phrase the question I wanted to ask. Frank yawned and turned toward the cushions, so I settled on directness.

"He says he still has the desire. How do you tell him to shut it down?"

Frank rolled back toward me. I got the thousand-yard stare again. "It's not desire that Hugo has. It's muscle memory. We think we're meant to do one thing, and when that thing ends, we don't know how to cope. I was a boxing trainer, and then I wasn't. I own a bar now. That was my next thing. Hugo, he's just got to find his."

Frank nestled into my couch and began snoring. I got up, set a blanket across his girth, and retreated to my bedroom to wrestle with my own slumber.

12

For sheer spectacle, I've never seen anything like what happened in Billings the day we returned from Barcelona.

I was first up the Jetway, and the concussive beat from inside the terminal rattled that tin can. It was tittering laughter and the brass band blowing through some practice notes and the hum of anticipation and the smell of carnival popcorn. I expected something big. Marlene had tipped me off when I'd called from JFK between flights. "It's unbelievable what's happening here," she'd said, and there I was, always with something better, saying, "It's unbelievable what happened in Spain." There are so many things I regret saying to her, and that—a stupid, tossed-off line that one-upped her—is one of them.

On our last connection, the flight from Minneapolis, Frank leaned in all casual and said to Hugo, "I think there's this little to-do planned back home." Hugo nodded in his self-assured way and went back to feigning sleep, the only way he could keep the well-intentioned folks who shared our flight from queuing up at his aisle seat, seeking pictures or autographs.

As we crested the ramp, it was me, then Frank with his coat over his arm and a newspaper jammed in his back pocket, and finally Hugo with a duffel bag over his shoulder.

The terminal looked like a glitter bomb had gone off. Streamers hung from the ceiling tiles and poster board signs clung to the walls, every letter a different color: "Welcome Home, Champ." "Hugo Hunter, Our Hero." "He's a Knockout!" We stood there for at least a second or two, blocking traffic off the plane, before recognition registered with the gathered throng and they finally lurched into action. The off-key notes of the "Rocky" theme blared out, and this surge of humanity came at us, all hands and mouths and a garble of congratulations.

It was easy enough for me to slip by. I wasn't the object of their attention. I retreated to the side and found Marlene and kissed her, then knelt in front of her and rubbed her belly. "Trimear wants me to ride down with Hugo," I said, and she teared up but nodded vigorously, the bravest face she could show me as I disappointed her again.

I looked back at the commotion and found Frank, who had sidled off to the edge of the scrum. I saw Hugo make eye contact with him and give the universal raised-eyebrows signal of "Where the hell is she?" and Frank nodded and plunged into the squirming mass.

"I'll get a ride home," I told Marlene. I was gone before she answered, pulled to the periphery of the crowd surrounding Hugo.

"What're you going to do now, Hugo?" one guy asked him.

"I'd like to sleep, sir," Hugo said, looking him in the eye, showing the confidence of a boy-become-man that he hadn't exhibited before Barcelona.

At last, Frank parted the crowd, coming up the middle, his right hand around the tiny left wrist of Aurelia, pulling her through. He twirled her into her grandson's arms, and Hugo held on to her.

"Where were you?" he said.

"Waiting at the back."

"Grammy, you don't wait on anybody."

"Oh, hush." She pulled away from him just a bit and ran her hands along his shoulders, straightening his Team USA sweatshirt. "These nice people came to see you. We'll have plenty of time to talk later."

Hugo slipped a finger under her chin and lifted it until their eyes met. "Did you watch me?"

"Yes," she said. "Every time."

"Came up one short," he said.

She smiled and shook her head. "Nobody here thinks so," she said, and Hugo hugged her again as the crowd went wild.

———

We rode from the airport in a white limousine, Hugo and Aurelia and Frank and me, and a Yellowstone County commissioner named Rolf Eklund. People stood on both sides of the road, holding signs welcoming Hugo home. Later, on the cusp of his first title fight, Hugo and I would talk about that day and that line of humanity just wanting a glimpse of him. "It didn't seem real," he'd say. "I've been down the steep drop of Twenty-Seventh Street so many times—lonely times, on my feet, pounding out the miles. To see all these people there, and to know they were there for me, it was stunning. I mean, I can't think of another word."

At JFK, I'd called Gene Trimear after hanging up with my wife, and he'd laid out the plan for me. We'd use my status as an insider to do a behind-the-scenes story on Hugo Hunter Day. That put me in the awkward position of trying to fire questions at Hugo while knowing full well the answers.

"Roll down that window, son, and lean out if you want to," Commissioner Eklund said.

I reached for Hugo's hand and stopped him from engaging the button. "I want to ask you a few questions before we get to the courthouse."

"Sure, Mark, fire away."

And so began the ping-pong of conversation around the limo, a frenetic, disjointed scene I tried to capture in print the next morning.

Here's Frank, nosing through the compartments in back. "Any whiskey?"

"No whiskey," Commissioner Eklund said. "The county can't be liable for that. There are some Cokes in there."

Aurelia: "Oh, this is so exciting."

Me: "Did you expect a greeting like this, Hugo?"

Frank: "I don't want a Coke."

Hugo: "I don't know what I expected. It's amazing."

Commissioner Eklund: "We're almost there, Frank. How about I buy you a drink later?"

Me: "What are you going to do now?"

Aurelia: "I'll have a Coke, Frank."

Frank: "You're on, Commish."

Hugo: "I haven't thought too much about it." (This, by the way, was a lie with a capital *L*. What Hugo was going to do next occupied his every thought, and Frank's, and mine, for that matter. Asleep on the plane, I'd dreamed about what was next and wondered if my marriage would survive it. Seeing the reception put on for Hugo, I couldn't help but think of what was next. Always, always what was next.)

Commissioner Eklund: "Would you just look at that!"

We were in the middle of downtown now, and the courthouse lawn looked like the scene of a rock concert—as if everybody in town had squeezed onto that patch of grass in a rollicking mass of anticipation and pompons. When Hugo stepped out of the limousine, a cheer like you've never heard went up. Following Hugo all those years, I came to know something about rowdy crowds. Nothing in

Barcelona, or anywhere else, could compare with what we heard right there that day in Billings, Montana. The hairs on the back of my neck prickled, and as I followed Commissioner Eklund, Hugo, Frank, and Aurelia up the stairs to the dais, I had to remind myself to breathe.

I found my way to the back of the gathered mass of dignitaries and ciphered out an angle for observation. Hugo took a seat near the lectern, between Mayor Ted Stanton and Commissioner Eklund. The grass, already burned up from the summer heat, was trampled by the massive glob of humanity that crowded the stage. I looked down the line at Frank and Aurelia. He managed to tolerate the suit he was wearing, while she looked like an angel, an embodiment of grace. It's fair to say I loved her. Even fairer to say I harbored a bit of a crush on this woman nearly forty years my elder. When I was younger, older women had a wisdom about them that attracted me—not necessarily in sexual ways, and certainly not that with Aurelia. It was an appeal to the mind, an intoxication that comes from recognizing a true sage.

Both of them wore the lopsided smiles and faraway eyes that I'd seen before. Frank bore the same look after the semifinals, after Hugo beat the guy from Germany and they knew he was going to win a medal. That's when everything began to get so crazy around them, when Hugo went from a minor curiosity to—well, to whatever he was that day in Billings and in subsequent weeks and months, damn near everywhere you looked. Frank's visage in Barcelona said "How in the *hell* did this happen?" The expression in Billings said the same thing.

I moved closer, stepping sideways through county and city officials, to get nearer the action.

Mayor Stanton rapped Hugo's left knee with his fist and said, "Awesome job out there, kid."

"Thanks."

"You know, I knew your mother. Did you know that?"

"No, sir."

"A wonderful woman. How long has she been gone?"

"Seven years."

"She'd be proud of you today."

"She was proud of me every day, sir."

The mayor got a funny look on his face, just for a moment, like food had gone down the wrong way or something, and then it cleared. "OK," he said. "Let's do this."

He stood, reached into his pocket for some notecards, and stepped to the lectern. The crowd broke out into chants of "Hu-go! Hu-go! Hu-go!" and drowned out his first few words. He kept fumbling around, trying to get things going, and still the chant came: "Hu-go! Hu-go! Hu-go!"

Hugo turned around in his seat, looked at me, and said, "That's my name. Don't wear it out."

———

Darkness hugged Billings tight when Aurelia, Frank, and I stepped outside her house that evening, leaving Hugo blanket-covered on the recliner, bagging all the sleep he'd missed during a fortnight in Spain.

"Better enjoy this crisp air while you can, Aurelia," Frank said. "In another month, you'll be smelling nothing but sugar beets cooking." He cast a hand south, toward the plant that looms over the South Side.

"I like it," she said, settling into a chair on the porch. She pulled a shawl tight around her shoulders. "To me, it's the smell of home." While I appreciated Aurelia's embrace of one of the defining aspects of her neighborhood—and, really, what choice did she have?—I had to go with Frank on this one. On a day when the wind was blowing out, I could smell that sickly sweet air, something on the order of meat halfway between edible and spoiled, all the way up in the Heights. I spent much of the fall, every year, on the precipice of nausea.

Frank eased down into the chair next to Aurelia's. I sat on the railing opposite them.

"The kid gave a good speech," Frank said. "Said the right things, thanked the right people."

Aurelia clasped her hands and brought them to her mouth. "I'm amazed at how grown-up he seems. Frank, you took a boy to Spain and brought back a man." She reached down and grasped his hand, and even as she did, a storm cloud crossed her face. "I wish Helene could have seen him. She was the orator in the family, you know. I saw a lot of her in him today. It usually comes in little bits, something he'll say, a way he'll cock his head, and she'll be there. Today was different. She was more fully there, if that makes any sense."

Frank nudged Aurelia. "Can you believe Stanton?"

"Oh, whatever," she said, brushing his arm away. "He's the mayor. Of course he'd be there."

"Yeah, but—"

"Wait," I said. "What?"

"Nothing," Frank said, a little too fast, a little too abrupt. I might have let it go if not for that.

"Come on," I said.

"Just leave it be—"

"Well, there's no chance of that, Frank."

Aurelia held a finger to her lips and craned her head to make sure Hugo was still in slumber. She stood up and glared at Frank. "Come out into the yard, you two."

We followed her out to the edge of the lawn, under a lamp spraying the street in gold.

"Well," she said to Frank, "you brought it up. You want to tell him?"

"Tell me what?" I said.

Frank moved in close to me. "Mark, I hate to do this, but I'm going to have to ask for your word that this is off the record. Off the record, out of the atmosphere, out of the solar system. You got me?"

I held my arms out, an innocent. I hated it when people did this to me. It made for a convenient joke—"Hey, watch what you say around the newspaperman, or he'll make you famous for all the wrong reasons"—but it came at a considerable cost to my comfort around other people in social settings.

"You want to pat me down for a wire, Frank?"

"I'm serious."

"So am I."

"OK, boys, enough," Aurelia broke in. Then, in a whisper: "Mayor Stanton is Hugo's father."

I looked at Frank. He nodded grimly.

"Does Hugo—"

"Absolutely not," Aurelia said. "My daughter loved that man. Loved him enough to retreat when Stanton said he didn't want to be with her, that he wanted to return to his wife. Loved herself enough not to be made a fool. They were over and done long before she found out about Hugo. She didn't tell him about her son, and she saw no reason to tell her son about a man who didn't want them."

I struggled to sort it all out in my mind. Ted Stanton was one of the most powerful and wealthy men in the state, a former oilman who was about to use the mayor's job as a springboard to a county commission seat. Some people figured he'd be governor someday. The economic disparity alone was enough to make a connection with Hugo dubious. Here was a hardscrabble kid from the poor South Side, and his daddy lived in splendor on the West End. And still, armed with this knowledge, I could picture Stanton's mug shot that commonly ran in the *Herald-Gleaner*, those penetrating green eyes that stared back from the newsprint, and I could see the similarity to the eyes of the boy I now knew to be his son. The galaxy of freckles sprayed across Hugo's nose was a match, too. It was the black hair, thick as a house painter's brush, and the fractional-Native complexion that separated Hugo from his father's image. This apple fell far from the tree.

"So Stanton doesn't know," I said.

"Nobody's ever told him," Aurelia replied.

"How many people do know?"

"Three, including you. Now."

"What's with all the questions?" Frank asked.

"Nothing. I'm just trying to get my head around it. You know, the mayor sat up there and talked to Hugo about his mom. I just thought—"

"No," Aurelia said. "I don't think so. He's a blowhard, so maybe he was just trying to show off. I don't know. We haven't said anything, and we don't want anything."

I looked at my watch. Nearly midnight. "Speaking of fathers," I said, instantly cringing at my awkward segue, "this daddy should have been home hours ago. Frank, can you give me a lift?"

————

We were nearly to my turnoff in the Heights when I broke the silence.

"I still can't believe it."

Frank gripped the steering wheel. "We shouldn't have said anything."

"Why?"

"It's not a good subject. It's a distraction."

"Frank, I'm not going to say anything to anybody."

"I'm just saying that it's not good."

I leaned back in the bucket seat. "I will say, it's a hell of a story." In the corner of my eye, I caught Frank agitating. "Potentially. Theoretically."

Frank said nothing, the clearest possible sign that he was pissed.

"Frank, there's so much interest in Hugo. You were there. I don't have to tell you. There's going to be a lot of people who want to tell his story. Maybe—"

"What?"

"I don't know. Maybe you ought to consider how to handle all of this, in case it gets out. Could be dicey for Hugo. Could be dicey for the mayor, too, if he doesn't know."

He pulled into my driveway and shut off the ignition.

"I have one job, Mark," he said. "That's to get him through this next year without any damage coming to him. He made a promise to Aurelia that he'd finish high school before we'd start his career, and he's gonna honor that promise. I'm gonna honor that promise. So don't talk to me about handling anything where Hugo's concerned, OK? I'm on it. And just to be clear: fuck Ted Stanton."

"I never suggested that you—"

He cut me off. "I'm tired, Westerly. Just forget it, OK? Go see your wife. You gotta stop hanging around guys like me."

I climbed out of the car and tapped the roof twice, thanking Frank for the ride. He backed out of the driveway and left the neighborhood the way he'd come in.

I hauled myself up the driveway toward the porch light. On the door, a sheet of yellow legal-pad paper flapped in the night breeze. I reached for it and pulled it close.

It was Marlene's line-perfect cursive.

I guess we'll see you tomorrow then.

13

Aside from handing a tip to Bobby Olden that Hugo was, in all likelihood, finished as a fighter, I spent the next several weeks disengaged from him and the Feeneys. Olden's story came and went, a tidy enough account. Hugo wouldn't commit to being done. He acknowledged that it didn't look good, and that at the minimum he'd have to wait until the Babcock fight series started again in the autumn. Trevor Feeney cast things more definitively: "The end comes for every great fighter. And that's what Hugo was: a great fighter."

In what must have been the biggest indignity of all for Hugo, Billings and its people took the news without breaking stride or, frankly, seeming to give a damn. I've seen that kind of wandering interest a hundred times. There's nothing in the world we won't grow tired of.

As for me, it wasn't that I'd grown weary of Hugo. I'd just been taken in by the simple, sweet distraction of Lainie Vermillion.

I wouldn't have laid odds that it was possible I'd see her nearly every day, that I'd even want to, but that's what happened. I called her that first night she asked me to, before Frank showed up at my place soused, and told her I had a day off coming and I'd like to take her to dinner. She countered by asking me to bring a bottle of wine to her place, a little bungalow near the park, so she could cook for me. I left her house that night with a chaste kiss on the lips and an urgent need to get home and rub one out. Within the first week, she told me she didn't like my smoking, and instead of saying "tough shit, lady," as I'd have surely said to anyone else, I stopped. Well, I mostly stopped. I still stepped outside the *Herald-Gleaner* with Trimear between editions and blazed up while I listened to him carp about his recalcitrant twenty-six-year-old son who's got Crisco for brains and better by God put that degree to some use and get out of the basement and holy shit did the world not need another friggin' English major. It would take an English major to know, I supposed. Even so, I barely raised those Camels to my lips, instead letting long lines of ash fall to the sidewalk before I mashed the husk out on the building and dropped it into the trash.

In the days immediately after my first date with Lainie, I faced the long work stretch that Trimear had warned me about when I took the night off to watch Hugo. The district basketball tournaments bounced into town, and I couldn't get away. So Lainie came to me, bringing me hot dogs and sitting with me on press row between games, the banter between us easy and light. It would be unfair of me to make any comparison that casts a negative light on Marlene, because God knows I alienated her a baker's dozen different ways, but she never cozied up to what being a newspaperman required of me if I wanted to do it well. Lainie got it from the beginning.

On our second proper date, I stood in Lainie's kitchen, cutting carrots for a salad, when I realized that the night was likely to end with me in her bed (or if not that, with the biggest case of blue balls I'd ever experienced). I knew then that once I'd had her, I'd only want more of her, that all the borders I'd erected with other women would be made porous. I couldn't face that without unburdening myself.

"Where did your son go to middle school?" I asked her. Tony, a rig hand, was on his two-weeks-on cycle in the oil patch, and I hadn't yet met him.

Lainie stood at the stove, stirring the rigatoni. "Castle Rock. Why?"

I set down the knife and faced her. "He might have known my boy."

"But you said—"

"That I don't have kids. Yeah. I don't. But I did. I had a kid."

She turned down the burner, took my hand, and led me to the couch in the living room.

"Tell me," she said.

"Von Eric Westerly," I said, and I swear, I felt like I'd breathed him into the room just by letting his name out. Into my mind came a crashing jumble of thoughts—what he might look like if he'd lived, what I would say to him if I had the chance, whether he'd forgiven me for what I'd done.

"He'd be twenty-one in October, about the same age as Tony. He only made it to twelve."

She brought my hand to her lips and kissed it. I closed my eyes.

"What happened?"

There is no good answer for that question, simple though it may be. What happened is that I fathered a son who was smarter than I was the day he was born, who was headstrong (where the hell did he get *that*?), who had his own sense of what was what, a sense that in his budding adolescence had increasingly put him opposite of me in matters of familial harmony. What happened is that I came home for dinner one night, pissed off about something I can't even remember, and lit into the boy over the major infraction of leaving the skateboard I'd just bought him in the yard for any young scofflaw to take. What happened is that right there, like a hanging judge, I'd dropped a penalty on him that I couldn't possibly make stand, something so wildly out of proportion to his transgression that Marlene laughed in her incredulity and thus drew her own ration of my wrath. What happened is that Von ran for the door, grabbing his skateboard out of the front hallway, where I'd put it, and tore out into the dusk. What happened is that I chased him to the top of our hill, the perfect place to see him tucked low on that skateboard, whooshing down into the thicket of lanes below us, his hair blown back by the wind. What happened is that I went back to the house and lingered in the front yard, burning through my smokes and waiting for Von to come back to us. What happened is that he never did.

"He got hit by a car," I said. "Three days in the hospital. No brain activity. I wouldn't let them let him go. I told the doctor I would fucking kill him if he let my boy die."

I sniffled. I stared at the ceiling in some futile hope that my filling eyes would drain back into my head. The rest came in a whisper. "You know how that goes. Calmer heads prevailed. They didn't do anything I hadn't already done."

Lainie squeezed my hand. "Mark, no. It's not—"

"Yes," I said. "It goddamn sure is."

She moved into me, her hips and her hands and her head taking up the spaces adjacent to mine, until there was nothing between the end of me and the beginning of her. She cupped my neck in her hand and brought my head to her shoulder and I breathed her in, and then I broke down.

The skateboard was fine, not a scratch on it. That night, my son lay crumpled and broken on some poor bastard's lawn. We never brought him home, but the skateboard came back and got propped up in its usual spot in the hallway, because we were too overtaken by our grief to do anything else. Someone who divines meaning from mundane action might suggest that we put it there in some desperate hope of turning things back to that last moment when Von might have decided to stay, or I might have decided not to scold him the way I did, or Marlene, shouted into silence by me, might have intervened and saved us all. I have enough guilt and shame about all of that on my own. I didn't need to objectify it.

It was, simply, something he loved, and we loved him, and he was gone and it was still here. It was something he'd left us. The same thing with his bedroom, just across from ours. In those blurred days after Von's funeral, I'd find Marlene in there, sitting on the edge of his bed, staring at the walls. The sour stink of our adolescent boy lingered in that place. She'd sit on the bed. I'd stand in the doorway. And silence and memory and the perpetual parsing of the things we should have said but didn't or the things we shouldn't have said but did—all that taunting shit gathered between us and carried us away from each other.

14

Hugo rang my doorbell early on the morning of my next day off. It's weird to say so, because Billings with its hundred thousand souls isn't a particularly large town in the scheme of things, but seeing him there on my porch threw me for a loop, as if he'd ventured into a foreign zone. He hadn't been out this way since Von was still with us, since before Marlene left, and I realized I'd managed to put him in a box. If I were downtown or on the South Side, Hugo fit into the picture. Here, not so much.

"How'd you get here?" I asked him.

"A buddy dropped me off. It's cold, Mark. Can I come in?"

"Christ, yes. Come on."

Hugo pushed into the living room, a place he knew well in some distant, other time. There was a rawness to his movement, an agitation. He didn't sit. Instead, he ground a path into the carpet with a fast-twitch walk.

"I don't have much in the fridge," I said. "I can scare up some coffee."

"No, thanks." He didn't look at me, but the pacing continued.

"Have a seat," I said.

"In a minute."

I sat down. I thought maybe that might induce him. No dice.

"Mark," he said at last. "You know anything about books?"

"Paper, binding, glue. Haven't cracked one in who knows when." I pointed at my bookcase, a static piece of furniture in my house these last few years.

Hugo stopped and looked at me. "Huh?"

"I'm just kidding."

He came over and sat down on the couch opposite me. Now I had his full attention, his eyes bearing down on me, sharp and focused. Intimidating, if you want to know the truth.

"What I meant was, have you ever written one?"

I tugged at the collar of my robe. "Hell, no. I wouldn't know where to begin." The truth of the matter is that I wrote the equivalent of a book damn near every couple of months, it seemed, but that was easy. Everything happened in front of my face, and I regurgitated it in five-hundred-word chunks.

"I want to write a book," he said.

"Yeah?"

"Yeah. And I want you to help me."

I laughed at the idea of my being helpful with such a thing, and he cringed, and in covering up I cracked a joke—"I could write a book about grabbing ass"—that just made it worse.

"I'm serious," he said.

"Tell me what you're thinking," I said.

"I don't know. My story. A cautionary tale. Something like that. I've got a good story. I need help with the words, though."

Shit, yes, he had a good story. That had never been in dispute. I'd been approached by a publisher back in the immediate post-Barcelona days about writing a quickie Hugo biography. It wasn't so much for my blinding literary skill as for my fairly unfettered access to Hugo. I'd dropped the subject after Frank Feeney snorted. "Biography? He's goddamn seventeen years old. He's barely lived."

The living wasn't a problem now. The focus and motivation after all his other short-circuited aspirations, I feared, would be.

"So . . . motivational?" I asked. "Or biography? Maybe both?"

"I don't know. I mean, I think I can tell people what it's like when, you know . . ."

"Things don't work out?" I finished for him, and he looked wounded.

"Yeah."

"Hugo, I don't know. I'm not the best person for something like this. I don't know jack about getting a book published."

"Yeah, but you were there. You know the story. I trust you."

"When did you get this idea?" I asked.

"A while ago."

"When?"

"I've been thinking about it since, you know."

I knew. Since Frank had pulled the plug on him that day after our trip to Billings Clinic.

"Are you prepared to be honest about everything?" I asked.

Hugo leaned in, and those eyes cut deeper into me. "What do you mean?"

"Well, there's some not-so-good stuff."

"Yeah?"

"Some stuff I've never heard you acknowledge. Publishers like that stuff. Did you read Andre Agassi's book?"

Hugo shook his head.

"He came clean about some things. He also came up with some details about things that were common knowledge. Ernest Hemingway talked about how writing is opening up a vein and bleeding onto the page. You prepared to do that?"

Hugo seemed to shrink with every word, something that didn't surprise me. It was typical of him, really. He got an idea into his head, became fixated with the result, and didn't think through the process of getting there.

"I'd like to try," he said.

I stood and walked over to the bookshelf. I scanned the rows and plucked a few books down. The Agassi memoir. Some others, too, either autobiography or biography. Ali. Keyshawn Johnson. Jack Nicklaus. I gave them to Hugo.

"Some research. Read them, get a feel for the form," I said.

"So you'll help me?"

As if he had any doubt. As if I could tell him no.

"I'll do what I can," I said. "I want you to do the writing—"

"No, Mark, I need you to—"

"Hold on," I said. "Just listen to me now. I want you to write some stuff for me. Don't worry about order or making it all fit together or whatever. Just write what you're feeling, on whatever topic. Bring it to me, and I'll check it out. If I think I can help you, I will. You understand?"

"Yeah, great," he said. "That's awesome."

"No guarantees." I tried to effect a stern look in the face of the easy Hugo charm.

"Right. I got you," he said.

I came out of the bedroom not fifteen minutes later, fresh out of the shower and with the day's clothes on my back. I found Hugo at my kitchen table, a dozen pages deep into the Agassi book, and I thought, well, maybe there's hope for this idea.

You've always got to have hope.

15

I didn't hear much from Hugo in the weeks that followed, just assurances that he was reading and taking notes. Meanwhile, the seasons rolled on for me the same as any other year, with the only difference being my mounting dismay at how quickly time seemed to be moving. I made it through state basketball and wrestling, the variances in Gene Trimear's moods, and advancing gray in my own hair. Life, by any measure except the loss of time, was better than it had been in a long while.

The weather kissed us with kindness and warmth in early spring. You can't count on that in Billings, but if you don't like what you're getting in the way of weather, you can burn off fifteen minutes on some other pursuit and the outlook will change.

The inconvenient math of opposite schedules kept Lainie and me apart more than we'd have liked, but we had a standing Friday golf date. We'd move the venue around—Yegen, Pryor Creek, the rinky-dink little par-three course where she'd beat me even more soundly with the negation of my lone advantage, length off the tee. In this game, we had another way to get close to each other, not that we were having any trouble in that department. Most of the time I felt like a giddy teenager.

Lainie said she'd picked up the sport from her late husband, Delmar, a three-time state amateur champion. He taught her well. I grew accustomed to standing in sand traps, unleashing a blue blast of profanity at my ball after a failed attempt to get it onto the green, while she squatted over her own three-foot par putt, trying not to laugh aloud at me. And I'd look up at her there, pretty as could be and hell-bent on making me smile, and my frustration would just cut and run. Somehow, I'd done something right to be with her.

Rain chased us into the Pryor Creek clubhouse on an April afternoon. I sawed on a steak sandwich while Lainie did the crossword. A hand on my shoulder broke the peace.

"Hiya, Mark."

I looked up and into the face of Hugo's son. It was disquieting. I hadn't seen Raj in a couple of years, at least. The resemblance to his daddy had only blossomed with time.

"Jeez, Raj, here, sit down." I pulled out a chair, and he poured himself into it. "This is Lainie, my—" I looked at her. We had no terms. She reached out her hand, and Raj shook it.

"Your what?"

"I'm his girlfriend," Lainie said. "He keeps wanting to say wench, but we're slowly breaking him of it."

I swatted her with the newspaper. "Shush, you."

I sat back down. "You playing golf?" I asked Raj, feeling an immediate flush of foolishness at the question. My grasp of the obvious was airtight.

"Yeah, meeting some buddies."

I leaned into the table, voice a register lower. "You've heard, I guess."

Raj sat back, lacing his fingers behind his head. "Yeah. Saw it in the paper. He called me a couple of days later."

"I haven't talked to him in a while. What's he doing?"

Raj gave me a searching look. This wasn't our pattern. For years, I'd been the one who gave him information about his old man on the sly. I nodded my head toward Lainie, my distraction from my usual interests.

"Working for Feeney, I guess. It was a short conversation. You know how it is."

"I do."

Lainie cut in to save us from the conversational cliff. "What do you do, Raj?"

"I'm at Rocky Mountain College."

"What are you studying?"

"Education, but I think I'm going to try for my master's and become a PA."

"PA?" I said.

"Physician's assistant," they said in unison.

"Good school," Lainie said. "My husband was the golf coach there."

And so it began. My girlfriend—girlfriend!—and Hugo's son had found common ground, and that pretty well cut me out of the conversation. I gladly ceded the floor to them.

It was just as well. They prattled on, fast friends, veering from literature to string theory. I'd toss in occasionally, but mostly I sat back and listened. The reminders that life moves on were all around me now. Here was Raj, forever a little boy in my own sensibility but now fully a man. Here, the woman who'd prompted me to move past my insecurities and history and try again. Even so, I felt the inexorable pull toward the past. My mind, even more keenly attuned to thoughts of fathers and sons since I'd unloaded to Lainie about Von, headed off in the direction of Hugo. I wished he was here for this moment with his boy. I wished, too, that I hadn't willingly given up time with my son. There was nothing to recapture.

Excerpt from the introduction of
Hugo Hunter: My Good Life and Bad Times

When I was in high school, there was a popular song titled "Don't Know What You Got (Till It's Gone)." It was a sappy, cheesy song by a hair-metal band, and it concerned romantic love. But the sentiment applies equally to just about anything, and now, with my fighting career over, I find that it's true for me, too.

I had three chances at greatness as a boxer. You could argue that the first, in the Olympics, came through for me. I won that fight. Everybody knows it, and I was as celebrated for the injustice of my loss as I would have been for a victory. As a pro, I twice had a shot at winning a world title, and I squandered both of them. If there's anything I truly regret about my career as a professional boxer, it's not the money I lost or the fact that I can't throw a left hook the way I used to. It's that I didn't bring my best effort to those two opportunities, and as a result they are lost to me forever.

Think about this: If it's love you want, you can keep trying until you're dead and buried. If you're an actor, you can keep going to auditions until you finally get that part. If you're a writer, you can keep pounding out words until finally they're arranged in the proper order and your book gets published. All it costs you is time and effort.

But if you're a fighter—if your aim is to get in the best possible shape and go into the ring and inflict violence on another human being—you have a limited amount of time to do that while the flesh is as willing as the mind.

I will never have that chance again. I will never know what it is to raise my hands in victory while a championship belt is fitted around my waist. I will never hear the words "world champion Hugo Hunter."

I don't feel sorry for myself. I'm not owed any of that. The opportunities were there, and I did not take them.

I find it difficult to live with this sometimes.

16

Von died on May 8, 2005. Twenty days later, I kissed Marlene on the forehead—she didn't move, didn't look at me—and then carried a suitcase and my computer bag down to the end of our driveway to wait for a cab. A jet bound for Vegas stood on the tarmac at Logan Airport, and I was due to board it.

If you'd asked me two years earlier if Hugo would have a second chance at a title, I'd have laughed at your silly ass. By my estimation, that opportunity was nearly seven years in the rearview, buried under false starts, halfhearted proclamations of readiness, struggles to beat guys who weren't qualified to wash Hugo's trunks, and a monkey on his back that nearly wiped us all out.

It's a funny thing, though. For all that Hugo squandered in his prime—the endorsement deals, the headlining bouts, the money, oh, Jesus, the money—he regained his reputation, at least, when he got clean and came out punching. Frank, convinced that he finally had Hugo's attention, put him on an ambitious schedule when the calendar clicked over to 2004—fights every two or three weeks, first against a few regional tomato cans to build up his confidence, then progressively against tougher opposition until he could

regain a world ranking. After that, Frank reasoned, the opportunity would come. After two years of cooling my heels, back on the
high school beat while Hugo tried to get clean, I returned to the
traveling Hugo Hunter show. As much as people loved him when
he was this exotic-looking teenage wunderfighter, they seemed to
be even more aboard for a story that promised redemption. My
corporate overlords at the *Herald-Gleaner* could squeeze nickels
until Abe Lincoln screamed, but even they recognized this. I had
carte blanche to go where Hugo went.

The maneuverings to push Hugo back into prominence also
came with a change in weight. Age and maturity had taken Hugo
from lightweight in his amateur days to welterweight as a pro. Frank
and Squeaky set about adding yet more bulk to Hugo's frame, lift-
ing him another class higher, from 147 pounds to a threshold seven
pounds heavier. Frank reasoned that Hugo would carry his superior
speed to the next level without giving up too much in the way of
power.

After Hugo knocked out Lennie Flatbush, a rugged Irishman,
in December 2004, word came down: he'd get his shot. He'd spent
the previous year fighting eighteen times and winning every bout.
Everything looked ascendant. In February, he signed the contract:
$1.2 million for Hugo, $3 million plus a share of the pay-per-view for
Mozi Qwai, the undisputed junior middleweight champion. This was
a big opportunity for Hugo, a chance to own an entire boxing division. Hugo and Frank and Squeaky went into training. Hugo sparred
for hours against handpicked partners, trying to get a handle on the
particular challenges posed by Qwai, an evasive southpaw. I buried
my son. We met up on the charter flight to Nevada, greeted each
other like the old colleagues we were, and flew off into the morning
sky with the hope of finding something better.

Hope is a son of a bitch, anyway.

———

I can go back and watch the tapes of most of Hugo's fights, even now, knowing everything. I can sit there, break them down, watch in wonder at how he could draw another man in, goad him into throwing a punch, then evade it and invoke his own toll of leather. I can appreciate the movement, the grace, and, most of all, the work I know he put in to get there.

I've never looked at the footage of the Qwai fight. Seeing it in person was enough.

If you thumb back through the media accounts of the fight, you'll draw a different conclusion from it than anybody in Hugo's camp did. *The Ring* magazine called it the forty-seven most boring minutes of the year. *Sports Illustrated* said it made a senate subcommittee hearing look like a rock concert. And while it's true that there were no big momentum shifts, no moments of uncertainty, no junctures that required a sportswriter's favorite phrase, "gut check," what I saw was horrifying, not stultifying.

I watched Qwai beat on the kid for twelve rounds—just pound him side to side, back and forth. Lefts and rights and uppercuts and whatever else he wanted to throw. Everything landed. Hugo, proud if outmatched, threw enough punches in return to keep the referee from intervening, which just made everything worse. Afterward, Hugo's face was like a piece of fruit bloated by the sun—ears cauliflowered and swollen, eye tissue split apart, cheeks purple and green and brown from the bruising.

Frank, talking to me in the hallway after the main press conference like he always did, called attention to Hugo's carriage, because there was no way he'd acknowledge for public consumption what had really happened. "Did you see how far apart his legs were?" he said. "That's the sign of an old fighter."

"He's not even thirty," I said.

"It's a damned hard-run thirty, though. An old-man thirty. That kid is long gone."

I must have winced, thinking that I'd have given anything for Von to see thirty.

"Oh, damnit, Mark. I'm really sorry, man," he said.

———

What Frank didn't want on the record was this: It wasn't the nearly thirty years that mattered. It was the previous twenty-eight hours.

There's a superstitious art to breaking training when you're a fighter. When a crew finds something that works, it will follow that script forevermore—or until there's a slump so bad that all conventions must be challenged. Frank liked to finish training ten days before a bout and send Hugo home to sleep in his own bed, under the careful watch of Aurelia. Then, the week of the fight, the whole crew would board a chartered flight to the venue and set up camp in a hotel for all the sideshow stuff—the joint press conferences and the stare downs and the *SportsCenter* features. The night before the fight comes the weigh-in, and then an eerie quiet settles over everything until the fighters enter the ring.

The morning of the weigh-in, Frank put Hugo, stark naked, on a medical scale he'd had delivered to his room. He balanced the weights and read it off: 158 pounds.

"Shit, kid, that can't be right. Step off the thing and let's try again."

Down Hugo stepped. Frank reset the balances. Hugo climbed up again.

"One hundred fifty-eight." Frank pulled a hand through his hair. "You're four pounds over, Hugo. What the hell?"

"Must be the scale."

Frank peered at the certification. "Says it was calibrated this month." He jabbed a finger at Hugo's belt line and then turned up the volume. "Four goddamned pounds."

Hugo shrugged.

Frank looked fit to kill. And then, the import of the moment clear, he moved with alacrity to do the only thing he could.

He made Hugo choke down a couple of water pills, which set him to peeing every ten minutes or so, wringing the water out of him. What a diuretic couldn't do, a little old-fashioned sweating could. Squeaky put an out-of-order sign on the sauna door, and the crew shoved Hugo in there to wring him out.

To keep his strength up, Frank fed him every couple of hours—sliced up pieces of New York strip that Hugo was told not to swallow. He'd chew and chew, leaching out the juices and nutrients, then spit the rendered flesh into a bowl.

A little before seven that evening, we all headed downstairs to the ballroom for the weigh-in. Frank had a good poker face, but you could see he was addled. All the work of the year preceding would be undone if Hugo didn't make weight. If that happened, a few options—all equally undesirable—came to the fore. Qwai, with everything to lose, could call it off. Hugo, with little left to gain, could do the same. Or they could go forward with a nontitle, cross-weight fight for less money and in front of some seriously pissed-off fans.

"Think light," Frank told Hugo, imparting the last advice of a desperate man. "Blow all the air out of your lungs before you step up there."

Hugo did more than that. After Qwai came in at 154 on the nose, Hugo stripped off his underwear there in front of God and everybody, exhaled, then mounted the scale.

"One fifty-three point seven," went up the announcement.

Hugo lifted his arms and flexed.

Frank looked like he'd keel over.

———

We flew home a few hours after the fight, grim and silent. *SportsCenter* played back-to-back on a TV in the McCarran Airport terminal as we waited to board, looping analysis of what we'd all witnessed. The second time we heard Teddy Atlas call Hugo "a complete disappointment—here's a guy who had everything at his feet and just couldn't be bothered to scoop it up," Frank stomped through the empty seats in a rage. "Turn it off," he yelled at everyone and no one.

Once we were aloft, I tried to sleep, but like always, it wouldn't come on my terms. Memories of Von crashed into me, and for once I yearned for the controlled chaos of a high school game, some bit of constant action that would attract my attention and force me out of my own head.

Von hated sports, one of the more dramatic manifestations of the differences between us. When he was alive, I took it as a mockery, a perpetual reminder that my hopes didn't count. The day he was born, I did a jig outside the birthing room. I had a boy. My boy. I'd teach him to score a baseball game, lay down a bunt, tackle a man, throw a jab, hook a bowling ball, hit a fade in golf. Hell, I'd even teach him to kick a soccer ball, if that's what it came to.

What I got, instead, was an enigma. As Von grew, he developed interests outside mine. Marlene taught him to bake—and she was wondrous at it, so, you know, good for them, having that bonding time. He lived on Harry Potter books and *Lord of the Rings* movies and online role-playing games. Marlene told me once that maybe I ought to dip a toe into his world, that I might surprise myself and enjoy it. By the time she said that, we'd fallen into a grudging tolerance of each other, and so my answer was so flip, so cruel, that it drives me out of bed some nights to the dining room table, where I stare into a bottomless cup of coffee. "The hell you say," I said.

———

While I accounted for my losses on the flight home, Hugo balanced the ledger of his life and found it wanting. I could hear him and Frank talking in the seats in front of mine.

"No fight offers," Hugo said, as much a question as a declaration.

"I don't know where we go from here," Frank said.

A pause. "I thought, you know, after we got the title—"

"We didn't get the title," Frank said.

"Yeah, I know. What I'm saying is, I thought there'd be defenses coming, unification bouts, more money."

"All thoughts you should have had before you ate yourself out of your shot."

That one hurt, even from where I sat.

It was quiet again. Say what you want about Hugo's impulses— and that night, you could have said plenty—but he plotted a tight course where Frank was concerned. Frank demanded that kind of deference years earlier, and it stuck.

"You remember what I asked you to do?" Hugo said.

"I do."

"We need to hold off on that. I'm going to need that cash."

"No."

"What?"

"No. Absolutely not."

"Frank, it's my money."

"Yeah, it's yours. And you've told me what you want done, and I'm going to do it. You gave me power of attorney—"

"Not to ignore what I want."

"—after all that shit went down in California, you said, 'I need some backup here,' and you told me to set up an account for Raj, and goddamn it, Hugo, that's what I'm going to do."

"But don't you understand, I—"

A week or so later, when we could finally talk about it, Frank told me he heard a reverberation in my throat, an animal's growl, as I came over the back of the seat at Hugo. I cuffed him in the ear, split that cauliflower wide open, and it spilled blood and pus. Frank scrambled into the aisle and looped an arm around me, carrying me to the back of the plane. Squeaky, in the seat ahead of Hugo, tangled up his arms and held him back from going at me.

Frank had me pinned against the bulkhead, his chest rendering me motionless. He spoke in my ear, soft words only I could hear. "Not this. Not now."

"What's your problem, man?" Hugo shouted at me, wriggling against Squeaky's hold.

I was hysterical, the flash of violence having spun my emotions out of my control, my voice pitching into a scream. "It's his fucking kid, Frank. His fucking kid."

Frank drew me into an embrace, still talking to me. "Yeah. And he's mine. I need you to sit down." I lunged again, and he drove me into the bulkhead. "I'm telling you, Mark, sit down."

I couldn't dislodge Frank, and my burst of energy abandoned me as quickly as it appeared. I sat. Frank went back to his seat next to Hugo, while Squeaky dabbed his broken ear. I sat with my eyes cast toward my shoes. I wanted to cry, but I was all cried out from the preceding days, nothing left in my heart or my tear ducts that I could offer. I looked at my shoes and I waited to get home. The balance of the flight passed without incident or another word. I waited for Frank, Hugo, and Squeaky to exit, then I shuffled out behind them, hanging well back. In the empty terminal, I used a pay phone to call a cab.

Once outside, I sat on the curb and waited for my ride. Billings, below me at the foot of the Rimrocks, cast its light against the black spring sky. The wind kicked up, and I rocked against it, shivering. Across the parking lot and the road, atop the Rims, lay the places I'd gone to when I was young. It was an all-purpose venue for the invincible—a place where you could get drunk on cheap beer with your buddies and send crushed cans skittering down the sandstone walls. Or you could find a nook for solitude, you and the sky and the rattlesnakes, and contemplate the universe.

I'd met Marlene there, at a blow-off-the-steam-after-graduation kegger. She came with another guy, a mook who had no concept of the beauty she'd graced him with. I knew, I knew it completely, and she left with me. We got married, and you know how that turned out.

The cab came. I knocked the driver's queries back across the net, one by one.

"They run flights this time of night?"

I looked at the digital dash display glowing in the dark. "Private charter."

"You some kind of big deal?"

Breathe in. Breathe out. "No."

"Where'd you come from?"

"Vegas."

"Gambling?"

"In a manner of speaking, yeah."

"Win big?"

"Lost it all."

Things got quiet after that. In my driveway, I peeled off the fare plus a not-so-big-shot tip and handed it over the seat, then got out.

"Next time you'll do better," he said.

"Yeah."

———

I stepped through the front door and flipped on the hall light. The illuminated path led to the living room, where I again flipped a switch.

Couch gone. Love seat still there. One recliner gone. I looked into the dining room. Three chairs instead of six.

"Marlene?" I was calling to a ghost.

The bedrooms revealed the same King Herod touch. Our bed, still there. Von's bed, gone. White squares on yellowed walls where half the pictures came down. The chifforobe gone, and Von's upright dresser pulled into our bedroom.

I returned to the dining room and found a stack of papers with a sticky note affixed to them.

Mark—

I took $8,731 out of savings, half of what was there, in addition to the furniture and other items. I will take nothing else. It's your house—you paid for it, and I don't want it.

If you'll sign the papers at the places marked, this will be over, and I think that's best for both of us.

I will call you when I'm ready. Please don't call me.

Good luck (that sounds stupid),

Marlene

P.S. Sorry about Hugo. I know how much you love him.

17

Interstate 94 unfurled in front of Lainie and me, leading home after our golf game.

"Why don't you have bench seats?" Lainie asked.

"I don't know. Why?"

"Because I want to come over there and snog you."

I arched an eyebrow. "I could drive faster. We could be snogging on your couch in fifteen minutes."

She poked me in the ribs. "Not likely, mister. You have to go to work. And I have a rigorous day of . . . well, I'll figure something out."

"Why don't I have bench seats?" I lamented.

"Exactly." Lainie giggled. I reached for her hand.

"Raj is a nice young man," she said. "I didn't know Hugo had a son."

"Probably by design. I think Raj's mother would like as few people as possible to know that."

She squeezed my hand. "Come on now. Don't be glib. Tell me."

———

When Hugo left for Barcelona, it was with the intention to come back to Montana and complete his final year at Billings Senior. By then, it was pretty well accepted that college wasn't an immediate part of his future, that he would see what he could do as a professional fighter. Even Aurelia, who never got comfortable with his fighting despite her key role in setting it in motion, knew it. But she extracted a promise from Hugo: graduate, then turn pro.

What happened at the Olympics threw infinite complications into that plan.

Every Olympics has its prepackaged stars, the ones the national media has identified as the most compelling. In 1992, it was the "Dream Team" of NBA players on the US basketball squad, Jennifer Capriati on the tennis court, Carl Lewis on the track, Greg Louganis in the diving competitions. Hugo was the star nobody saw coming.

"It started with some of the European papers," I told Lainie. "They were struck by his looks and his story. They've got kind of a fetish about the Old West over there, and here's Hugo, this seventeen-year-old kid with the odd name, he's from Montana, he's got Indian blood and these green eyes. Plus, he's fun as hell to watch fight, or at least he was."

By the time Hugo got to the final, the whole world seemed to be watching him. And then came that awful decision by the referee, disqualifying Hugo. It's been more than twenty years now, so at some point the hope evaporates, but you just wonder if anybody will ever make that right. It's not as if the evidence is open to interpretation—even today, you can call up the video on YouTube and see for yourself. It's not fair to Hugo. Hell, it's not fair to Juan Domingo Ascencion, who will always have a figurative asterisk next to his title as an Olympic gold medalist.

"But here's the weird part," I told Lainie. "That loss, the way he lost, was the galvanizing force. If Hugo had just knocked Ascencion out and won the gold, he would have gotten a lot of attention, had some of the same opportunities and all that. But by being robbed the way he was, he got even more. It's an American thing, you know:

justice denied is justice doubly deserved. So when we came back, Frank Feeney had all these business cards spilling out of his suit—media consultants, people who wanted Hugo to pitch their products, that kind of thing. And we come off the plane and there's Aurelia, and she's saying, 'Hey, school's about to start,' and we're . . ." I held my right hand out at an upward angle, then let it droop.

"Your dicks went soft?" Lainie said.

I chortled. "Such language, young lady."

"That's what that means."

I snorted again. "Well, yeah, OK, in a manner of speaking. We were keyed up, you know. I mean, it was just a heady time. Before Hugo, I spent most nights typing box scores into the computer system. I knew I wouldn't be doing as much of that anymore. And you can imagine what kinds of things must have been going through his mind. It was hard to dial it back for nine months. Impossible, as it turned out."

I turned left into Lainie's subdivision.

"Hurry, hurry, hurry," she said. "Tell me about Raj and his mother."

I held her hand again. God, how I loved to touch her. "In due time. I'm gonna shag you first."

She pointed at the dashboard clock. Three p.m., the start of my day on the second shift, was coming up fast. "You'll be late for work."

"I don't care."

I pulled the car into her driveway. I took her hand again, and I led her inside. I had things to do, and after that, a story to finish.

———

Hugo couldn't go anywhere in Billings without being mobbed. That's the thing people don't get now, when he's an old, sad story. At seventeen years old, he was pretty much a shut-in. He'd go to school, and there, at least, the teachers and principals had some semblance of control over how much he could be hassled. Then he'd go home. Some afternoons, he'd wander over to Feeney's gym and work the heavy bag, run, shadowbox, but even that was confined to what it took to keep him semisharp. Sparring? Hell, no. With so much at stake, there was no way Frank would risk injury. And Frank was smart enough to know that he couldn't train Hugo the way you do with an active fighter—it's too arduous without some imminent reward. So Hugo went a few times and gave pep talks to the youth boxing team Squeaky was starting to build from the groundswell of interest in the sport after Hugo's Olympics, but that grew tedious, too.

I reached out and swept Lainie's yellow hair behind her ear. She lay naked on the bed, on her stomach, watching me as I shook loose the memories.

"He was bored as hell, Lains. Who wouldn't be? It's different for a kid, though. You can't just say, 'Hey, lay low till spring, and it'll be fine.' You know? Adults have more patience for that kind of thing. Hell, I've been hanging on for twenty-six years, trying to outlast Gene Trimear. But Hugo, he wanted to get going—right now. I couldn't blame him."

She clapped a hand on my stomach, sending me bolt upright.

"Ouch."

She laughed. "You're telling me everything except the story I want to hear."

I propped myself up on my elbows. "Look here, missy. I'll have you know that I am a professional storyteller."

"Windbag."

"I beg your pardon."

"You're a professional bag of wind." She scooted up and pecked me on the lips. "But you're cute, so I'll cut you a break. But tell me."

"Oh, right," I said, kissing her in return and swinging my feet to the floor. Truth is, I enjoyed her interest in Hugo. It would have been difficult to satisfy her advancing interest in me if she didn't want to know about him. Still, I started talking in double time, to tease her over her fixation and make her wait for the payoff. "So, anyway, Hugo met this girl Seyna and got her pregnant and dropped out of high school and started fighting after all, and her parents hated him, and soon enough she hated him, too, and it ended badly, and it was uncomfortable for everyone involved. The end."

I stood up.

"Wait, wait, wait," Lainie said.

"I have to shower. I'll be late for work."

———

A half hour later, Lainie rested her arms on the window frame of my car, leaned in, and kissed me good-bye. "That was a mean trick, telling the story that way."

"Hey, you didn't want to hear it the way I wanted to tell it." I gave her a wry smile, and she squinted in mock indignation.

"Is Trimear going to be mad?" she asked. I loved how, already, she referred to my boss by his last name, like I did. It was so deliciously dehumanizing.

"Of course," I said.

"Good. Will you tell me the whole story later?"

"Maybe."

"I'll be good." She unhooked two buttons on her shirt.

"You vile strumpet," I teased. I reached out a hand to cover her cleavage. "I really do have to go. I tell you what. Let's have dinner at Feeney's tomorrow. You can meet Hugo—"

"Again."

"Right. And Frank. Maybe they'll tell you the story themselves."

"Will they tell it more directly than you do?"

I dropped the car into reverse but kept the brake engaged. "Of course," I said. "They've never been paid by the word."

18

How I came to despise Gene Trimear didn't happen spontaneously or with malice aforethought. It dribbled out in indignities and violations big and small. But none was so damaging to our relationship as the time Trimear tried to take the Hugo Hunter beat away from me, soon after we returned from Barcelona and everything started to change.

I would like to think he didn't do it out of spite, but Trimear has been enough of a brazen bastard over the years that I'm not willing to foreclose any possibility. A week or so after the Olympics, I sat down with him and mapped out what I thought the upcoming year looked like in coverage terms while we waited for Hugo to finish school. I figured there would be the occasional straight news story—an endorsement deal, or something on Hugo's coaching little kids or whatever—and that we could supplement it with a longer feature story every six weeks or so where we caught readers up on Hugo's life, real behind-the-scenes stuff that they weren't going to get anywhere else. Frank, who was eager to keep Hugo in the news while waiting out the months before he could fight again, had already promised me access to him. I even had what I thought was a great title for the series: *The Fallow Season of Hugo Hunter.*

"I like the idea," Trimear had said then, "but I think we need to be more expansive in our thinking."

"Expansive?"

"This is the biggest sports story we've ever had," he said, a truth that needed no enunciation. "A lot of these guys would like a part of it. Hell, I'd like to write some of it—"

"You never write," I said.

"*Almost* never," he said. Oh, right, I forgot. He wrote memos. "But I'd like to write about this. So would some of the others."

"Well, Gene, I sort of had this plan that—"

He reached out and patted my notebook, the one I'd shown him, the one full of my scribblings about how we could do these stories. "It's a great plan. A great plan. I'm just saying that we ought to spread it around a little."

"How?"

"Same as anything. Do you cover every Billings Senior game? Hell, no. Does Landry cover every story out of Rocky Mountain College?"

"Most of them," I said.

"Most, but not all. Nobody has the market cornered on anything around here. We go with the best guy available."

I got my back up. "I *am* the best guy available."

His neck started bobbing. "Everybody in this department is qualified to cover this story," he said.

"You said the best guy."

"I know what I said." The bobbing sped up. "Look, I'm not going to discuss it further. Thanks for the good work on this. We'll see how well we can divvy it up."

It might have ended there if not for Frank and Hugo. Trimear's boss at the time, and mine as well, a wide inhabitation of flesh named Rick Westphal, was all aboard the spread-it-around plan, even thanking me for my broad-mindedness when we ran into each other in the men's room.

But Hugo's camp would have none of it.

Landry came back one day from trying to talk to Frank about Hugo's training regimen, and he told Trimear, "Son of a bitch wouldn't talk to me."

"Why?"

"Said he was too busy."

Trimear looked over at me. I bore down on my advance story for some high school football game. "You know anything about this?" he asked.

"Feeney can be pretty testy," I said.

A few days later, Landry tried catching up to Hugo after school. Same deal. He came back and told Trimear there'd be no story.

"What did the little jerk say?"

"Said he couldn't talk unless Frank said it was OK," Landry told him.

"What did you say?"

"Said I couldn't get hold of Frank."

Trimear handed his phone across the partition to me. "Call Feeney."

"Is this my story now?" I asked.

"Just call him."

I dialed the South Side gym. Squeaky answered. I asked for Frank, who picked up in short order. He must have been sitting right there.

"Hi, Frank." I cupped the receiver and mouthed, "What do I say?" to Trimear, who whispered back, "Ask him why he's been holding out on us."

"Um, Frank, my boss wants to know—that is, he sent a reporter over to talk and—"

"Put him on," Frank said.

I handed the phone to Trimear, who couldn't even choke out a hello. I watched his face turn about seventeen shades of crimson. After about twenty seconds, he said, "Got it," and he hung up. His head bobbed like that of a walking pigeon. He motioned me into the adjacent conference room. Once we were in there, he drew the curtains on the three sides that looked out on the newsroom. It was just the two of us.

"It's your story," he said, moving up on me. "I find out you're behind this or connected with it in any way, I'll can your ass. I'm not kidding."

I tamped down the urge to laugh at him. Truth was, I hadn't said a word to Frank or Hugo, so I was safe there, but I also knew that this was a tricky situation with Trimear. No matter how wrong-headed he'd been, we were in a situation where his authority was being directly contravened. An angry boss is a dangerous boss.

"Thank you, Gene," I said. "I'll make you proud."

He stepped back. "Another thing: I don't like your title for the series. *The Fallow Season of Hugo Hunter*. What does that even mean?"

"Well, he's facing this year of—"

Trimear held up his hand. "I know what *fallow* means, numb-nuts. I'm just saying, it's all la-di-da. We'll go with something simple, like *Catching Up with Hugo Hunter*."

"That's real good," I said. Placation became me.

"Damn right it is." Trimear opened the door and ushered me out. "Get to work."

Excerpt from *Hugo Hunter: My Good Life and Bad Times*

I can't be anyone's paragon of knowledge about love. What love is, how to get it, how to hold it, how to live with it, how to get over it—I could point you to a million works of art that would address the subject better than I can. I'm not going to waste your time here.

I will say this: The first time I fell in love, with Seyna, was the best. I'll say that even knowing what I know about how it unraveled. She got the best part of my heart, before it was beaten up and bruised and made to hide from love. Everything in the world was a wonder then, something to be discovered. I was seventeen years old and in love for the first time, and it seemed then that every day had dawned for me. That's the way to be in love. It doesn't last, of course. Life eventually kicks you in the teeth and makes you start dealing with it on its terms. But for that brief moment in my life when all I wanted to do was love Seyna? God, yes. I'd relive it in a second. Just to feel that way again.

I wonder sometimes if it's a cruel cosmic joke that first love comes when we're too young and too immature to handle the ups and downs. Seyna and I were just kids when we got married; I hadn't even had my first professional fight. And then, in short order, we had a kid and I had a fight career that was taking off, not to mention the attendant fame and how that pulled me in all directions, including away from her. I don't blame her for the unhappiness that resulted, nor do I blame myself for how I reacted to that unhappiness. We weren't old enough to realize what we were throwing away, or old enough to realize that if we hunkered down together, things might change.

Sometimes I wonder if I met Seyna today, without knowing her or the baggage of our past, whether we'd get along. Would there be a spark that, for us as teenagers, turned into a passionate flame? Would we even give each other a second glance? There's no way of knowing, which is what makes the questions so intriguing.

Our marriage produced a son, Raj, who makes us both proud. If he's the only thing that came of it, that's enough for anybody.

But we could have had so much more.

19

Frank Feeney managed to pack the place Saturday night. Lainie and I squeezed into a corner spot at the bar, and I flagged down Amber, Frank's niece, and asked her to bring us a couple of Slumpbusters.

Couples and single drinkers held a line against the bar. In the middle of the room, at the tables, larger groups rumbled in laughter and chatter. I dug it when Billings got this way, in that sway between winter's frozen blasts and the coming heat of summer. People were ready for some action, some fun.

Lainie leaned into me. "Loud."

"Yeah."

"So much for talking."

"Overrated anyway."

I slipped a hand to the small of her back, and then lower. I couldn't keep my mitts off her.

"Where's Hugo?" she said.

I swept the room but didn't see him. Didn't see Frank, either. I tugged at Amber's cuff when she passed.

"Where's your uncle?" I hadn't seen her in a while, long enough to not remember the last time, anyway. She was like so many other people these days—a marker against which I measured how quickly the days passed me by. The braces and scatterings of acne I remembered had ceded to a lovely young woman and, it was now obvious, the de facto manager of Feeney's.

"In the back room. Birthday party." Amber pointed the way.

"Hugo here?"

"Yeah," she said. "He's in there, too."

I took Lainie by the hand and pulled her through the obstacle course of tables toward the pub's north side. Before Frank bought it, the building had housed an insurance office. The contractor he'd hired had suggested tearing out the walls of the conference room and expanding his floor space, but Frank decided to keep it. He had this idea that he could rent it out as sort of a downsized ballroom, but Feeney's never became that kind of place, much to Frank's bemusement. Instead, his pub took on the flavor of downtown and brought in a clientele that was a little bit of everything—bankers, surgeons, ditch diggers, college students—sitting side by side and disappearing into their suds. Frank's grand ballroom sat mostly unused, except for a monthly poker game that I didn't frequent, what with my need to hold tight to my scant salary as a small-time sports reporter.

A red felt curtain, heavy and dust-laden like one you'd find in an old movie theater, separated the ballroom from the hallway. I tugged back a corner and peeked in.

"Hey, Mark Westerly."

The voice and the face startled me, the familiar in an unexpected place, like finding a zebra in your backyard. The editor of the *Herald-Gleaner*, a twenty-eight-year-old interloper I and the rest of the newsroom knew as the Diploma. "Hey, William Pennington."

Frank sat to the right of my boss. Hugo, in a too-small sport coat that I recognized from the Qwai news conference, stood off to the side of Pennington. Pennington's wife and twin six-year-old girls looked at me, smiling.

"Come on in, Mark," Pennington said.

I clenched my hand tighter around Lainie's wrist and brought her inside the curtain with me. I nodded at Frank and Hugo. "Fellas."

"Who's this?" Pennington asked.

Jesus, it's like I was a little kid with no manners. I introduced Lainie, and everybody did the "so nice to meet you" bit, with names being exchanged all over the room, until Hugo snapped his fingers, pointed at Lainie, and said, "You're the Billings Clinic lady."

"I am," she said.

Hugo feigned a couple of punches at me. "You old dog."

"Listen, we didn't mean to intrude," I said, pointing to the half-eaten birthday cake on the table. "We'll let you get back to your party."

"Nonsense," Pennington said. "Have a seat. Hugo here was just telling me about the old days. You're part of the story."

———

I am not part of the story—not the way Hugo told it that night, anyway.

After Lainie and I crashed into the room, Hugo picked up the thread. It's 1997, London, where we went for his first chance at a world title. Five long years—interminable, in their own way—had gone by since the Olympics in Barcelona, and Hugo had been chafing for nearly two of them, threatening to dump Frank if he didn't get a title shot, and they were damn near at a breaking point. But Frank had followed a plan, a precise formula that kept Hugo's workload small but steady and allowed him to grow into a fully realized man, not the flashy teenager he'd been in Spain. At twenty-two years old and with a 20-0 record, all of them knockouts, Hugo was ready. We all were. And the guy standing between him and the championship, a light-hitting Brit named Rhys Montrose, didn't have much of a chance of stopping Hugo. The week of the fight, Hugo stood as a 5–2 favorite on the Vegas boards.

"I'd had a bad year," Hugo was saying now, with everybody else paying rapt attention and with me trying to keep a poker face as I parsed his words, trying to figure out how he was going to finesse a tale I knew he didn't want to tell completely. "Got divorced. That was tough. But I'm telling you, Mr. Pennington, I was in the best shape of my life. It was my time."

As strained as things were between Frank and Hugo on that trip, I'd never felt closer to him. Seyna's leaving had left him wounded, and her taking Raj had poured salt in it. But Hugo still got visitation with his boy, and in the run-up to the London trip I'd taken to inviting them to our place for Sunday dinners so Raj and Von could play in the yard while Hugo and I talked sports and Louis L'Amour books, the only two things other than family either of us cared much about. By that time, Marlene and I had found a chilly détente in our marriage, a place where we experienced little strife and no joy, and Hugo's regular presence in our home warmed up even that, at least for a little while. She enjoyed the buffer between the relentless white noise of living with me, and he treated her with kindness, just as you'd expect from a man raised by women.

"How long were you married, Hugo?" Pennington asked.

"Four and a half years, sir. Seyna always said it felt like no less than fifteen. I guess I'm pretty hard to live with."

I squeezed Lainie's hand under the table. She might get her story yet.

"She was pretty hard to live with, too, just for the record," Frank threw in, correctly.

"I'm sorry," Pennington said. "Go on."

"Right," Hugo said. "So we're there in London—me, Frank, Mark, everybody—and we do all the press conferences and the weigh-in. There was a lot of interest, wasn't there, Mark?"

"I'd say so."

"Anyway," Hugo continued, "we get to the night before the fight, and I usually sleep like a baby, but I'm up and down, up and down, all night. I can't get to sleep. My mind, it's going, all the time. I don't know if it was the time change or what, but I'm just wired." I wondered, at that last word, if anybody else picked up the same connotation I did. It was damn near a Freudian slip.

"Long story short," Hugo said, "I'm going back to bed, trip over a rug in my hotel bathroom and try to stop my fall, and I break my arm on the marble floor. Cracked it through the skin. I'm done. No fight."

"Oh, wow," Pennington said. "You know, I remember hearing about that at the time. I was in my freshman year of high school, I think. I don't know. I'm sorry to say I wasn't paying that much attention. But I sure loved watching you in the Olympics."

Hugo bowed with magnanimity. "I appreciate that. It got a lot of attention, just because of how long I'd been waiting. I guess I was a little snakebit there. When I look back on it, that was the crucial moment. I had some troubles after that, some of them my own fault, but I think, if that fight had gone off and I'd won, things might have gone a lot differently. What do you think, Frank?"

"No doubt about it."

"Mark?"

"Well, you know, Hugo, ifs and buts." At that, Lainie pinched my leg under the table. I brushed it away. I had my reasons to be dismissive.

"So what are you doing now?" Pennington said.

Hugo shrugged. "You know, still punching. Frank's letting me talk to people here at the pub about the boxing days. I might do some coaching. Something will come up. Might even fight again."

"Really?" Pennington said. "Even after that stuff a couple of months ago?"

"Maybe. I don't know."

I looked at Frank, and Frank looked at the floor.

Pennington stood, and his family followed his lead. "Well, in any case, I wish you luck. Seems like boxing's heyday is a thing of the past. I keep hearing about this mixed martial arts stuff."

"You can't help what you love, sir," Hugo said.

"Indeed you can't." Pennington shook Hugo's hand, then came over and shook mine. "See you in the office, Mark. Don't get used to these Saturdays off." He laughed, more to let me know I'd been stung than to suggest he was kidding.

"See you, Bill."

———

We sat around awhile after that, just the four of us, while Amber stopped by a few times to keep us stocked in beer. Lainie, not knowing the terrain and the fault lines the way the rest of us did, charged right in on Hugo.

"I met your son the other day," she said.

"Oh?"

"Raj is looking good," I told Hugo. "Have you seen him lately?"

"A few months ago, I guess."

"He told us we could find you here."

Hugo nudged Frank with an elbow. "Frank's idea. I'm the entertainment, right, Frank?"

Frank fidgeted. He'd been fixing a gaze on Lainie that was a little too hard for my taste. Frank's talents didn't run toward diplomacy, and clear back to 1992, when Seyna had first shown up in Hugo's life, he'd taken a hostile view of subjects involving her. The invocation of Raj qualified.

"I'm paying your bills now. I figure you'll damn well earn it," Frank said.

Lainie jumped in again. "And he lives right here in Billings. That's a shame you don't see each other more." This time, I pinched her knee. She slapped at my hand. "Well, it is."

Frank stood up. "I gotta get back at it. Nice meeting you, miss," he said to Lainie, and he nodded at me as he exited. "Mark."

"Did I say something wrong?" Lainie asked.

"Ma'am," Hugo said, "when it comes to Frank, it's not so much what anybody says, it's just that if you say anything for long enough, he'll end up getting ticked off. I wouldn't worry about it."

I broke in. "The thing is, Hugo, we ran into Raj, and I was telling her about things with you and Seyna, only I didn't tell it in the right way—"

"He is literally the worst storyteller ever," Lainie said.

Hugo laughed. "Hey, I've been reading him since I was a kid. You don't have to tell me."

"Bunch of damn comedians in here," I said. "So, anyway, she likes your son—"

"And I'm wondering why the distance between you, when he's such a great kid," Lainie finished. "I'm nosy like that."

Damn, she was cute. How else to explain the sheer brazenness of her approach?

Hugo, perhaps taken in the same way I'd been, didn't seem fazed. "I can talk about that," he said.

Excerpt from *Hugo Hunter: My Good Life and Bad Times*

Even before I went to Barcelona, I didn't have much in common with
my peers at Billings Senior High School. I was a poor South Side
kid, someone who preferred spending time at my grammy's house to
hanging out at the mall or making out up on the Rimrocks.

After I came home from the Olympics, I enjoyed more attention,
but in an odd way, my isolation from other kids my age simply grew.

It was easy enough to figure out why adults were suddenly interested in me and my story. It was a vicarious thrill for them to see an
Olympic athlete and to hear me talk about what happened there in
Spain. Kids my age, by and large, weren't as interested. I was one of
them, and so what if I went to another country and won an Olympic
medal? That didn't make me any better than them, they reasoned.

It might surprise them to know that I agreed with them. I just
wanted to come back, put my head down, and do well enough at
school to graduate. I didn't need or want confrontations over whether
I was too full of myself. After I went to a football game that fall and
autograph seekers swamped me in the stands, the quarterback of
the team confronted me in the hallway at school and demanded
that I stay away from the team's games. I get it. He didn't want to be

overshadowed. I didn't want to overshadow him. He thought I was the adversary, but I was on his side.

That's the thing about fame. If you have it, it's almost never on your terms. You become what other people—people who don't really know you—imagine you to be. And if you don't live up to that, if you disappoint them in some way that you don't even see, you lose credibility in their eyes.

It took me a long time to learn that lesson. A long time and a lot of lost friendships and money.

20

Unless you've lived through something similar, it's hard to understand what a constrictive place Hugo's hometown became after the Olympics. The Wheaties people put him on their box of cereal in November of that year, and he couldn't even escape his own image when he tagged along with Aurelia to the grocery store. He stopped going to football games or any other extracurricular school functions because the attention he received detracted from the other kids—and in fairness to them, they had reason to be upset by that. But if you're going to give those people a pass under the auspices of kids being kids, you have to give Hugo some credit for recognizing how divisive his presence could be.

By winter, he was just gutting it out, trying to break through to graduation and into the clear.

One of Hugo's few outlets was the movie theater. He took to rolling up late, after the previews had started, and quietly buying a ticket. He'd stand at the back of the theater during the show, then walk to the front and out the door before everybody else tumbled out. Two, three times a week, that's how Hugo Hunter moved unseen among the people of Billings.

And that's also how he met Seyna Wynn.

At Feeney's, Hugo told us that it started with a wisecrack from Seyna, who was in the ticket booth when he arrived for a late showing of *The Bodyguard*. "I wonder how much I can get from *National Enquirer* for telling them that the great Hugo Hunter watches wussy movies."

"I probably fell for her right there," Hugo said. "All the girls at Billings Senior who wanted to date me, they were kissing my ass. I hated that. Seyna, she got tough with me. She had some moxie to her."

Soon enough, Hugo wasn't buying movie tickets anymore, just waiting on a bench outside for Seyna's shift to end so they could do what a goodly number of Billings kids have done for as long as a town has spilled out below the Rimrocks. You drive up to the top of the butte, overlooking the city lights below, and you find yourself a spot that belongs only to you, at least for a night, and you get busy being young and reckless.

Seyna was a smart girl—a smart-ass, yes, but well educated, too. What she lacked was some direction. A year older than Hugo and already out of high school, she worked a mindless movie theater job as a protest against her father's idea that she go east like her mother before her, pull down a degree from Smith College, and go on from there to the corporate world. The Wynns were, and remain, big movers in Billings. Samuel, her father, owns the Mercedes dealership and sits on a half-dozen boards that touch on damn near every aspect of civic life, and Barb, her mom, runs the city's preeminent public relations firm. Seyna, following the playbook of disaffected youth clear back to time's beginnings, rejected all of that. In Hugo, she found someone to tweak her old man, who was downright apoplectic at the idea of his well-groomed daughter ending up with a bastard son of the city's gritty South Side. In Seyna, Hugo found someone who valued him outside his tightly controlled sphere of school, home, and boxing.

"We were good for each other," Hugo told us, and it struck me that he probably still believed this, despite everything that followed. Even so, Seyna and Hugo weren't good for anyone else who cared about either of them.

Frank's reaction proved typically blunt: a girl could mess up everything. She could take Hugo's mind, his legs (Frank, an old-school man if there ever was one, equated sex with depletion), his hunger, his edge. "I remember Frank telling me, direct quote, 'The goddamn Beatles weren't shit after Yoko came along,'" Hugo said. "And I told him, hey, at least John was getting some trim."

"You womenfolk do kind of ruin everything good," I said, nudging Lainie.

"I'll remember that tonight when we get home," she said.

We all chuckled at that—even me, the guy who stood to lose the most—and then Hugo turned serious. "The first time Sam and I were alone, he offered me money to leave her be. Ten grand."

It sounds like something out of a bad TV movie, which I suppose is why it happens in real life. People see that kind of thing and then lean on it when their own sense of control is threatened. I'd never heard of the first offer of cash—it amazed me how, even now, new information about Hugo came to light—but I knew well the second one, a decade later, when Hugo was penniless and in recovery, and Sam Wynn dangled cash in exchange for his abdication of parental rights. I've taken a few trips around the sun and seen that people are mostly good and bad, rarely pure either way, but that move was unadulterated evil. Sam Wynn took what Hugo loved the most and needed the most and forced him to choose. When Hugo asked me what he should do, I told him that he needed money now but would want to know his boy forever. I told him that it sickened me that he even had to ask.

"I can't even—wow," Lainie said.

"I laughed at him," Hugo said. "I laughed right in his face. I had these endorsements kicking in—I didn't have the money yet, it was all in this trust for me, waiting till I graduated from high school. That was my deal with Grammy, but it was mine. I told him, 'Dude, I'm going to make a million dollars. What do I need with ten grand?'"

"Mark says you didn't finish high school." Damn, Lainie could be direct. Hugo couldn't hide the wound, and she scrambled to set it right. "Sorry. I didn't mean to make it sound so harsh."

"It's OK." Hugo was quiet now, his jovial retelling reduced to the stark realities of what actually happened. "No, I didn't finish school. Only promise to Grammy I never kept. I had my eighteenth birthday in March, and we found out Seyna was pregnant in April. She made it clear that she'd keep the baby, which is what I wanted, too, and her folks told her that she wasn't welcome if I was part of the deal." His eyes drew back their focus, as if fixated on a spot miles from where we sat.

For Lainie, and hell, for me, I finished the story. There was no way to get from there to where we were now without the last details of Hugo giving up on being a boy and facing up to being a man.

"I got a call from Frank—it had to have been the first week in April, because I remember I was wrestling with our tax return—and he said, 'We're going out to Las Vegas to sign the contract on Hugo's first fight.' So I called Trimear and told him, and that was that. I started following this guy around."

I smiled at Hugo. He spread his arms wide as if to take in the whole room. "And look where it's led us," he said in that happy, booming voice of his. And then, just like that, he grew quiet and looked at the table.

Lainie reached out and took Hugo's hand and held it, her thumb working the grooves between his knuckles.

21

Night covered us on the drive back to Lainie's place.

"His life is a tragedy," she said.

I turned left on Main and headed for the Heights. I think a lot of people might skim the surface of Hugo Hunter and end up where Lainie did. Hugo inspired bleeding hearts. From where I sat, it was hard to be definitive about cause and effect. After a while, the disappointments—those of happenstance, and those of his volition—tended to run together.

"In some ways, I suppose," I said.

"In every way. That story about her dad offering him ten thousand—"

"Lainie, he took the money."

"Wait a minute. What? He said—"

"Not the first time. Later. He was broke and in rehab, and Sam offered to pay his debts if he gave up his right to see Raj. So he did it."

I broke off what I wanted to say further about that subject in particular. It pissed me off at the time, and it sure as hell pissed me off later, when I'd have given anything to have a son I could bargain over. To talk about it would only introduce anger and confusion that

I'd spent a good number of years burying. I instead made a straight line toward generalities.

"Look, it's just hard to be in the business of feeling sorry for Hugo," I said, "because every piece of bad luck—and there's been a lot—can be paired up with an instance where he just made a dumb decision for the wrong reasons, or made the right decision at the wrong time. I think Frank has him pegged right. He's the kind of guy you'll do something for again and again, because you genuinely love him, even when you know you'll end up being disappointed eventually."

Lainie let go of my hand. "That's pretty cynical."

I reached for her, but she was having none of it. Failing placation, I defended myself. "Well, I am cynical. Mark Westerly, cynic, glad to meet you." I laughed. She didn't. "And in Hugo's case, it's well earned."

"Show your work, then."

"Lains, this is silly," I said. "I've been around the block a few times with this guy. I probably got too close to him, to tell you the truth. He's my friend. So's Frank. I probably never should have let it come to that."

"What do you mean?"

"I should have kept some distance, some detachment. I can't be objective. Not about Hugo."

She stepped into that opening. "See? That's exactly what I'm saying."

"Yeah, yeah," I interrupted, "but you're not objective, either. You look at him and you see this lost kid, or maybe you see some chance to fix him. This *kid*, Lains, is thirty-seven years old, and he is where he is mostly because of his own screwups. But you—you think you can make it better somehow."

I bit the inside of my lip. I'd said too much, too harshly. I gripped the steering wheel hard and pulled into her subdivision.

"I'm sad for you," she said.

"Oh, Jesus."

"No, really, I am. Aren't you lucky that no one holds you to the standard you have for him?"

"Oh, Jesus."

"Stop saying that."

"No, look." I pointed dead ahead, at her car sitting in her driveway. Broken glass sparkled on the concrete, put there by holes blown into the back and side windows. I reached into my glove box and pulled out a flashlight, and we exited the car for a closer look.

The front window of the house, a checkerboard of small panes, was dotted with entry holes. Lainie fumbled with her keys, trying to get the door unlocked. Once we were in, we found pellets scattered across the front-room carpet. Little lead pellets, like the ones for the air gun I'd bought my son on his eleventh birthday.

"What the hell?" I said.

Outside, it became obvious that the whole neighborhood had been hit. Lainie and I walked up and down her street, finding some of her neighbors outside in their pajamas, assessing the damage, as perplexed as we were. Others, we woke up when we saw what had happened to their cars.

The knowledge that Lainie's house wasn't alone closed the case on one pressing question—who the hell had it in for her?—while inspiring another: What kind of jackass drives around shooting out car and house windows? There are some real knuckleheads in this town.

I put in a call to the *Herald-Gleaner* and told Gregg Eddy, our nighttime cops reporter, that we'd counted in the neighborhood twenty-five car windows and about half that many houses shot up. Similar calls were coming from all over town, he said—West End, South Side, the central business district. Whoever was doing this, or the many whoevers, had gotten around that evening. "Quiet night up until about an hour ago," Gregg said. "I don't know if I can get up there, but mind if I use your numbers?"

"Sure, go ahead," I said. "Could be more damage on other streets, too. We haven't been anywhere else."

"Cops'll know. Thanks, Mark."

We sat on the front stoop, waiting for an officer to get to Lainie's place. I told her I'd stick around to talk to the police. She told me to go home.

"It's been a long night," she said. "I'd just as soon be alone."

"Look, if this is about—"

"My heart hurts a little, Mark. I just need some time to think."

"What about the mess in the house? I'll help you clean it up."

"No," she said. "It'll keep. The police might want to take a look. Go on home. OK? I'll call you."

Fear took hold of me. I regretted my nonchalance about Hugo. She could see it didn't reflect well on me. "Don't shut me out. Not about tonight."

She smiled, only I couldn't tell if it came from warmth or pity. My guts were playing Twister.

She leaned over and kissed me. "You just need a little more work," she said. "A little more time with me, and you'll be a damn good man."

22

I saw Marlene one time after she left. Her eminently fair division of the household left nothing to contest. We simply had to show up a single time in court to affirm that our wish was to not be married anymore—and in the absence of so many other wishes I'd have preferred, I didn't see how I could deny Marlene that.

She showed up early. I showed up early, too, because I knew she would, and I didn't want to disappoint her again. We had a few minutes alone, together, in the anteroom. She clutched a small blue purse on her lap. I fiddled with my tie. I hate ties. She looked beautiful— just a little eyeliner and blush, something she rarely put on for me, enough to notice without being stopped in your tracks. I liked it.

"You look nice," I said.

She choked more life out of that purse. "Thank you."

I didn't say anything else. When it was time to enter the courtroom, we went in silence until compelled to speak. We said yes—or, rather, we said no to each other—and we signed our names and we left. She took the elevator. I took the stairs. She went out the north doors and to her car, I presume. I went out the west doors, crossed two streets, and poured myself into a seat at a bar. Frank and Hugo came around to check on me, and to buy me a few. Good friends, those guys.

———

There's the occasional night—it's almost always a night—when I've had too much beer and not enough recent companionship, and I pull out the tattered memories of life with Marlene and rearrange them and almost convince myself that we had a chance. We didn't, of course. The fights between us, from the start, exceeded all reasonable concept of proportion. They never turned physical. It might have been a relief if they had. Instead, we bypassed the usual ramping up—minor disagreement yields to raised voices yields to bitter recrimination—and proceeded directly to the ugliest, most damaging things we could say to each other. At times, it felt like a crazy-making game to me. Could I take away her will to battle me, then save everything by reversing course and telling her I loved her? Could I say I was sorry and make it stick? Whose feelings would be trampled first? Who would come home in the nastier mood and inflict it on the other? It was such an ugly brand of brinkmanship we played that each of us, on the eve of the wedding we had planned just so we could double down on our dysfunction, faced the concern of our respective best friends—but we insisted that yes, we wanted this marriage. We would be better. We would do better. That was the lie we told ourselves, and the lie we believed for a long time.

That lie carried us, man. It carried us through my early years at the *Herald-Gleaner*, when we'd bridge the last week of a month with ramen noodles and found pennies, even as we took up battlements in our ceaseless fights about how thin our margins were. It carried us through the belief that a child would somehow bond us in all the ways we couldn't manage on our own. When the child came and our division only grew, we lied to ourselves and said we just had to figure out how to make it work now that everything had changed. And we believed it anew.

We couldn't be saved. That's the truth I came back to every time I thought about those years, which was far too often. I could rearrange the order of things, fixate on small moments of kindness and laughter and read something bigger into them, but the pathway just wasn't there. I tried to tell myself that it was no one's fault, that no one had to take the blame for it, but that was another lie.

Von changed our marriage. That seems a self-evident point. Two plus one equals three, and the mathematics alone shift the variables. What I mean is that Von made it better, at least for Marlene. He made it tolerable for her, because he was the realization of the only dream she ever asserted for herself in our marriage. Thus, he made our existence together tolerable for me, too, because I was all about the path of least resistance. Where before I hung on out of some warped sense of testing my endurance, as if it would have been some mortal failure to give in and say to Marlene, "You know what, this isn't working for us," once Von came burping into our lives I stayed in because it required less effort than being honest with myself, or with her, or with our boy.

Had Von lived, had he come home that night he was so angry with me and I with him, had he snubbed me on the way to his room and kissed his mother and seen another sunrise, Marlene and I might be married still, living alone in the same bed and the same rooms.

I still have two pictures of us. One we took in early 1996, when Von was three years old. He sits between us, smiling for the camera with an eagerness he probably never showed again, and Marlene and I sit there, close enough to touch, and we present our son to the world. We're wearing sweaters, all three of us, but we look good— we're not the garish families you see on the comedy websites, the ones with costumed dogs and pleather Santa suits. We match our son's enthusiasm, and if someone were to draw an inference from that photograph, it would be of a happy, contented, growing family. We were none of those things, which just goes to show that you can never assume knowledge of what goes on in someone else's house on the basis of how things appear from the outside.

The other picture is just me and Marlene, 1985, the only one of our engagement photos that we had blown up so we could put it on the wall. She left it behind, so either she wanted me to have it or she couldn't bear to keep it. I hung it in Von's room so I wouldn't have to see it, wouldn't have to think about how different and promising the world looked to us back then. Everything that Von left behind went with Marlene. Where he played and slept became just a room, filled with boxes and items that didn't fit in a house where I lived alone.

That night, after I left Lainie at her place, the dream woke me up, and I could still catch the tendrils of it—Von and Hugo, wrestling on our living room floor, with me sitting in the recliner, frowning at them over my newspaper and Marlene in the kitchen, watching them in wonder, every bit of it playing in my head just as it actually happened. I shuffled out to the bathroom and put some water on my face, setting back the haze and emerging more in the moment. I walked down the hall and opened the door to Von's room, and I flicked on the light. The bulb, in the socket for years and never engaged for most of them, flickered and went dark. I propped open the door and let the illumination from the hallway spill into the room, and then I stood before the much younger Marlene and me. In the half-light, I could make out only the outlines of our forms. Our teeth, though, couldn't hide in the shadows. Clear as day, I could see the two upturned smiles, beaming and white and youthful. I tried to remember the day of the photo shoot, where we'd gone, the time of year, but the details had ridden out long ago. It was like digging through the morgue at work and reading a forgotten story I'd written years before and being surprised by how active and fresh it seemed. Like it had happened to someone else.

It wasn't really Marlene I was thinking of. It wasn't me, either, at least not the version of me that was nearly thirty years gone.

I thought only of Lainie and how time was drawing short. Eventually, and probably soon, she would figure me for the fraud I was.

Excerpt from *Hugo Hunter: My Good Life and Bad Times*

Frank Feeney used to tell me that I had to work up a reason to hate my opponents, if only for the minutes we would spend together in the ring. Hate, he said, would focus me on the task at hand—namely, inflicting more violence on my rival than he could inflict on me.

I never hated anyone. Not even Juan Domingo Ascencion, who has a gold medal that belongs to me.

What I did, instead, was rely on a competitiveness that borders on maniacal. In a boxing match, there can be only one winner. It had to be me. If there were some reward beyond the victory—say, a gold medal—that had to belong to me. I'm this way with anything, as it turns out. Checkers, Yahtzee, Ping-Pong, you name it. If there's victory at stake, if one person is going to win and one is going to lose, I want to be the winner. No, wait, scratch that. I don't *want* to be the winner. I *have* to be the winner. When you play-wrestle with a child, you're supposed to let the kid win. I never did. I'm that kind of competitor. Is it healthy? Probably not. Can I do anything to change it? Probably not.

The only two times that drive to win failed me, as it turned out, occurred when I was set to fight for world championships. Both times, I was involved with something beyond the fight game, a mon-key on my back. Both times, I was a failure in the eyes of the sporting world.

Try living with that.

23

The pellet-gun vandals stayed busy for the next two nights. Reports of shot-out car and house windows came in from the far West End, Blue Creek, Emerald Hills, the Heights—every neighborhood and enclave in Billings, it seemed. Monday morning, I trundled out to the driveway in my robe to fetch the morning paper and saw that my neighbor Bob Dilfer's car had been relieved of its driver's-side windows. That sent me on a frantic reconnoiter around my own property, which turned up clean, thank God. I went back inside without saying anything to Bob. It might make me small and petty, but I couldn't face Dilfer's yammering on about his damned Prius that early in the morning.

In the *Herald-Gleaner*, both in the daily dinosaur of a print product and the Wild West of our online forums, the nightly bursts of thuggery were being cast as a Most Alarming Trend. The mayor and the police chief held grim-faced news conferences to assure the citizenry that Everything Possible Was Being Done. The Diploma commissioned a web chat with Chief Roscoe Hamer, and the website crashed under the weight of folks crowding in to express their fear that our fair burg was going to hell. About the only people who seemed happy were the owners of the glass repair places, which were enjoying a windfall to the tune of nearly $250,000.

———

Lainie called me twice Sunday, and I ducked her both times. I wasn't ready to talk, and I wasn't ready to talk about why I wasn't ready to talk. I like my life in compartments—work here, home here, social life there, with the pathways between them known only to me. Lainie was breaking down that discipline, crossing boundaries, learning things that I wasn't ready to tell her, things I might never be ready to tell her. I'd spent more than twenty years finding a place of peace, or at least bearable unease, on the subject of Hugo, and she was already challenging my position there. What would she do or say when she found out more? I wasn't sure I wanted to know the answer.

Monday night, I was back on the desk at the *Herald-Gleaner*, and she called me again. Nowhere to hide.

"Take me to lunch tomorrow?" she asked.

"I can do that."

"I missed you yesterday."

"Yeah, busy."

"OK. Noon then? At the clinic?"

"That'll be fine."

We said our good-byes, and I hung up. I sat staring at the phone, wanting a do-over on the whole exchange. The Diploma came barreling out of his office, relieving me of that thought.

"Damn, Mark, I need you to roll on this," he said. "Miles and Eighth. Cops think they have the vandals."

I looked around the office. Just the copy editors, me, and Pennington. Everybody else was at dinner, I guess. "Where's Eddy?" I asked.

"City council meeting. Get going. Cops are there now. Grubbs is heading over to shoot it."

It had been years since I did a cop beat, clear back to my intern days at the *Herald-Gleaner*, before Trimear brought me aboard full-time with the sports staff and long before he figured out that he didn't like me all that much. I remembered now how much I craved the adrenaline rush of a spontaneous, unpredictable story. Put back on the job by the Diploma, I fractured a fair number of traffic laws whipping my Malibu through downtown and up into the asscrack of midtown Billings.

Near the intersection of Miles and Eighth, the strobes crossed my face, bathing the inside of my car in blue. I jammed it into an empty spot on the street and tumbled out to stand among the ten or twelve gawkers who had congregated on the corner.

In the middle of the street, a gray sedan sat at an angle, the left front tire blown out and the front end splattered with bullet holes. The cops had three men face down in the nearest yard, and across from them, two other officers talked with an older guy, maybe fifty-five or sixty, in a pair of basketball shorts and a sleeveless T-shirt. He gesticulated with a fair amount of fervor. The cops nodded as they followed the line of his hands.

My cell phone buzzed, a text from the Diploma: *TV going live. What's up?*

Finding out, I typed and sent.

Tweet as soon as u can.

I nudged the guy next to me and nodded at the scene. "What happened?"

"Old guy came out shooting, I guess."

I crossed the street. One of the cops talking to the older guy peeled off and walked toward me, hand up. I showed him my work badge.

"What happened?" I asked.

"Still sorting it out, but looks like those guys over there"—he motioned at the scene across the street—"picked the wrong house to hit."

"How so?"

He started laughing and then, perhaps realizing the impropriety, walked it back to a broad smile. "Damnedest thing. So those guys roll up and start shooting out windows in this guy's garage. Problem is, he's in there. Bigger problem is, he's got an AR15—"

"I'm sorry, an AR . . ."

"Big freaking gun. Semiautomatic. The guy was in there cleaning and loading it. He'd just finished when Team Loser over there started in. So he hits the garage door opener, comes striding out, and starts blasting away."

"Jesus."

The cop laughed. "Yeah. It could have been a bad scene. He wasn't aiming to kill, just neutralize. I imagine those boys are going to need a change of underwear."

"Will he be charged?"

"Not our department. I doubt it, though. He's legal to own the gun, no record, he was defending his property. Plus, if these guys are who we think they are, what jury would convict him?"

I thanked the officer and hung back a bit to get Pennington's tweet posted. I pictured the twitterpating back at the office over what passes for journalism these days: "Homeowner shoots at suspected pellet-gun vandals." I flagged down Larry Grubbs, who was snapping pictures on the other side of the street, and filled him in. We agreed that the gold standard would be getting Dirty Harry Homeowner to talk with us. We would have to wait for the cops to finish with him.

While Larry uploaded raw video to the office, I crossed over to get a better look at the perps. One by one, the arresting officers lifted the guys to their feet and moved them toward the patrol cruisers. I braced myself for recognition. They were all young men, muscular, the kind of knuckleheads with whom I was likely to be familiar.

The first two didn't register with me, but the third one sure did: Cody Schronert, last seen beating on Hugo Hunter. Such a promising young lad. He looked at me and offered a smirk. I just shook my head.

———

The Diploma made sure he splashed my story six columns wide across the front page Tuesday morning. The circulation manager told us later that he'd had to refill the boxes on several Billings street corners and at gas stations around town. Online, people went nuts for the story. Three days later, it remained our most clicked- and commented-on piece, an honor generally reserved for when some country cracker writes a letter to the editor bashing Mooslims and asserting his rights granted by a document he's never actually read.

Miles Avenue Homeowner Stands His Ground Against Vandals

By MARK WESTERLY
Herald-Gleaner Staff

Three Billings men with a pellet gun and some bad intentions picked the wrong house to vandalize Monday night.

Artie Bispuppo, 57, of 801 Miles Ave., was in his garage at about 7 p.m. when the small panes of glass on the garage doors started to shatter. As it turned out, Bispuppo had been cleaning and loading an AR15 semiautomatic—"My baby," he called it—in response to a wave of property vandalism that has gripped the city in recent days.

"I had a pretty golldang good idea who was doing it," said Bispuppo, who described himself as a "freedom-loving, Second-Amendment-saving son of a gun" and a longtime Billings resident. "I was going to be ready if they came here. Kind of hoped they might, actually. It worked out, didn't it?"

What happened next, as described by Billings Police, surely gave the vandals the shock of their young lives. Bispuppo triggered the automatic garage door opener and came striding out to his driveway, where he strafed the car carrying the three men with 15 bullets that took out the front tire and left a trail of holes on the car's front end. When the car stopped, Bispuppo turned the gun on the three men and held them there while police responded to a neighbor's phone call.

Arrested at the scene were Michael Ray Russo, 19; Andrew William Marchant, 21; and Cody Reese Schronert, 21. Schronert, in the news recently for defeating Olympic silver medalist Hugo Hunter in a boxing match, is the son of well-known Billings personal-injury lawyer Case "the Ace" Schronert. Reached by phone at home, the elder Schronert said he had no comment.

So far, the three men have been charged with willful destruction of property in the Miles Avenue case, but Sgt. Ben Blakeley said more charges are likely to follow in more than 150 cases of auto and home windows that have been shot out in Billings in the past few days.

While Blakeley said police don't relish the idea of citizens taking the steps that Bispuppo took Monday night, the Billings man isn't likely to face charges. A state law known as the "castle doctrine" holds that Bispuppo was merely defending his home, Blakeley said.

For his part, Bispuppo said he had mixed feelings about what happened on Miles Avenue on Monday. On one hand, he said, actually using the AR15 left him "a bit stressed out." But he also called on other "responsible, God-loving, criminal-hating" people to take an active role in defending their homes and lives.

"We outnumber the punks," he said. "But the punks seem to win. Not this time, bubba. Not on my street."

———

At lunch, Lainie reached over and took my hand. "I read your story this morning."

"Thanks," I said. "I'm glad it's over. What did the insurance people say?"

"Small deductible. No big deal. Car glass has been replaced, and they'll be out to do the house windows Friday. I went ahead and gave the police the figures. They said it would be helpful with the prosecution."

"Little assholes."

"Yeah."

I watched Lainie eat while I pushed some macaroni salad around my plate.

"I'm sorry about the other night," I said. "I'm sorry I didn't call."

She looked up at me. "No, I'm sorry. I got a little emotional about him, and the instinct for protection kind of kicked in. You know?"

"Yeah." I squeezed her hand and plunged in. "It's just that... there's a lot of stuff about that subject. A lot of stuff I haven't said. A lot of stuff I'm not sure I can say. I want to tell you, but I'm afraid of what you'll think of me if I do."

"About Hugo?" she said.

"Yeah, about Hugo. About me."

Lainie let go of my hand, laced her fingers and ground them together for a few seconds, and then she reached for me again.

"When I pictured saying this to you, this isn't where I thought it would be." She laughed, a little chuckle that dribbled off. "I'm going to say this thing, it's very hard for me, and then you can decide what you want to do."

I nodded.

"I love you. OK? I didn't think I would again, not after Delmar, and I didn't want to, but I do."

"Lainie, I—"

"Wait. Let me finish. And because I love you, there isn't anything you can say to me about what you've done before I met you that will change that. OK? If it's time you need, time I have. If it's secrets and you can't part with them, that's something else. I'm not saying I won't love you. But secrets make everything harder. Everything. You understand what I'm saying?"

"Yes," I said, the briefest acknowledgment I could muster so I could get to what I really wanted to say, what I'd been dying to say before she said it first. "I love you, too, Lains."

"Good." She smiled. The whole damn world lit up. "That's the right thing to say."

"I want to tell you," I said. "I think I'll need to get drunk to do it."

"Beer?" she said.

"Tequila. Lots and lots of tequila."

"I'll be waiting up for you tonight. First bottle's on me."

———

I drove northward toward home, up the face of the Rimrocks to the little parking lot below the airport. Summer was pushing toward us now, dislodging spring. I walked down along the concrete trail and took a seat on a bench overlooking town. Behind me, joggers, bicyclists, and dog walkers plied the opportunities of a warm, clear day.

I traced my life through the bramble of streets and neighborhoods below me. There, in the central part of town, where Lewis Avenue meets Fifteenth Street, sat the house I grew up in. I slid my eyes left, moving east, to the oil refinery where my father, a pipe fitter, worked from 1960, three years before I came along, to 1989. We never connected much. I was bookish, like my mother, and Dad never saw the work value in what I did, chronicling others' lives instead of living my own, by his estimation. My memories are buffeted by the knowledge of how difficult it was for us to have a decent conversation. Some people say time does something about that, downsizes recall into something easier to take. I haven't found that to be true where Dad is concerned. I'd have liked to talk to him about Von. Maybe I could have understood him a little better when my own son seemed so unlike me, when our conversations were so eerily reminiscent of what I'd gone through with my own father, but Dad was gone by early 1991.

Closer to me, almost close enough to touch it seemed, lay Montana State University Billings—Eastern Montana College when I went there. I found the big brick building, dead center in my view, and I went three windows up and four over. My first dorm room. The roommate I'd been saddled with and despised, an awkward kid from Geraldine, was now the majority leader of the state senate. How the hell did that happen?

Now I telescoped in to the South Side. I found South Park, the big patch of grass in Billings's oldest, poorest neighborhood, an oasis among the iron-barred gas station windows and halfway houses and tenements. The trees obscured my view of Hugo's house on the southeast corner of the park, Aurelia's house before that. Well tended, at least as long as Aurelia was here, although not so much these days, when neglect pervaded so much of our lives.

The first time I went there, it was to see a boy. Now he was a man. A grown-ass man, Hugo liked to say. So much had changed. So little, too. Who would have thought twenty years ago that Hugo and I would both still be here, still punching?

Excerpt from *Hugo Hunter: My Good Life and Bad Times*

If there's a sports adjective I despise, it's *snakebit*.

Unfortunately, it's one often applied to me.

Here's the problem with it: *Snakebit* suggests that factors beyond your control have conspired to defeat you. That you were motoring along, minding your own business, doing everything right, and some variable injected itself into your contest and you lost because of that.

What a bunch of nonsense.

Certainly, you could argue that the Olympic final qualified for such a description. I had Juan Domingo Ascencion beaten dead to rights, knocked out, and I did so legally. The gold medal that was rightfully mine went to him because of corruption. That's an outside variable, to be sure.

But still, I could have knocked him out earlier, when the end of the round wasn't so imminent. I could have played it safe, not pressed, and taken a decision that was surely mine. There were things I could have done.

Mostly, I object to *snakebit* because no athlete wants to think he doesn't have control of everything in the field of play or, in my case, in the squared circle. To admit that you're powerless against your circumstances goes against everything you've worked for and the considerable sense of self required to get in there and trade punches with another man.

Interestingly enough, submitting to a higher power and admitting my weaknesses is the only way to stay even in a fight against the toughest opponent I've ever known.

It's a continual chore to reconcile those contradictions.

24

Hugo had one thing right in that mess of lies he told William Pennington at Feeney's: if he'd come to a different end against Rhys Montrose in London, the landscape of his life would look different today. I've seen enough in my time to not be too confident about whether it would be better or worse—worse, perhaps, given how self-destructive Hugo could be even without the money and fame that would have come with a world title—but I'm all in on different.

The hell of it is that Hugo had never been better or sharper. Squeaky and Frank took him to the cabin on Flathead Lake in the summer of 1997 and set to carving out the best version of Hugo. He spent July through September up there, chopping wood, running on mountain trails, sparring. By the time camp broke, he stood at his mandated 147 pounds, but the distribution was different—hips narrowed, shoulders broadened, more power rippling through the core of him. If there's any such thing as an indestructible boxer, we had it that summer in Hugo. He was a piece of iron, impossible to bend. Frank broke camp a day earlier than planned, partly to account for the cross-Atlantic trip that awaited, and partly because, in his last sparring session, Hugo was untouchable. That last word is a sports writing crutch, but in this case, I mean it literally: Dave Runson, a good fighter in his own right, a guy who got into the lower half of the welterweight rankings, could not land a punch on Hugo. All summer, he'd been mimicking Montrose—the upright, move-ahead style, the sticking left jab, the overhand right that was the Brit's only power punch. By summer's end, Hugo had him locked down. There'd be the jab—stick, stick, stick, stick, finding only Hugo's gloves—and then the right would come, and Hugo would already be gone, slipping to the side and digging hooks to Runson's body.

When we boarded the plane in Billings, bound for Minneapolis and then JFK and, finally, Heathrow, I'd begun to see the wisdom in Frank's grow-him-slowly approach to Hugo's career. At twenty-two, Hugo was a full-on man and a full-on wrecking machine, and Frank probably figured that the extra helping of rage Hugo felt at having to wait so long would only help matters. I almost felt sorry for Montrose, who had no idea what was coming for him.

————

We touched down in London on October 5, seven days before the fight, to give Hugo a chance to acclimate to the difference in time and place, and to allow for the promotional responsibilities he faced. That was the part Frank barely tolerated—the endless on-camera interviews and pushy fans and set pieces engineered by the fight promoters—but Hugo, as always, lapped it up. He wasn't quite the curiosity he'd been the last time he was in Europe, no longer the soft-featured kid with the killer name and the dashing ring style. The name still stuck, of course, and the manner inside the ropes had grown even more devastating, but hardness had set into the face. Hugo looked like a guy you wouldn't want to tangle with, right up until he started talking, and then you belonged to him. Flames sprung up behind his eyes, his mouth lifted at the corners, and he'd turn so engaging, regardless of subject, that a room full of journalists would feel as though he were speaking only to each one of them.

Our flight landed in the early morning hours, but we still faced a scrum of cameras as we moved out of customs. Hugo signed a few autographs while Squeaky minded crowd control.

We at last fell out into the street. Rainwater collected in great puddles on the asphalt, a harbinger. It rained every day we were there, a persistence of water that cast a gloomy pall over London day and night, filling our senses. The limo driver, a puff pastry of a man, greeted us and loaded the bags into a bottomless trunk.

———

I hadn't slept much on the flights. I was a white-knuckle flyer, truth be told—too pragmatic not to do it and too damned scared to relax—and had stayed up for long stretches, reading the Richard Hugo book of poetry that Hugo had slipped me before we took off in Billings. I'd been so moved by the gesture, and it's hard to talk about the why of that even now. I felt as though Hugo—our Hugo—was sharing with me some intrinsic part of him, this poet who'd unknowingly given him a name, the mother many years dead who had looked into his eyes and seen a world in verse.

Somewhere over the Atlantic, I read "Farmer, Dying," and I cried there in my seat, Squeaky asleep next to me, Frank and Hugo in slumber in the row ahead.

It's hard to remember now exactly why it caught me the way it did and leveled me right there in business class. I thought of my old man, who left the farm in Carbon County to come to Billings—a small town by the world's reckoning, a metropolis to any rural Montanan. He never talked much about it, but the lines I read between had been visible enough. Dad was the only son of his own parents, and his leaving had sealed the deal. The farm passed on when they did. Another light went out.

It wasn't just the literal parallels. A sense of leaving pervaded that trip. I'd walked out of my own house with an admonition to Von to mind his mother if he couldn't find the respect to listen to me, another hectoring of the boy that lives on in my head, ready to taunt me at random. Hugo and Seyna were divorced—her father had pushed for annulment, a bridge too far by Hugo's estimation, because you can't annul a kid—but still squabbled over little Raj. Even Squeaky had pulled himself away from a new wife and a house he was building in the hills east of town. The house that Hugo built.

We'd all calibrated our own lives to this moment for Hugo, and we all expected transcendence. In retrospect, that was probably unfair, both the expectation and how we came to it. Hugo was just a man, susceptible to the fall like anybody else. And what right did we have to claim intrusion on our own lives when we so readily attached ourselves to his? Nobody made us do that. We went along willingly. Eagerly.

———

Wembley Stadium—the old beast, not the new one that stands in London now—hulked on the horizon, dark and menacing. As we drew closer, the banners, fifty feet high at least, revealed themselves. Hugo, right hand cocked, staring down at us, green eyes boring in. Montrose, standing at an angle, proper and prim. They hung off the top of the stadium and unfurled toward the ground.

The driver brought down the partition. "Impressive, aren't they?"

Hugo leaned in. "What do you think of Montrose?"

"He's a good bloke."

"But as a fighter?"

"He's a good bloke."

Hugo laughed and fell back into his seat. "Diplomatic," he said.

The driver tossed a quick look back at us and then put his attention on the road. Our hotel loomed. "If you don't mind my saying so, sir, we're all keen on Rhys."

"As you should be," Hugo said.

"It's just that a boxing champion is special to us. We don't get many of them."

I looked at Hugo. He smiled like a cat.

"I understand that," he said. "I'm still gonna kick his ass."

It was unusual talk for Hugo. Sure, he could trash talk with anybody—taunting Juan Domingo in Spanish perhaps the most prominent example—but he tended not to carry it out in public forums in such a blunt way. He knew the game. He'd talk up his chances to the press, go chin to chin with an opponent at a weigh-in, that sort of thing. But he wasn't braggadocious, and he didn't set out to embarrass anybody anywhere but in the ring.

The London trip was different. The gauntlet of cameras at the airport, the limo driver, people on the street who approached him—Hugo told them all, in indelicate terms, that he was there to lay a whupping on Rhys Montrose. It did not go over well with the stiff-upper-lip British. The *Guardian* called him an ugly American, and an unoriginal one at that, saying John McEnroe twenty years earlier had brought a better brand of brattiness to these shores. Montrose, a lower-middle-class kid from Stoke Newington who'd made up for a lack of artistry with superior craftsmanship, opted against matching Hugo's rhetoric. "He can say what he wants, but I'm the one with the belt." It played well with the folks at home, but it didn't exactly set *SportsCenter* afire.

The night of the weigh-in, after Hugo had come in at 147 pounds and then invited Montrose to go at it right there for free, I sat on a pub stool with Frank and asked what in the blue blazes was going on with his guy.

"I figure it's nerves," he said, staring into his half-empty glass.

I studied Frank's face. His jaw throbbed from the grinding of his teeth. Nerves, my ass.

"What's he got to be scared of? This guy's a cream puff."

"I didn't say scared," Frank said, pouncing on my words like a dog attacking a pork chop. "That's your word, not mine. I said nerves."

"Come on, Frank."

He drained the last of his beer. "It's nerves. It's that simple. He's waited a long time for this—too long, he says—and he's overcompensating. Once he gets in there tomorrow night and works up a sweat, he'll be fine. I gotta go."

———

The hotel room phone woke me just after four in the morning on fight day. I'd been cascading through a pleasant dream—one long lost to me now—and the ringing sent me headlong into the black-gray of awakening.

I picked up, my heart kicking in from fear. Had something happened back home?

"Yes?"

"Mark."

Hugo.

"What the hell?" I said.

"You gotta come get me."

I tried to sweep away the remnants of sleep still sandbagging me. "What? Where are you?" Seven hours earlier, I'd been there for bed check. I'd watched him and Frank say their goodnights as Hugo sat down to a New York strip steak. The weigh-in attained, he was now adding back protein and carbs to fortify himself for the battle ahead.

"I have no fucking idea," Hugo said. "Somewhere in East London, I think. We crossed the river. There's all these flowers around."

"Flowers?"

"Fucking plants, man. Flowers. Petals and shit. All these people setting up booths and flowers."

"Where are you calling from?"

"A phone booth."

"Step out and ask somebody where you are. Jesus, Hugo, why aren't you upstairs in bed?"

A primal scream came back at me. "I'm standing here staring at my picture in the newspaper. I am not fucking getting out of this phone booth and talking to anybody. You come get me right fucking now. East London. Shitload of flowers. Figure it out, Mark."

"I'll get Frank."

"No! No. Do not get Frank. You come alone. Come get me, please." I swear to God, Hugo started crying right there on the phone. "Come get me."

"OK. Hang tight. I'll find you."

The connection went dead. I got my ass moving.

———

The concierge called a cab for me, and when I told the driver that my friend was somewhere in East London with a lot of flowers, he said, "Columbia Road," as if it were the simplest thing in the world, like telling me the time and the temperature.

Even in the dark and the rain, with few other cars on the road, the drive took nearly fifteen minutes. I stared out the window at the passing buildings and watched the first hint of daylight scratch at the sky. The driver minded his business, and for that I was thankful. He no doubt figured that an early, frantic ride to a place I was only guessing at didn't portend anything good.

The driver made a turn and the headlights flashed on a phone booth. "That your friend?" he said. Hugo was unmistakable. He wore the same button-front shirt and slacks he'd had on at the final press conference for the fight. He cowered as the lights fell on him.

"Wait here," I told the driver, and I scrambled out of the car and over to the phone booth.

I took off my jacket and gave it to Hugo. "Put this over your head."

I led him to the car, and we climbed in.

"Everything all right?" the driver asked.

"Yeah, fine," I said. "He got into a little scrap."

"Need a hospital?"

"No, just take us back."

The cabbie backed up. As he turned and looked through the rear window at his progress, I watched the Columbia Road vendors and their incessant motion, scurrying about as their stands took shape. Flowers of every color and size you can imagine, and a few you can't, filled in the open spaces and cast shadows like monsters on the buildings that lined the street, lit up by the headlights.

And then, just like that, we turned and darkness fell on Columbia Road again.

It was as if we'd never been there.

_____

It all spilled out upstairs, in Hugo's room, the whole sordid mess.

"I couldn't sleep," he said. "I went for a walk." The walk, he said, led to a pub that led to a table full of young Englishmen, which led to a late-night car ride, which led to a dank basement on Columbia Road.

"And you've been doing cocaine," I said.

"No." The single word was meek, halfhearted.

"The ring around your nostril says yes."

A thumb and forefinger flew to his nose, grasping it. He rushed into the bathroom. I badly wanted to follow and start in on him, but I stood my ground.

"Shit," he said from the bathroom. Running hot water blew whispers of steam into the room. "OK, this is OK, this is going to be OK."

"Hugo—"

"If I can just get some sleep, I'll be all right. This is nothing."

"What about the drug test?" I called in to him.

"Already had it. Passed. I'm good."

I walked to the entryway. Hugo had his shirt off and his face lathered. He scrubbed at it with his hands.

"Jesus, man, don't you read your own contracts?"

A sideways glance found me in the mirror. "What?"

"Drug tests before and after, Hugo. You're screwed. You are so unbelievably screwed. Even if you win, you're gonna lose. Cocaine stays in your system, what, three days? Four? It doesn't matter. You're screwed."

I don't think anyone ever hit him with a heavier punch. Hugo shut off the water. He took a towel and cleared the soapy residue from his face. He walked toward me, and I vacated the doorway so he could pass. At the end of the bed, he dropped anchor and sat, silent.

I approached on tentative feet. "Let me go get Frank," I said, soft and low. "Maybe he can figure a way out of this."

"No."

"Hugo—"

"No."

"He's gotta know."

"He can never know about this."

I stood there, tried to think of an angle I could take that would make Hugo see what he needed to see. He stood and undressed. One by one, the buttons came undone on his shirt, and he tossed it to the floor. He shimmied out of his slacks and piled them up, too. Socks came off and were balled up. He went to the dresser, opened a drawer, and removed a pair of gym shorts and a T-shirt. He climbed into those.

Now he walked past me, toward the bathroom.

"Listen—" I said. He didn't stop.

I don't know how to explain the next part. Something deep and compulsive, something I couldn't ignore, moved me toward the bathroom. Fear. Foreboding. Whatever you want to call it, I felt as though I had to be there.

Hugo sat on his knees on the marble floor. A towel encased his right arm, held at an acute angle above his head. In his mouth was a balled-up washcloth.

"No!"

Hugo closed his eyes and crashed his hand against the floor like a pile driver. The snap of the bone was sickening, and his neck and face and eyes bulged red, the washcloth holding his scream in. He toppled over onto the floor.

I ran to him and fell to my knees at his side. I cradled his head and removed the washcloth from his mouth. Tears ran from his eyes to my lap in broken-dam rivulets. His right arm twisted beneath him, still wrapped in the towel, at a grotesque angle.

"Are you stupid?" I said.

Hugo's words came in gasps. "Help me up."

I climbed to my feet and lifted him with me, but I nearly went down again when I saw the arm, now freed from the towel. A bone, gray-yellow, poked from the flesh. The towel lay at our feet, soaked with blood.

"Take me to the bed," Hugo said.

I maneuvered him as best I could, each movement putting stress on his injury. He gritted his teeth to hold back a scream.

"Hand me the phone."

I complied, setting the receiver against his shoulder while he trapped it with his head. I didn't want to, but my eyes kept returning to the jutted bone that pierced his skin. "Jesus, Hugo."

Hugo looked up at me, fingers from his good hand reaching for the phone's buttons. "You better get out of here now."

25

Lainie stood at the stove and beat eggs into submission. I sat across from her in Delmar's terry cloth robe, still a bit uncomfortable in it even though she had insisted that it was fine, her pragmatic assertion being that Delmar, two years dead of cancer, wouldn't need it anymore. Modesty won out over discomfort, I suppose. My only other choice was to sit there naked. I'm not into crimes against humanity.

"So Frank never found out?" she said.

"No."

I'd filled her in on the aftermath of Hugo's horrifying act, about going back to my room, unable to breathe, trying to pretend like I had no idea what was happening three floors up, what Frank was discovering, what machinations had been set in motion. Frank bought the story that Hugo had tripped and fallen, and the compound fracture and necessary medical attention had served to keep us in London for a few extra suffocating days before we came home.

The fight, of course, was canceled. Rhys Montrose held a press conference and praised Hugo, said he would be more than happy to give him another shot when he healed up, but that never happened. Three months later, Montrose made a mandatory defense against Mozi Qwai and lost by a second-round knockout—nice guy though he was, Montrose was surely a pushover—and Qwai went on to seven successful defenses of the belt before moving up in weight and capturing that title, too. Meanwhile, Hugo dealt with the myriad problems that were only just coming into view.

It's strange to think of that. Had Hugo beaten Montrose (as we surely knew he would) he'd have been compelled to face Qwai at the peak of his powers, not as the compromised but capable fighter he was seven years later, when they really did go the twelve rounds.

What I hadn't told Lainie, and what dug at me now, was what London did to me. Or, rather, what I did to myself in London.

She poured the eggs into the melted butter in the pan, and a sizzle went up.

"I'm a fraud," I said.

She ran a spatula through the eggs, beginning the scramble. "Don't be silly."

"I am. There are lines you don't cross, Lains, and I crossed all of them that night. I became part of the news, and then I helped bury a story."

"You tried to do right by someone you care about."

"Caring is a crossed line, too."

She put a wicked stare on me. "See, when you say things like that, I'm just not sure what to think."

I flushed with stupidity. I was beginning to find in Lainie a strange dichotomy. As my love for her grew, so too did my recognition that she wouldn't let me get away with blatant overstatement without showing my work. There would be no unsettled resignation from her. Accountability sucks.

"What I mean is, it's a slippery slope, getting that close to someone you're covering. Feeling the way I did—I do—about Hugo paved the way for me to compromise myself in a moment like that. I didn't do him any favors, and I discredited myself, even if I'm the only other one who knows."

Lainie slid the eggs onto my plate and then pushed a cup of coffee across the bar to me. "You helped him avoid humiliation."

"But I didn't do him any favors. It wasn't a one-time thing. A year later, Frank pulls him out of a crack house in LA—"

"You couldn't have known that would happen," she said.

"It doesn't matter."

She came around the bar and sat next to me with her own plate. She leaned in and nuzzled me under the chin, and I slipped an arm around her back and pulled her in. It was just her and me and the Aqua Velva leavings of her dead husband.

"It matters," she whispered. Then, a little louder, this: "You can make yourself crazy, refiguring it all after the fact. You did what you thought was best at the time. You helped a friend. That's what matters."

———

Just before six a.m., as the neighborhood began to stir, we crawled back into bed. Lainie had a day off that she pronounced fit for all-hours sleeping. I had one hell of a tequila-induced headache I needed to burn off before reporting to the *Herald-Gleaner* in the afternoon.

I made like a cocoon around Lainie, our naked bodies fitting together as if our symmetry had been a grand design. I grew hard even at her casual touch. She felt me and said, against the current of onrushing sleep, that she'd be ready in a few hours. Not more than a minute later, I listened as she purred in slumber, and I nestled my chin into her neck and breathed her in.

It's not that she didn't make sense. She always did. But her sensibility was underpinned by a practical way of looking at things that just didn't have much currency in the house-of-mirrors realm of journalism. I'd been conditioned to not express opinions on politics, not cheer for a good sports play, not take sides—indeed, in some endeavors I was compelled to present the dissenting side of incontrovertible facts. This is the folly of objective journalism as practiced at most newspapers, and certainly at unsophisticated rags like the *Billings Herald-Gleaner*. It attempts to subvert human nature.

And yet, even if I give myself a pass on all that, I can't say that what I did in London came entirely from a place of pity and affection for Hugo. Were that so, I might have assimilated it and moved on, in my own head, years earlier.

The truth is, I did it for me as much as I did it for him. Maybe more.

Had the full story emerged about Hugo in London, had he faced the shame and ridicule of a positive drug test, his career might well have ended there. Boxing forgives a lot—rapists and murderers are welcomed back if they can still throw a punch—but Hugo's circumstances were different. Frank, I'm certain, would have quit him on the spot, appalled at the reality that Hugo could undermine all of their hard work in a single night. Back home in Billings, Aurelia's tentative peace with her grandson's brutal sport would have been in jeopardy, and among us all, only she had the unilateral power to move Hugo to action—or, in this hypothetical case, inaction. When we found out the extent of Hugo's problem, when the destruction wrought by it was just as crippling but less collateral, Aurelia marshaled the support that helped him through rehabilitation and recovery. She recognized that the attendant activities of Hugo's sport—the training, the eating right, the focus of preparation for an opponent—mitigated against idle hands, and she gave her blessing and commandment for him and Frank to continue. A lot had gone by the wayside by then. But in London, a few years earlier? I don't know. Aurelia might not have countenanced that.

As for me, I've come to the conclusion that I didn't want it to be over.

If Hugo had been done, I'd have been forced to trade in expense-account dinners and Las Vegas and London for a grimy desk at the *Herald-Gleaner* and Friday night football games. I'd have had to listen to Trimear curse his Excel files and watch Landry sleep through a shift and laugh at Raymont's jokes. I'd have had to sit through interminable conference room meetings with a cavalcade of editors, each one convinced that we were doing it all wrong and that he could fix it, and each one just imposing new and constricting policies upon us. I'd have had to eat sheet cakes marking smarter colleagues' departures. I'd have had to stand in the newsroom and applaud politely while the publisher handed out logo T-shirts when we came in under budget for the fiscal year.

I'd already had to do a lot of that stuff, because Hugo wasn't always in training, but I certainly dreaded the thought of more.

And now, as I listened to the rising and falling breath of the woman I loved, I could be honest with myself: a sidelined Hugo meant I would be at home more often, forced to confront the emptiness of my life with Marlene and my distance from my son. Marlene often accused me of believing that neglect could solve anything, and my disagreement with her on that point came out in bullheaded ways. Why wouldn't it? She was right.

By protecting Hugo that night, I'd protected myself from unpleasantness, from accountability, from reckoning. And now, Hugo's fighting days surely done and Lainie pulling at threads I'd left alone for years, everything I'd held at bay was coming for me.

I sank my head into the nape of Lainie's neck.

How could she not see that I was a coward?

26

A couple days after Cody Schronert was shuffled off to jail, I came into the office after a track meet and headed to my desk to type up my story. A better one was already brewing in the newsroom. Sam Landry caught me coming in the door and filled me in.

"Ace Schronert is suing that guy you talked to, that gun-nut homeowner."

"Why?"

"Emotional trauma and distress, he says. He filed a suit saying that the guy—what's his name? Bisquick or something?—"

"Bispuppo."

"Right. Yeah, anyway, Schronert says that when the guy used that machine gun or whatever, he inflicted emotional distress on his kid. Suing him for three-hundred grand. Can you believe that?"

It was all too easy to believe, sadly, but that didn't do much to short-circuit the anger I felt rising in me. Artie Bispuppo didn't strike me as the most rational son of a bitch in the world, but he was a decent guy who'd done what all of us wish we could do to a petty criminal. He'd caught them in the act and brought humiliating

justice raining down. Now Ace Schronert, every bit the thug case his
son was, was looking to make a quick buck off him.

"Who's writing the Sunday column?" I asked. A prime piece of
the biggest sports section of the week went to the *Herald-Gleaner's*
sportswriters in a rotation—a full length-of-the-page strip of newsprint to make our case for something. All I knew was that I didn't
have the duty this weekend, but now I damn sure wanted it.

"Raymont, I think," Landry said.

I went across the room and settled into my chair.

"Hop," I said to Raymont. "What are you writing this week?"

He took off his headphones. The guy listened to Johnny Cash con-
tinually while at work. Better than listening to Trimear, I supposed.

"I don't know, Mark. Maybe something on the redistricting in
Class C."

"Can I take your spot?"

Raymont looked relieved by the request. One more thing he
wouldn't have to do. He nodded at Trimear at the adjacent desk,
across from me. "Ask Gene."

"Gene?" I said.

"I'm more interested in your story tonight." He glanced at the
clock above my head. "Getting late."

"Fifteen minutes and it's yours," I said. "Can I have the spot?"

He sighed. His head bobbed on that spastic neck of his. "Sure."

———

I turned my track story around in twelve minutes, a story I'd written
a thousand times before. Only the names and the numbers change.
Once I got the all-clear from Trimear that it was on the page, I set
to writing the Sunday column that Raymont had gracefully ceded to
me, and I zeroed in on my targets: Case "the Ace" Schronert and his
boy, Cody.

Before I commenced with ripping, I considered whether I ought to acknowledge that Cody Schronert and I had some history, a past that informed how I viewed him and gave me all the reason I ever needed to consider him a mindless little punk. A few years earlier, when he was still attending Billings Senior, I'd been at a practice to talk to Mack Hargroves, the football coach, for a story on the prevalence of wing-T offenses in the state. I remember that specifically because we were talking about Schronert—Hargroves going on expansively, the way he tended to, and me with my head buried in my notebook, taking down his dripping bits of wisdom—when a thrown football hit me in the back of the head. I wheeled around, dumbfounded, while Hargroves fetched the ball, pitched it back, and said, "You guys be careful now." I looked at the group of kids, and there was Cody Schronert, staring at me with this shit-eating grin on his face.

I turned back to Hargroves and tried to pick up our conversational thread, and bam—I'm hit again, behind the knees.

This time, Hargroves was pissed. "Damn it, Cody, I told you to be careful." I stared at the kid, and he just looked back at me, that grin never leaving his face. I knew. He knew I knew. And he didn't give a good goddamn.

It bothered me. It still bothers me. I took it because—here's that conditioning thing again—that's what I do. I'm not the story, and I don't intend to become the story by amping up a tense situation. I've had athletes stand as close as possible to me, lean in, breathe on me, and tell me I'm shit. Scream at me. It happens to all of us, eventually. In every case, I just delivered my words a little flatter, a little more monotone, a little quieter. I'm not the story.

But I'm also not some punk-ass kid's plaything.

I wondered if I should acknowledge, in print, that I hated Cody Schronert. And then I decided the hell with it. If I wrote this thing the way I intended, there'd be little doubt about my feelings on the matter of Cody or his bottom-feeding daddy.

27

If I'm going to call Gene Trimear a ham-handed hack—and I am, because he is—then I also have to give him credit where it's due. He wrote a corker of a headline for my Sunday column. Everything else related to it turned out to be a disaster, of course, but the headline was a thing of beauty.

A Dummy and His Dad: Misadventures of Cody, Case Schronert

By MARK WESTERLY
Herald-Gleaner Staff

If you're looking for a good example of the difference between class and crass in sports today—indeed, in any walk of life— you could do no better than one right here in Billings.

Back in February, we all got quite a jolt when Cody Schronert, a former Billings Senior High School running back, beat Olympic hero Hugo Hunter in a boxing match at the Babcock Theatre. Hunter hasn't fought since, and it seems a better-than-even bet that he never will again.

But let's take a look at where those two are today:

Cody Schronert, 21, sits under house arrest, charged in a three-day vandalism spree that did wide property damage across Billings and gripped the city in fear.

Hugo Hunter, 37—and believe me, that 37 matters, as the 21-year-old version of him would have had no problems with the likes of Cody Schronert—can be found most any night of the week at Feeney's, the pub owned by his former manager, Frank Feeney, where he entertains diners with tales of his life in the ring.

Affable despite a career's worth of heartache and a fortune lost, Hunter has the good sense to know that he was given an athletic gift, and though he certainly squandered some of his opportunities along the way, he is proud of what he's done and willing to share it with the people of this city he loves.

Cody Schronert has never wanted for anything. He was a child of privilege and is now a man of low character—and that's true regardless of whether he's found guilty of the crimes with which he's charged.

He's a bad apple. And if you want to know why, look at the tree.

Schronert's father, Case "the Ace" Schronert, is this city's most aggressive personal-injury attorney. If you see an ambulance in Billings, you're unlikely to have to look long before you see Case Schronert's Mercedes in tow, chasing down another payday. It's hard to move around this town without seeing one of his billboards. And that's fine, as far as it goes. It takes all kinds to make a society, and Case Schronert is happy to be a bottom-feeder, so we're probably all better off letting him be just that. I suspect we can all agree that it's a little unseemly to profit from others' misery, but if this guy weren't doing it, no doubt someone else would.

The problem is when Case Schronert flexes his ill-formed legal muscles on behalf of his immature son, and in so doing targets someone who is a productive member of our society.

By now, you've surely read about Case Schronert's $300,000 lawsuit against Artie Bispuppo, the Billings home-owner who brought Cody Schronert and his accomplices (alleged) to justice with his own legally purchased and legally fired gun. If that lawsuit doesn't make you sick, on a basic level, then I don't want to know you.

Let's be clear: Artie Bispuppo did what any of us would have done under similar circumstances. Have you ever come out of a store to find your car keyed by some miscreant? What did you say to yourself when that happened? Oh, if I'd only been there. Yes. It's what we all want: to hold someone accountable for his bad acts.

That's what Artie Bispuppo did. This city ought to celebrate him for it.

Instead, Case Schronert wants to take $300,000 from him. For inflicting "emotional distress" on his conscience-less son.

It's a travesty.

As for Cody Schronert, I'd suggest an immediate change of behavior and an infusion of humility and grace.

If he needs lessons, he can wander down to Feeney's and consult with Hugo Hunter.

After the case is resolved, of course. Until then, he can't leave the house.

Billings has never been so fortunate.

———

I'll cop to it: that last line gave me pause. Even for a bona fide critic of Cody Schronert, which I certainly was, it seemed a bit of undue celebration of someone else's bad circumstance. In the end, I left it for two reasons. First, I wasn't able to achieve objectivity where the Schronerts were concerned (interestingly enough, a point the Diploma would soon be making to me). Second, I figured if it struck Trimear badly, he'd just cleave it out of there. He'd certainly had no previous compunction about manhandling my work.

The morning the column hit the streets, my phone started ringing, and it didn't stop for more than a few minutes until early afternoon. Lainie came over with a box of doughnuts and coffee, and then she let me take her in the bedroom and do as I would—not a bad way to mark a Sunday morning. My e-mail in-box was jumping, too. The only dissent came from Case Schronert, who suggested, in a way that was just lawyerly enough to not be construed as an overt threat, that he would even things up. The key phrase he used was "assassination of character," and let me tell you, it was no easy trick to keep myself from making an observation about needing the presence of character first.

About the only person I didn't hear from was the Diploma, and that's how I knew I'd landed myself in a spot of trouble.

It was worth it.

———

Sure enough, just before noon on Monday I was summoned to the *Herald-Gleaner* for a chat with the Diploma and managing editor Mike "the Drone" Lindell. The Diploma's response was a terse "no" when I asked if Trimear would be there, and strange as it sounds, that scared me as much as anything. Trimear was a mostly useless human being, but he did have some value in explaining to overly curious executives just what it was that the sports department did, our rituals and idiosyncrasies. I'd lost count of the number of people who'd occupied the Diploma's office and wanted, among their first acts, to abolish the annual NCAA basketball tournament pool. Something happens to a journalist when he's elevated into executive-level leadership: it's as if he forgets all the irreverent humor and grab-ass that goes on in a newsroom and suddenly wants to run the place like a damned bank. Trimear had talked a succession of executives out of acts that would have obliterated morale even more than the general tenor of the business was already managing to do. I probably should have been more grateful for that.

The Diploma sat in his chair and leaned way back, like Ali on the ropes against Foreman in Zaire, his undergrad and graduate sheep-skins framing his head and supplying his nickname. The Drone sat in the chair next to mine, an uncomfortable proximity.

"We've had to mitigate a lot of damage from your column," Pennington said.

In the queasy car ride to the office, the topic of the talk had seemed bluntly obvious, so I gave myself no credit for insight. I'd used my driving time to imagine the Diploma's openers and what my responses might be, and this one, it turned out, called for mockery.

"It's unusual to hear the truth equated to damage," I said.

"Oh, spare me," the Diploma said, only his even delivery didn't betray the slightest bit of irritation, which was too bad. "There's a way to deliver the truth, as you call it, without being offensive, and without calling one of the most prominent people in town names—"

"Prominent?"

"—and a major advertiser, to boot."

I started in again. "Ah, yes, advertiser. Now—"

"That column was not to the standard we expect," Lindell said, and I swear to God, I wanted to lean over and puke on his shoes. I didn't like Pennington, but I respected him. I respected his intellect and, usually, his manner, even if his sensibilities sat in direct oppo-sition to mine. But Lindell? The worst copy editor I've ever seen—certainly the worst on the *Herald-Gleaner* desk—had risen to the number-two newsroom job mostly because nobody else wanted it, or wanted to carry water for the Diploma. Let me put it this way: Gene Trimear had more managerial bona fides in his short, fat, nicotine-tinged fingers than Mike Lindell had in his entire soulless body.

I scrambled to get my footing. "OK, Bill, look: I didn't call anybody any names."

The Diploma stared back at me, incredulous. "A dummy and his dad? I'd say your lack of objectivity about the Schronerts shines through."

"That was the headline," I protested, and immediately I wished I'd seized on the Diploma's incantation of "objectivity," which shouldn't be a factor, as opinions are all about subjectivity. "I didn't write that. Talk to Trimear."

Lindell again: "We have."

"Well, OK," I said.

The Diploma leaned forward, his hands on his desk. "Look, Mark, we're going to cut to the chase here, as it's already been decided. This is a serious incident, but you've been a good employee for a lot of years—"

"Meaning you can't find the juice to fire me," I said.

"If I were you, I wouldn't be too sure about my juice, as you put it. As I was saying, you've been a good employee, which means I hope this episode is an outlier. We've managed to set things right with Mr. Schronert, the column has been expunged both online and in our in-house library, and we'll be sitting you down without pay for five days. At the end of that time, you can report back to work."

He stopped there, looking at me, trying to suss out my reaction. I sensed there was more he wished to say, and I wanted him to just get on with it.

"OK," I said.

"OK," he said. "When you come back, there will be no more columns, at least not for a while. You can still cover regular sports news, but no more in-print opinions until I'm certain you're ready. That's up to me."

"The buck stops with you," I said.

"That's right."

"Starting now."

I fought with myself not to smile, as I surely wanted to at my tweaking of authority, like a good journalist. Instead, my face heated up as I watched the Diploma choke down my last flinging bit of insolence.

"You may start your five days away now," he said.

"Let me ask you something," I said. "We have editors here, right? Gene could have stopped this column. Hell, you could have, too."

"Gene's been disciplined. That's between us and him. And we will be reassessing our protocols for columns from now on. Thank you for pointing that out."

Lindell saw another opening to toss in a useless remark. "That's it, Mark," he said.

I got up and surprised Pennington by offering a handshake. He took my hand, a good, solid grip, and gave it two quick shakes and then let go. Lindell looked at me as if he wanted one, too, but I wasn't inclined to oblige. If my time was now my own, I figured I'd spend it sidled up to one of Frank Feeney's beer mugs.

Excerpt from *Hugo Hunter: My Good Life and Bad Times*

Frank Feeney is the father figure I never had, a truth that's made difficult by the fact that we aren't talking anymore.

From the time I was eleven years old, Frank's word was the law. He trained me, he watched over me, he led me to opportunities that would have never come my way without his presence in my life. He was a moral compass, a trusted friend, a rescuer.

I will love him forever.

And yet, there have been betrayals. Mine against him. His against me. One of the things you learn to do in recovery is make amends, to the extent you can, with those who have suffered from your addiction.

What I owe Frank remains undone. What he owes me remains undone as well.

It's the worst kind of stalemate.

28

I shuffled into Feeney's and found a seat at the bar. I had plenty to choose from. The lunch crowd had come and gone, leaving Frank alone in the place.

"Where's your court jester?" I asked him as I settled into my seat.

"Slumpbuster?" Frank said.

"Sure."

I watched him draw the beer, the glass tilted just so to form a right-sized head. When he served it, I thanked him and then gave him the look I'd perfected for reluctant sources. A gentle *come on now, I asked you a question.*

"Ah, hell, you know that kid," Frank said, sweeping the bar with a rag. "Always something new, always some shiny penny he's gotta pick up."

"So he's gone?"

"Gone from here, yeah. Some girl came in, talking him up. He comes to me the next day and says, 'Frank, I'm going to be in a play.'"

"A play?"

"Yeah, she's one of those artsy types or something. You know, with the theater down the street? She gives him this line about how he'd be perfect for this play they're doing, and so he comes to me and says he's gotta go to rehearsals at night. And I'm there saying, 'Look, asshole, if you're working here, you work here at night.' And he says, 'Come on, Frank, I gotta do this.' And I tell him, 'No, you gotta choose.'"

Frank rubbed his eyes and then laughed. "Well, he chose, I guess."

It would be a lie to say I was surprised. Oh, the circumstance was a little jarring. I don't think anyone who knew Hugo would think of him as a thespian. But that he'd up and quit a seemingly good situation—well, that was easy to swallow. It followed a pattern that had been well established since the end of his prizefighting days. Before working at the bar, he had jobs driving a delivery truck for an industrial laundry, putting up sheetrock, organizing the stock at a plumbing supply house, and sweeping the floors at Billings West High School. The operative word, in every case, was *had*.

"Well, he made a liar of me," I said.

"How so?"

"I talked him up in the paper yesterday. Said he was doing an honorable thing here."

"Yeah, I saw that," Frank said. "Thanks for the extra business. You ripped that guy pretty good."

"They sat me down, Frank. At the paper. Suspended me."

"For that?"

"Yeah."

Frank took my glass and topped it off, then set it before me.

"You know," he said, "I don't think I want to live in a world where you can't kick the ass of someone who deserves it."

———

Frank wasn't the person angriest with Hugo. His niece, Amber, had become smitten during Hugo's brief employment, against Frank's initial advice that she maintain some distance from him.

"The thing was," Frank said, "I was worried about something worse than this—I don't know what, exactly, but we've been around the block with Hugo a time or two, you know? But I gotta admit, he treated her well, and he was good to Jackson."

"Jackson?"

"Her little boy."

The night Hugo told Frank he was leaving, Amber apparently let him have it, both barrels. Told him he wasn't reliable, that she'd made a mistake letting her son grow fond of him, that he'd die alone. Frank's relaying of that last bit made me cringe. That's a tough pronouncement to put on anybody. Before Lainie came along, there were many nights I considered that my own probable fate.

"Hugo's going, 'Baby, baby, baby, it's just a play,'" Frank said. "And she's going, 'You don't get it.' She's right. He don't."

"What about this girl, the one who pulled him into the play?" I asked.

"Hugo swears there's nothing going on."

"Amber believe that?"

Frank snorted. "What do you think?"

I'll tell you what I thought. I thought that I could have stayed there all day and into the night, slowly putting away Frank Feeney's brew and my angst. I also thought, rightly, that Hugo wouldn't be the only lonely man in Billings if I didn't get off my ass and go tell Lainie what had happened at the *Herald-Gleaner*.

"Well, I guess I'll go figure out what to do with myself for a week," I told Frank. "Might be spending more time down here with you."

"You're always welcome," he said. "You know that."

I tried to pay the bill, but Frank would have none of it. "I figure you made me thirty times this just in referrals," he said. "Sorry about what happened."

I gave a sly salute and headed for the door. Before I hit the street, I turned back.

"What's the name of this play?"

Frank snorted again. "You're not gonna believe it," he said.

"Try me."

"Requiem for a Heavyweight."

29

I went down to the South Side to see Hugo. I'd neglected him for a few weeks anyway, but more than that, I didn't like taking any bit of news from Frank as gospel, at least where Hugo was concerned. It's an old reporter thing, to corroborate everything. I knew that all of us tended to cycle our experiences with Hugo through our own filters. Frank's were predisposed to disappointment. Mine were, too, but I told myself that I needed to be open to hearing Hugo's side of things.

A few years of neglect had done a number on Aurelia's house. Blue paint flecked away on the eaves above the door, and I remembered how Hugo had come home from Mississippi after losing to Coconut Olson, long after Frank had bailed out and Squeaky had been sent to the sidelines. It was a nothing fight against a young fighter, the kind of fighter Hugo had once been, and it came out the way things had been ordained. Olson got a victory that looked good on paper, and Hugo came home a busted, tired boxer and paid off his grandma's funeral bills.

Once he got back, he had climbed up to that bedroom and stayed for weeks. I'd gone to see him a few times, but he'd never come out to stay. He'd come down and he'd chat for a bit, and then he'd be gone again. Before Aurelia died, she had been on him about the house—"Hugo, can you paint it for me?"—and dutiful grandson that he was, he'd told her, yes, he'd do it, just as soon as he had the time. He promised.

Four years had slid off the calendar since she left, and still the promise went unfulfilled. It pissed me the hell off.

I knocked on the front door. Nothing. No stirring from the other side that I could hear.

I went around between the house and the garage, to the little concrete path leading to the backyard. On my tiptoes, I could get my eyes above the fence. Hugo sat in a weather-battered Adirondack chair, his back to me.

"You taking visitors?" I said.

Hugo lurched up out of the chair and turned around. He wore an old robe, molecules of terry cloth holding it together, and a T-shirt and a pair of basketball shorts that were only slightly less vintage.

"Hey, Mark, come on through." Hugo ambled over and lifted the latch for me. "Sit down, man." He pulled an old barstool across the patio and set it up opposite his seat. We settled in.

"Damn, you look good, Mark."

"Thanks. It's only been a couple of weeks since you've seen me. This isn't old-home week or anything."

Hugo chuckled and made like he was going to throw a punch at me, our old patter. "I know, I know. But you do look good."

"Thanks."

"I read what you wrote about me," he said.

"Yeah? You kind of made a liar out of me, didn't you?"

"You talked to Frank, I guess."

"I did."

"He's mad, I guess."

I took measure of him. He had a bit of a hangdog look, an expectation born of experience that Frank considered him a screwup. He wasn't far wrong.

"I didn't get anger from him," I said. "He just doesn't get it. It looked like you were doing well there, hanging out, entertaining people. He just—"

"Glory days."

"Huh?"

"You know," he said. "Like the Springsteen song. Frank was paying me to relive my glory days for the people who came in."

"Well, yeah, I guess."

"It's a sad song, though. You know? Like there's nothing better out there." He looked at me plaintively.

"But Hugo, the song is about a guy who topped out in high school. That's not you."

"It's not? Barcelona happened when I was in high school. That wasn't the top?"

"It didn't have to be. That's the point. You had possibilities. The guy in the song, he's just some schmuck drinking beer. You had a chance at something greater."

His face twisted, like he'd been gut-socked. I stopped cold. I was fixing him with an even sadder song.

"Jesus, Hugo, I'm sorry. I mean, there's truth, and then there's—"

He waved his hand toward me. "It's not like I don't know."

I scrambled for a different way in with him. "So, a play?"

He leaned forward, his hands flying around as if someone had jump-started him.

"Yeah. I'm Mountain Rivera."

"I figured."

"He's a washed-up old boxer."

"I know."

"It's a great part."

"Yeah, but you don't know anything about boxing."

"Screw you."

We busted up over that.

———

Hugo invited me inside for some coffee. I followed him through the back door to the kitchen. The place had served as the center of so many gatherings, it was like walking in on the ghosts of our younger selves. It was almost as if I could see Aurelia there at the stove, her back to us as she worked up a pot of stew or a pan of enchiladas— anything she had, really, to keep us there with Hugo, his family by extension. Frank would be in the far corner, knocking back the beer that Aurelia kept in the house only for him. Squeaky would sit across from Frank, deciphering a crossword and, later, sudoku, that crazy-ass Japanese number game, and he'd scold us once the roaring got too loud, as it always did. And Hugo would be in the middle of it all, at the table or Aurelia's side, listening to the chatter or helping his grammy. That it was all for him, he knew as deep in his bones as he knew anything.

Now, Hugo shuffled through ahead of me, nimbleness and athletic youth gone and not coming back. The order Aurelia imposed on things was gone, too, replaced by dust and papers and unpaid bills, the detritus of a life that Hugo claimed to be pulling under control. I didn't see it.

"Black?" he said.

"You know me better than that."

He poured the coffee, leaving plenty of room in the cup for doctoring. A three-quarters-empty jug of creamer followed, and I damn near drained it.

"Enjoy your nonjava," he said, toasting me.

"It's more a matter of color than taste," I said.

He leaned against the Formica counter. "You want to know why, don't you?"

I took in the first lukewarm mouthful and smacked my lips. "I'm always the guy who wants to know why. You know that."

"It's my mom." He cast his eyes down at his bare feet.

"What is?"

"The reason I'm doing the play."

I set my coffee down. Helene, cut down in her relative youth, was the great loss in his life, more so than even Aurelia, I think. In more than twenty years of knowing Hugo, I'd talked about so many things with him, it would be nigh impossible to catalog them all. But Helene—we only glanced off the topic of her, so profound was his yearning, so overwhelming the memories, so devastating the emptiness. I gave him my full attention and hoped he'd talk.

"I look through her stuff sometimes," he said at last, after he'd fought a silent battle in front of me to keep his emotions in lockdown. "She didn't throw anything away, I don't think. She kept old scripts from high school, playbills from college, letters she got from people she admired. She got one from Al Pacino."

"Pacino? No kidding?"

"Seriously. She wrote to him about *The Godfather*, and he wrote back, thanked her for her interest. There's all this stuff she loved, and I feel like I didn't get a chance to talk to her about it. So I'm doing this thing, because it makes me feel closer to her."

I wasn't going to argue with him. How could I? I couldn't plumb the depths of his yearning for his mother. All I could offer was perspective that perhaps he hadn't considered.

"Did you tell Frank and Amber about this?"

Hugo looked like he'd swallowed something sour. "He told you about me and Amber?"

"Yeah."

"No, I didn't tell them. I didn't really have it all worked out in my head. It's just something I felt like I had to do."

I stepped closer to him. "Well, maybe that's why they're confused and hurt. You know? They gave you a job, and Amber, she obviously cares about you, and they feel abandoned. Frank said everything new for you is shiny and irresistible, so—"

"Yeah, probably."

"See? I don't know, Hugo. I think maybe you just need to talk to them."

"Maybe."

"What are you doing for money?" I asked.

"I have a little. Something will come up."

"Well, let me buy you lunch, anyway."

———

I waited downstairs while Hugo showered and dressed. Being in the house, left on my own to wander a bit, was like randomly firing off my own synapses. I perused the bookshelf and came across a row of old *Reader's Digest* almanacs from the '70s, and in my head, I was back in 1993, looking at these very books in this very spot while I waited for Aurelia to get off the phone and come in and talk with me.

That year, a big national magazine had commissioned me to write a profile of Hugo, less from a sports angle and more from who he was as a person. This was after he met Seyna, so finding time alone with him proved a significant challenge. I'd started at the periphery and worked my way in. Aurelia made the digging easier.

That day, and deep into the afternoon, I got my first extended insight into where Hugo came from and who his mother was. It made me wish I'd known Helene. It also lent credence to my theory that nobody really gets what they deserve from this life, that it's all a question of what you can take while you have the time. How else do you explain how a woman of thirty-two, her whole life spread out before her with a boy who needs her, is taken by pancreatic cancer, as good as dead before anybody even knows something's wrong? Aurelia sat there, even-keeled through the most harrowing details, and talked about how you just pick up the remnants of what you once had, you go on, you keep living. Although I knew she was right, even then, before I found out on my own that there's no other way,

I kept thinking of Von. He was just a few months old then, and I fixated on how devastating it would be for him to lose his mother.

It was my most general question—"What was she like?"—that brought the deepest insight into the son Helene had left us.

Aurelia got this far-off look, as if she could see beyond the walls of her house and to the great world outside.

"She got every bit of living out of every minute she was here, and it didn't seem like she was even trying," Aurelia said, the only time in the many hours I spent with her that she teared up even a little. "She was like the Pied Piper. If she was around, you wanted to be with her. You might not know why, and she seemed unaware of the effect she had, but you did. When you're that open, and when people come to you like that, you don't always make the best choices." I knew, of course, what she was speaking of with that last phrase: Hugo's father. I also knew that topic was off-limits. The subsequent questions that I would ordinarily ask remained in my quiver.

Now, I ran my finger along the row of books, leaving a dusty trail in its wake. A thought, not fully formed, bubbled in my head. Something about cosmic juxtaposition, about how some things stand in place while the rest of the world changes all around. It was out of my usual range. I shook my head and tried to rejoin the moment.

Hugo, trampling down the stairs in a T-shirt and jeans, moved matters along.

"Don't just stand there playing pocket pool," he said. "Let's go get some enchiladas."

———

We ended up a few blocks away at Guadalajara, a hole-in-the-wall place on the edge of downtown jammed between a casino and what used to be an Army-Navy store. The restaurant, with its stomped-down industrial carpet, plaster walls, and Naugahyde chairs, drew a cross-strata of Billings—carpenters and bankers and lawyers and hair

stylists, all in snug quarters, eating mountains of old-style Mexican
food. We took up residence at a corner table and got a couple of nods
but nothing more. It was the kind of place you could go and not be
hassled, no matter who you were.

"God, I'm hungry," Hugo said. "I think I'm going to have one of
the *supremas.*"

"What are you weighing these days?" I asked.

He chortled. "Hey, screw you, Westerly. I should ask you the
same thing. You're looking a little thick around the ribs."

I had put on a good deal of weight, thanks to Lainie's work in the
kitchen and my increased appetite after ditching the cigarettes. "The
love of a good woman," I said.

"Love, huh? She's a nice lady."

"She speaks well of you, too, Hugo."

We loaded up big corn chips with salsa and ate like we'd skipped
a few meals, and then we jostled over the last chip. Not having anywhere to go later, I nursed a cerveza while Hugo filled me in on the
production. The curtain was set to go up in two days, and nerves had
gone to work on him.

"You ever seen the play version of *Requiem for a Heavyweight?*"
he asked me.

"No, just the Anthony Quinn movie."

"Yeah, I didn't even know there was a difference. I guess in the
play my character is Mountain McClintock, not Mountain Rivera.
We're doing the movie script. Director said there's more action in the
movie version."

"Interesting."

"Yeah. You know I'm going to have to wear a headdress?"

"I think I remember that," I said.

"I wonder what Grammy would think of that."

"She wasn't Native, was she?"

"No, but my grandpa was."

"Does it bother you?"

"A little."

I knew even less about Hugo's granddaddy than I did his mother, just that he'd come home from Korea, started a family, and died suddenly in his midthirties, a congenital heart thing that went undetected by the medical knowledge of the time. He left Aurelia with a house and a child and a stack of obligations, and as time went by, it was like she walled off that part of her life. I can't imagine that there weren't men who made their play for her—anybody who knew Aurelia knows what a beauty she was—but I never saw any, and Hugo never talked of any. She just carried on. You wonder sometimes how much loss can afflict one family.

"Are you going to wear it?" I asked him.

"Yeah, I think so. I think I can see my way clear."

"You know," I said, "I always admired how you didn't trade on your heritage when you were fighting."

Hugo perked up at those last few words. I tried to walk them back. "It is past tense, isn't it?" The moment took on a tension that hadn't been there previously. I mentally backtracked over the past few months, trying to catalog the news stories and the whispers and the declarations, and I realized that Hugo had never said, definitively, that he was done.

He leaned in, his voice low. "The doctor said I might end up with dementia or something if I keep fighting."

"Shit."

"Yeah. He asked me how many concussions I've had."

"What did you say?"

"I don't know. Nobody ever counted them."

"Shit."

"You got any other words, Mark?"

I shook my head. I didn't, really. I'd assumed all along he was done, and even so, hearing it straight out left me a little depleted. "So that's it, then," I said.

"Yeah. Hell of an ending, huh?"

I sat back and let our server set the food out for us.

"Maybe not," I said. "Maybe it's just the beginning."

———

We tumbled out on the street, and Hugo said he'd walk to the play-house, just a few blocks down on Montana Avenue. I told him I'd be happy to drop him off. I literally had nothing else to do.

"It's OK," he said. "I like walking. Might as well enjoy it before winter comes."

We shook hands, and then I did something that surprised me. I pulled him in and gave him a hug. Nothing awkward or embarrassing. A bro hug. It felt like the thing to do.

"You need any money?" I asked him.

"Nah, man, I'm good. Thanks, though."

I watched him ramble off, first a half block to the south, then a left turn. A few seconds later, he was gone around the corner.

"Mark Westerly?" came a voice from behind me.

I turned, and a manila envelope snapped against my chest. A young guy—younger than me, anyway—in black-framed glasses smiled at me and said, "Court papers. You've been served."

His deed done, the guy walked briskly in the other direction. I opened the envelope. Case Schronert had followed through with his threat and filed suit against me—just me, no mention of the *Herald-Gleaner* as a defendant—for libel. I was half inclined to wander down to the newspaper office and raise some hell, but I nipped that thought just as quickly as it occurred to me. Nothing good, for me, could come of that.

I could still see the process server at the north end of the block, waiting for the light to change. He turned and looked at me and got the stinkeye.

"You dick," I yelled.

30

Lainie bailed on work early to introduce me to a lawyer friend of hers, a guy named Larry Largeman. He operated out of a little rat nest of an office in midtown, in a strip mall that had gone up in the mid-'60s and had been permanently detached from its better days.

We walked into a labyrinthine office. No receptionist. No waiting room. A desk stacked high with papers. A hallway with a low ceiling jutted off to the left and terminated in a room with another desk, also groaning under the weight of paper and absent any sentient being.

"Larry?" Lainie called.

A muffled voice emerged from behind a closed door at our backs. "In the can, honey. Hold on a sec."

I leaned into her and whispered, "What is this?"

"Don't worry," she said. "He's good. Different. But good."

We heard the whoosh of a flushed toilet and the running faucet, and then Larry Largeman opened the door and sidled into the hallway. Largeman was not a large man—shorter than Lainie, in fact, who stood about five seven. He wore a business-issue short-sleeved white dress shirt, good-for-any-era brown trousers, and a pair of loafers that had worked the corners. I could see the ruins of a handsome man among the burst nose capillaries and bagged-out eyes.

He walked up to Lainie as if I weren't there and wrapped her in a hug. He nuzzled his mug against her neck and growled. Lainie laughed, and firmly pushed him away. A good move, that, so I didn't have to do it.

"You're Mark, then," he said, turning to me and offering a handshake. "Don't worry. I washed it."

I gave him a cursory shake and let go. He clapped a hand against my shoulder and said, "Come on in. Let's let the legal healing begin."

———

I gave Largeman the summons and hoped he'd make himself a copy before the original washed away in the sea of paper already swamping his desk.

"You'll have to excuse the mess," he said. "Secretary has been out since 2004."

He laughed. Lainie did, too. I ground my hands into little skin meatballs while Largeman read the paper.

"It's a sham," he said.

I blew out a blast of breath. "Well, that's good news."

"Of course, it's going to cost you a hell of a lot to identify it as such." At this, he laughed again, sounding like a strangling horse.

"How much?" Lainie said.

"You want me to handle this?" he said. I started to say no, but Lainie said, "Yes."

"OK," Largeman said, "if I figure in the prettiest-girl-in-Billings discount, the getting-to-know-you-Mark offset, and the fact that not too much work is coming through that door, I'll do it for two thousand to start, which I'll need today. Cash is preferred, but I'll take a check, since I know where you live." The horse laugh again. "That should do it, unless Schronert *really* hates you, in which case it might be more."

"Unbelievable," I said.

"I know," Largeman said. "Lawyers are scum."

I dug in my pocket for my checkbook. As I wrote the check out, Largeman leaned across the desk. "That's *L-A-R-G-E-M-A-N*. Largeman. Think thickness, not length."

Jesus.

I tore off the check and handed it to him. I'm a frugal guy, a function of my modest wages and my upbringing, and I'd managed over the years to tuck a fair amount away. I hated to see the money flowing the other direction, and for something so damnably stupid.

"OK, now, let me tell you what's up," Largeman said. "Schronert's going to have a hard time making the case for injury against you when he's been made right by the paper. They expunged this article, right? Probably gave him some ad space to sweeten the deal. That's what I'd do."

"Yeah."

"OK. I suspect this lawsuit was filed because he knew you'd be down here, or somewhere, today writing this check. I'll make a motion to dismiss. The thing is, these judges are so backed up—really, it's like constipation—that it may be a while before somebody looks at it close enough to see what a mockery it really is. In the meantime, maybe Schronert files a few amendments or add-ons, and we've gotta answer to those. He can play that game a lot longer than you, I suspect."

"Brilliant deduction."

Largeman didn't get the gibe, or didn't care. "Hey, it's what I do. You're gonna get the best representation two grand can buy."

———

The tension on the drive home should have imploded the windows. I drummed fingers on the steering wheel at stoplights. I worked my jaw at double speed, chewing on my trouble.

"What?" Lainie said.

"I'm supposed to feel better after that?" I didn't want to look at her. I hadn't thought Case Schronert was really going to go after me, and now that he had, I had some dingleberry carrying a torch for my girlfriend as a lawyer. I should have walked out of there.

"No. You're supposed to feel like a guy who's getting sued."

"That guy's a joke. I'm dead."

She reached for my arm, but I drew back.

"You are not dead," she said. "And Larry is not a joke. He's a lot of things, but he's not a joke. He's the real deal."

I smoldered on. "You don't seem like an objective source on that. What's the story with you and him?"

"Really, Mark? Jealousy?"

"I just want to know."

"Yeah, OK, you got me. I burn for Larry Largeman. It's so intense that I married Delmar and loved him and buried him and fell in love with you, but Larry Largeman is who I ache for."

"Jesus, Lains, I was just—"

"You're a dope."

We headed up into the Heights, toward Lainie's place, suffocating in silence.

"Larry was my boyfriend in high school," she said at last. "If I'd cast my future when I was sixteen, maybe I would have married him, but I didn't. He's brilliant, Mark, but he's a mess, too, and I think I always knew that about him and couldn't allow myself to get in too deep. But he'll do this, and he'll do it right. I promise."

I pulled into her driveway, next to the RV with the pellet-gun dents in the side. She and Delmar had bought it for an eventual retirement, and then he up and died before they could enjoy it. Life's a damn gamble, every day.

"I trust you," I said.

Lainie squirmed against the console and set her head into my shoulder. I pulled her into a hug and teased her hair with my fingers. Above the roofline of her house, I watched a gathering storm.

Excerpt from *Hugo Hunter: My Good Life and Bad Times*

In a span of about three weeks in the spring of 1993, these things
happened:

I dropped out of high school.

I took Seyna to Las Vegas and married her.

I signed the contract for my first professional fight.

I had that fight at Caesars Palace, on a card full of other 1992
Olympic boxers—Cordero Montez, Jimbo Duggins, Maxie "Rerun"
Robbins, and a few other names you probably remember.

To say that I was intimidated would be, perhaps, to devalue the
word. Rationally, I knew that I was set up for success. I hadn't been
in the ring for real since Barcelona, and my opponent that night, an
earnest if overmatched fighter from San Bernardino named Leland
Briggs, had been handpicked for me. That's how it is when you're a
hot young fighter making your debut. You get red meat served up for
your four-round opener. In the second fight, it's another opponent
on the descent and six rounds, and so on. Somewhere after the first
dozen, you start fighting guys who know what they're doing and can
put some damage on you if you're not careful. Leland Briggs posed
no danger to me.

And yet, as I stood in the tunnel waiting for the houselights to come down and the music to start so I could make my way to the ring, I felt on the verge of losing control of my movements and my bodily functions. I'd heard whispers in the press before the fight, wondering if I was just a flash in the pan in Barcelona who would get exposed in the pro game, where it's grown men and no headgear. I had no such fears. I was worried, no doubt about it, but it was rooted in other things: Is the rust gone? Can I set the pace early? Can I get up the stairs to the ring without falling down in front of fifteen thousand people?

Two things let me know I was OK. The first was seeing my sportswriter friend, Mark Westerly, along press row as I made my way to the ring, everybody screaming and the music blaring. I gave him a little nod and he gave me a little wink, and that calmed me considerably.

The second occurred in the first few seconds of the first round. The first jab I threw connected squarely with Briggs's chin, and I knew then that I was much faster than he was. I backed up after that and invited him in, and sure enough, I saw his own jab coming from way back. I slipped inside it and threw an uppercut to the stomach that knocked the air from him. A minute and thirty-seven seconds into the round, it was over.

I was going to be all right.

31

We collected our tickets at the box office and stepped inside the theater lobby. Lainie waved, and I looked up to see Raj standing against the far wall, under the placard listing the theater's benefactors. She grabbed my hand and we walked over.

"What are you doing here?" I said. I was mildly surprised. Raj tended to keep his distance from Hugo. Force of habit, I suppose.

Lainie jabbed me in the side. "I invited him."

God, I could be dumb sometimes. "Good," I said. "Going to be interesting."

Raj fiddled with his tie. The kid—hell, any kid—was more comfortable in T-shirts and khaki shorts. I gave him credit for making the attempt.

"Does he know I'm coming?" Raj asked Lainie.

"He doesn't know *we're* coming," she said. "No extra pressure, right?"

Lainie reached for my hand, and then for Raj's. "Come on, men. Let's go see a play."

———

Any hesitations I had about Hugo's headlong dive into theater—and I had many, starting with his base irresponsibility of leaving his job at Feeney's—eroded when I saw him on the stage that night. We sat in a middle row, just out of the reach of the footlights, and we watched him. The few novice moves I picked up on, like a nervous glance at the audience in his first scene, fell away quickly and yielded to a display of remarkable control. I'm not a theater critic. Far from it. But for my money—$17.95 plus a $5.00 lukewarm beer at intermission—Hugo became tragic Mountain Rivera. The performance had verisimilitude, it had depth, it had pathos. It occurred to me, as I sat there, that beyond the obvious parallels between Hugo's character and his real life, he had been prepping for this role for a long time. Hugo knew how to sell a show, and he was doing it again there on the stage.

Traveling all those years with Hugo, I had occasion to see and meet some famous people. Athletes. Actors and actresses. A few politicians, although most of them stay away from overt blood sports. Some surprise you with their physical dimension, because you're used to seeing them bigger than life and reality right-sizes them. Some aren't as glamorous as they're made out to be. Some are even more devastatingly attractive. My point, I guess, is that the one commonality is their fame alters how they move through the world. A famous person—at least a famous person whose face is his currency—can't hide in plain sight. I'd seen that with Hugo in Billings, and years earlier everywhere else. A current goes through a room or a city street when someone famous enters the scene. The chemistry changes. The way others comport themselves is transformed.

At some point in Hugo's performance, he stopped being who he was and became who he was playing. I grasped Lainie's hand and leaned over and said, "My god. He's wonderful." She smiled, and I looked beyond her, to Raj, lost in the art his father was making. It was a glorious night.

———

We went over to Feeney's after the show—Hugo; Lainie; Raj; me; and his director, Joelette, who'd approached Hugo about the play originally and most assuredly was not his lover, since she was accompanied by her partner, Hannah.

We took a high-top table and grabbed some menus. Hugo looked like he had been lit up from inside. He threw an arm across his son's shoulders and said, "It's great to see you, bud."

Frank swept by and asked what we were drinking. I ordered a couple of pitchers of Slumpbuster.

"We're doing a pulled-pork sandwich special," he said. "Fries, tots, or salad on the side. Eight ninety-nine." He kept looking sidelong at Hugo, who noticed.

"Frank," he said, his eyes still caked in makeup designed to make him look older and broken.

"Hugo." Frank nodded and left.

"That was weird," Joelette said.

"Forget it," I said. I figured I'd talk to Frank later, tell him what a revelation Hugo had been. In a week and a half, the play would be over and Hugo could get back to work at the bar. Surely that was still doable. This didn't have to be a major impasse.

Frank dropped by again with the beer, and I poured the glasses one by one and sent them around the table.

"You old enough for this?" I asked Raj.

"As of ten days ago," he said.

Hugo slapped his forehead. "Shit. I forgot."

I shoved the beer across to Raj before this could derail us. "Belated birthday beers are the best," I said.

"Pretty pithy poetry," Lainie said, leaning into me.

"Enough," Hannah tossed in. "I'm thirsty."

I lifted my glass. "To Hugo."

"To Hugo!"

———

Through dinner, I watched Hugo and his son. It was strange—beautiful but strange—for me to see them together again after so many years of dealing with them as separate entities. Raj had done some growing up in my house, when I still had a family there to wrap around him. Sam Wynn's checkbook had managed to disengage that closeness, but it hadn't stopped Raj, over the years, from stopping me at some school sporting event and asking about his old man. I'd always been glad to oblige, even when the news wasn't so good. I was subversive like that.

Now, they dropped in and out of the table conversation, a rollicking, rolling stream, and confided in each other in between. I couldn't hear them over the din, but it was plainly deep and honest, the gesticulations carrying import, the attentiveness carrying investment, the intimacy carrying love. I leaned right and found Lainie's ear. "Look at them," I said.

She turned and smiled at me. "I know."

"You did that. That happened because of you."

She wrapped an arm around my back and pulled me in.

———

Our dishes cleared away, Hugo clapped his son on the thigh and said, "I'm gonna hit the head."

"Too much information, Pops, but OK."

Hugo eased off the barstool and moved around the table, giving Joelette and Hannah shoulder squeezes. When he got to Lainie, he drew her in and planted a kiss on her cheek. I got the sock to the arm. Anything more would have been inappropriate for the venue.

We watched him head off toward the men's room with a hitch in his get along, and I turned back to Joelette and said, "How did you know?"

"Know that he'd be a great Mountain Rivera?"

"Yes."

"I didn't," she said. "Honestly, I thought he'd sell some tickets."

"Don't ever admit that," Lainie said, laughing. "Take the credit."

The metallic clatter of silverware hitting the tile floor brought a shattering silence to the bar. I saw Raj's face go slack, like the muscles in his jaw had been severed, and I turned to see Hugo, kneeling on the floor with Amber, reaching for the forks and knives that had scattered across it.

"Leave it be," Amber said, her voice stretched thin by anger. "You've done enough."

"I just—"

"Leave it!"

Frank, who'd been at a table near the door, came hustling by and said to Raj, "Come get your dad."

When they reached the scrum, Frank leaned over and cupped Hugo under the arms and dragged him up. Raj took things from there and guided him back to our table.

"Take him outside and wait for us," I told Raj. Hugo looked spent, dazed, like he'd evacuated from the moment.

"What just happened?" Joelette said.

I couldn't believe I'd missed it. Over the course of an hour or so, Hugo had gotten himself drunk. Hell, we all probably had a little too much. Problem was, only Hugo among us couldn't handle it. From there, the course had been predictable enough.

Around us, the other customers slipped back into their own worlds and conversations. "We'd better pay and get out of here," I said to Lainie.

I was settling the bill with cash when Frank came by.

"You shouldn't have brought him," he said.

I looked my old friend in the face. It was twisted, emotional, irrational.

"We were celebrating," I said. "He's gone now. No big deal."

"A dozen other places you could have gone," Frank said, voice rising. "Why here?"

"Because you're his people," Lainie said. I turned to look at her. She was every bit as pissed off as he was.

"Lady," Frank said, "who the fuck are you?"

That tore it. I took a swing at Frank, an act dumb as dumb could be. Had Hugo been there, he might have instructed me on the need for a strong defense to back up one's offense, but he wasn't, and I didn't, and the lights went out quickly after that.

32

I awoke in the frayed gray tapestry of morning on Lainie's sectional, Hugo's socked, stinky feet in my face. Raj sat erect in the recliner across from me, his head thrown back in slumber.

"Raj."

I tried to blink my eyes into focus. They hurt. He didn't stir.

"Raj."

Hugo's son swatted a hand across his face and turned his head away from me.

"Raj."

He shook his head now and blinked awake. "What?"

"What happened?"

"You don't remember?" Our voices were whispers. Hugo flopped over and ground himself into the back of his part of the sectional.

"Hugo," I said. "I remember . . . my fucking head." I passed the fingers of both hands under my eyes and found the welt. "Did Frank punch me?"

"That's what that lady said."

"Lady?"

"You know, your lady."

"Lainie."

"That's what I said."

"No," I said. "Never mind."

"Here's an idea," came Hugo's voice, a low hum. "How about both of you shut up?"

We all broke into giggles at that. Hugo rolled again on the couch and then sat up. I did the same, and the rush of blood to my head set off a new round of pain.

"What are we doing here?" Hugo said.

"My question exactly," I said.

Here came Raj with the answers. "Well, let's see," he said, pointing at his father. "You were drunk." He moved the finger to me. "And you got punched out by an old man. Me and your lady got you both in the cars and brought you here. We're the brains of this crew, apparently."

"Stop saying 'your lady,' dude," I said. "This isn't the '70s."

Raj just grinned at me.

"Frank took a swing at you?" Hugo said.

"I think the fair thing to say is that I took a swing at him first."

"Why?"

"He insulted my lady."

We all cracked up again.

"I just wanted to tell Amber I missed her," Hugo lamented.

"She didn't get that message, Pop," Raj said.

I touched the lump under my eye, and pain shot through me again. "I can't believe Frank punched me."

"How's it feel?" Raj asked.

"Like I got hit by the right hand of God."

"Impossible," Hugo said. "Frank fights at a much higher weight than God."

We cackled loudly at that one, until I shushed us. "Don't want to wake up Lainie. Which reminds me: What the hell am I doing out here with you whipdicks? I'm going to bed. You guys need anything?"

Hugo lay back down on the couch. "We're good, Mark. Sleep tight. Keep your chin tucked next time."

———

By the time Lainie and I awoke four hours later, the Hunter men were gone, leaving just the two of us for breakfast. I got my first good look at the dent Frank had put in me. The lump was about the size of a robin's egg, a grotesque, angry purple.

Lainie, behind me in the bathroom, draped her arms across my chest and kissed my ear. "That's the most chivalrous thing anyone's done for me."

"Well, you know me."

"Maybe the dumbest, too," she said.

I grabbed one of her hands and pretended to bite into it. "Don't mess with me, lady. I'm dangerous."

She clapped my shoulders and stepped back. We watched each other in the mirror.

"I like those guys," she said.

"Yeah. Me, too."

"Three men, each of you an only child," she said. "Interesting."

She smiled at me in that warm, knowing way of hers, a way that suggested she didn't have anything more to offer than that oblique observation. It was only later that I figured it out, that Hugo, Raj, and I had imposed our own dynamics on our disparate existences. There's family you're stuck with, and family you choose. For us, it was the latter course.

Those guys mean everything to me.

33

The night before I went back to work, Von came to see me in my slumber. We were all together again, me and Marlene and our boy, and Von talked to me about a brother he had on the way. It didn't compute, in the dream or in the immediate aftermath, when I jolted awake and lay there next to Lainie and her woodcutter snores, trying to make sense of it.

Marlene never got pregnant again. It was an unspoken understanding that a child had done little to improve things between us, save for sucking some of the uglier exchanges out of the air. We weren't good partners, but we weren't monstrous to each other, either. We weren't going to subject a child to that. And when we lost Von, that was the end for us. The indifferent hand of circumstance had taken away our hearts and given us the final shove.

And yet, between the folds of sleep, my son had come to me and talked to me of family. He appeared as he had the last time I saw him alive, that moppish brown hair, those sturdy, steady eyes that gave him the mien of someone much older. He talked to me of commitment and of follow-through, of the notion that anyone can live with anyone else when times are good, and that the measure of things is taken when it's easier to walk than to stay. He didn't tell me I'd failed him and his mom. His manner was gentle, advisory. But I knew. He knew. It was inescapable.

In my dream, I sat still for the comeuppance, because . . . because he made so much damn sense. Because his twelve-year-old mouth yawped out the wisdom of elders. Because I think sometimes maybe I'm forgetting what he looked like and sounded like, and he'd come to remind me.

And then he was gone, and I was awake, and the night spilled into the window above our heads, and I shook Lainie awake and told her I needed to tell her something. And Lainie, God love her, came flying into that sudden moment. "Tell me."

I started with that morning at the clinic, when I first saw her and I couldn't think of anything else. I started with the kindness in her face that drew me in, and the tartness that leveled me, in a good way. The best way.

"I don't know what you thought of me—"

"I thought you were adorable," she said.

"—but I knew I had to talk to you, and then once I talked to you I knew that I had to see you again."

"Yes."

"And it's been everything, Lains. Everything. I don't know what these last few months would look like if it weren't for you."

She slid against me. "I know."

"You're smart like that."

She smiled. "You're lucky to have me."

"I am, at that."

———

I wrapped myself around Lainie and kissed her neck as she fell back into the sleep that I knew wouldn't be coming for me again. Once the wheels start turning, that's it. My day begins. I've heard that the

difference between real life and fiction is that things happen in fiction because of other things, while real life is just a series of human
events, some related, some spontaneous. I don't know. I'm a chronicler, not a philosopher. I try to leave it to other people to make cosmic sense of it all.

I'd had two families in my life, the one I was born into and the
one I tried to build. Dad was gone. Mom, too. Von. Marlene had
taken her $8,000 and the remainder of her dignity and lit out for
God-only-knows-where. It would have been easy enough, lying there
next to Lainie and holding on for dear life, to wonder why so much
loss should be visited on me, but self-pity wasn't in my viewfinder.

And then my scattered thoughts shifted, coagulated, and I wondered if Von wasn't telling me about another duty I had. I thought
of Hugo and those who had been taken from him. More than that, I
thought of the losses he didn't even know about. I remembered the
day Ted Stanton died—it had to be four or five years back now. It
was big news in Billings, and I read the story in the *Herald-Gleaner*
the next morning about his bombast and his political acumen and
his wealth, and I remember wishing I could call up Hugo and talk
to him about this man who had supplied half of his genetic mate-
rial. I couldn't, of course, because I'd made a promise to a woman
who a year later would also be gone and who loved Hugo more than
anyone.

But there was more than just that. The obituary mentioned a
son, an Edward Stanton Jr., and that same son came to work at the
Herald-Gleaner not much later. He was a nighttime maintenance
man, a bit odd, kept to himself—unless something was broken, and
then he was unfailingly reliable. I couldn't remember a single conversation with him, not a single interaction, but when he was in the
same room with me, I would steal looks at him and try to find Hugo
inside him—a damned difficult proposition given his height and his
girth, much more in keeping with his old man's dimensions than
those of the famous half brother he didn't know.

I never managed to shake the unfairness of it all, that I should know such things and Hugo should not—and that I should know only because Frank Feeney got a little loose-lipped one night, prompting him and Aurelia to swear me to secrecy.

So, great, I knew. I remember once being proud that I knew, that I'd been confided in. That's the juice for a newspaperman, being in the know. That means you're good. That means you're trustworthy.

It was all bullshit now.

I shook Lainie again. I had more to say.

From page two of the *Billings Herald-Gleaner* Local section

The Billings Playhouse stage production of "Requiem for a Heavyweight" has hit a snag: Olympic medalist Hugo Hunter, who plays the lead role of boxer Mountain Rivera, has dropped out of the cast.

"He didn't say much," said director Joelette Carson, who had the idea of casting the former boxer. "He said there was another opportunity he had to take now. It's OK. We have a capable understudy and will move forward."

Hunter's deft performance, his first onstage, came as a surprise and helped establish the production as a hit. Drawing on his own past as a professional boxer who never quite made the big time, Hunter packed an emotional wallop with the role, just months after his career ended, seemingly for good, in a loss at the Babcock Theatre.

34

I dragged through the front door of my house Monday morning after seeing Lainie off to work. She'd twisted my arm and kept me at her place with the promise of a late movie and a later breakfast, and hey, I'm not made of stone.

The work cell phone I'd left plugged into the wall after my curt one-week dismissal blinked urgently. I dropped the newspaper on the countertop, fetched the phone, and punched up the voice mail. I was surprised to hear Larry Largeman's whiskey-sour voice.

"Hey, bud, give me a call. I think we're home free."

The "we're" threw me a bit. I still wasn't sure if I was ally or dupe. I dialed the number.

"Largeman," came the answer.

"Westerly."

"Hey, bud. I took care of your case."

Still with the vagaries. The only words I wanted to hear were "it has been dismissed" or "Case Schronert has dropped it." Everything else was just a possible variation on bad news.

"What's that mean?" I asked.

"It's over. It's done. No more lawsuit."

That was more like it.

"What happened?" I asked.

A gargle came through on the other end. "Listen, Mark, do you suppose you can come in today so we can talk about this at more length?"

"What? Why?"

"There are ears in the cornfield."

"Huh?"

"Eyes in the potato patch."

"Are you having a stroke or something, Largeman?"

He coughed, and I held the phone away from my ear. "Goddamnit, I don't want to talk about it on the phone," he said. "You're a lousy hint taker, you know that?"

I ignored it. "I can come by around eleven."

"That'll work."

"See you, Largeman."

———

With time to burn, I headed to Hugo's place. I'd read the paper and gone through my usual bit where he's concerned—surprised, but not really. I needed to find out what was going on. It did me no good to get on the phone. Hugo monitored his calls, and whether he wanted to talk with me was beside the point. I wanted to talk with him. It was an old trick of mine, this ambushing him wherever and whenever I needed to. The thing was, once you got face time with Hugo, he was so exceedingly polite and eager to please that he'd engage on any topic you cared to bring to him. That affability was golden to the newspaperman I was. I absolutely exploited it, which I suppose makes me craven and insensitive. Whatever. It got me stories, and that was the coin of my realm.

I didn't need anything beyond the small pile of newspapers on Hugo's lawn to know something was amiss, that he hadn't been home in a while. I pulled out my phone and queued up a number. A few minutes later, I had a lunch date with Raj Hunter.

————

Unease scratched at me on the drive to Largeman's office. In twenty-plus years of dealing with Hugo, I'd come to know something about his unpredictability, and none of it was very good. Some of it I had buried deep. In '98, the year after the disappointment in London, Hugo up and announced that he was moving to Los Angeles to be with his new girlfriend, that Ashley Lane character who made all those well-received period pieces in the early '90s but was more a straight-to-video vixen by the time Hugo sank balls-deep into her. So there he went, bought himself a house in the hills and a couple of cars, and what could anyone do? He was twenty-three, it was his money and his life. Frank and Squeaky exacted a promise that training would still happen at the place on Flathead Lake, and Aurelia put on a brave face, because that's what Aurelia did. I'd try to call every month or so to play catch-up, but Hugo was hard to reach.

What happened out there, in the end, was no big secret. Cocaine, fights with the paparazzi, drunken car crashes. That's the stuff in the public record. Fourteen months after Hugo left us, Frank and Squeaky were on the coast, pleading with a judge to let Hugo come home and get cleaned up. All the trappings of a fast-expiring fame, gone. His money, gone. At that point, I was socking money away for Von's college education, any stray dollar I could catch, and it burned my ass that Hugo could be so cavalier with something I worked so hard to bring into the house.

————

At Largeman's office, I sat alone and waited until he emerged in the wake of a toilet flush and running water and offered a handshake.

"It's OK," he said. "I washed."

"It's an old line, Largeman."

"Yeah, but reassuring people of cleanliness never gets old."

He signaled me to take a seat, and he settled in behind the desk.

"So, no more court case," he said, pushing across the document that verified this. "Best two grand you ever spent, right?"

"I guess. Why'd he relent?"

"He knew a superior legal mind when he saw one."

"Come on, Largeman."

He chuckled and tried to pull me into his mirth, but I'd have none of it. Finally, he sighed and set his hands on the desk.

"OK, look," he said. "Your fundamental concern should be this lawsuit, and it's gone. I'm gonna tell you the rest, but whatever you think of it, remember this: I did what I said I would do. I got rid of it."

"OK." Fewer words are better when you're bracing for literally anything.

"So I was thinking that the best way to squash this thing was to short-circuit it. Do you like to go to court?"

"Never been, other than my divorce."

"You're a lucky bastard, other than your divorce. I hate court. It's boring. It has rules and stuff. I didn't want to do that. So I started thinking about Case Schronert. If you're that guy, you've got a rep-utation, people know you, you've got some history. And a guy with history is a guy with secrets. That's just a fact of life."

"It is," I said. I started to feel a little squeamish.

"Case Schronert's secret is that he likes to shack up. A lot. With several women who aren't his wife. You want to see pictures?"

"Jesus," I said. "You followed him? You took pictures?"

"Hey! Remember what I said: you're off the hook."

My head began to spin. "You blackmailed him?"

"I did not blackmail him." Largeman was actually indignant. That took some gall. "I convinced him of my superiority as an inves-tigator. I suggested to him that if he did me a favor, I could do some good work for him. It's called revenue streams, buddy boy. You think I'm going to be able to retire on your two thousand clams?"

"Still." That's all I could say amid the mental processing and low-level nausea.

"You're making me feel bad," Largeman said, putting on the full pout for his own benefit. "I'm good at this. Finding out information is what I do. We're not so different, you and me, except that you announce your presence. I'm more comfortable being the fly on the wall."

"I'd say we're completely different."

Largeman came around the desk and offered a handshake, which I accepted. He had washed up, after all.

"I can understand why you'd say that," he said, "but we're really not. We're in love with the same woman. The difference is, my love for her exists somewhere else in time, before I became what I am. You get her now. You lucky son of a bitch."

Excerpt from *Hugo Hunter: My Good Life and Bad Times*

I've come to learn a few things about the way fame changes people. I'm not talking about me. Those changes are evident to anyone who bothers to look. I'm talking about the way people react to fame when they're in the presence of it.

Imagine losing your private life when you're only seventeen years old.

When you're approached by someone with something nice to say, imagine looking at that person and wondering what he or she wants. That's a terribly cynical outlook, and yet it's inevitable, too.

Imagine being asked, repeatedly, for just a few minutes of your time. If you say no, you're an asshole. If you take the time to explain that if you gave a few minutes to everyone who wanted it, that none of your minutes would belong to you anymore, you're an asshole.

In many respects, I was fortunate. Other than the months I was living in Los Angeles, falling in deep with drugs, I never ran with an entourage. Frank and Trevor Feeney kept a tight circle with me. My only family was Grammy, so I didn't have a lot of people coming to me with their hand out. I've lived almost exclusively in the town where I grew up, and people here gave me a certain amount of latitude (although, on the flip side, they're also more likely to tell me flat out that I'm a disappointment to them).

Last year, after I bubbled into the news again, and again for all the wrong reasons, a Hollywood producer approached me. He wanted to make a reality TV show out of my life. We never got far enough along in our talks to discuss money, so maybe I'm an idiot for having turned him away. I just didn't want to enter that cauldron again. Reality TV? No, thanks. For me, plain old reality has been difficult enough.

35

At lunch, Raj filled in the details that wouldn't have been in a newspaper story.

"He's on a rig in the Bakken," he said. "He left a couple of days after—well, you know, after all that stuff at Feeney's."

That clarified everything and exactly nothing. The most pregnant question of all: How does a guy go from greasepaint thespian to grease monkey rig hand in a week? Raj didn't have all the answers, but he closed the gaps that were within his reach.

"I took Pop to my apartment that morning after we woke up at your place," he told me, leaning into his plate of nachos. "Did you see him getting drunk? I didn't see it. Too much going on."

"I didn't see it," I said. "I should have."

"He didn't want to go to his house," Raj said. "He said he was still hungover, so I was like, 'I got a couch.' My roommate was all, 'That's Hugo Hunter on our couch.' Yeah. My dad."

"What'd Hugo say?"

Raj sat back in his chair. "You know, the same stuff. He was sorry. He needed to get his shit together. I've heard it before."

"We all have."

"Yeah. So he called a day or so later and said he was getting a lift to Williston, that there was a rig job waiting for him. He said he loves that Amber woman and that he had to grow up."

"Did he say where he'll be?"

"No. He said he'd call me every couple of weeks and stay in touch. You want me to let you know if I hear from him?"

"That'd be great, Raj."

"No problem. He said he really felt like this time it was going to work out for him."

"What'd you say?"

"I wished him luck. What else could I do?"

Nothing. It wasn't a question that demanded an answer.

"I hope it works for him," Raj said, "but I've got my own stuff going on. You know?"

I reached across the table and snared a nacho off his plate and popped it in my mouth, and I shrugged.

I can't say I was surprised by Raj's attitude, though I was sorry to hear it. That's what Hugo tended to do. He'd grind on you and grind on you with his dreams and schemes, and by the time he came up with something that might work, you were too exhausted to invest more than middling hope in it.

The fact was, the oil field sounded like a half-decent idea to me. It had its dangers and cautionary tales, sure, but it also had things Hugo badly needed: a job and money. I also couldn't discount the potential benefits of having his time and attention focused. That's how boxing had first beguiled him and then held him close. When he was doing it, when he was turned intently toward a goal, he was, at once, more of a danger to his opponent and less a danger to himself.

Raj had made the simple and sane decision to protect himself. He'd let hope in—he had youth on his side and could make that investment freely—and he'd gone on with his own life. I had to concede that, whatever I thought of his mother and his grandfather, he'd been raised well. I could sit there and condemn their actions, which

I'd witnessed and which I believed I could see in full, but I couldn't say anything negative about the results. And given the time that had passed us by, perhaps it was time for me to let it go.

36

Nobody at the *Herald-Gleaner* took my weeklong interlude as an opportunity to clean the joint up. I returned that afternoon to the same old workspace in the same old dingy corner of the office and with the same old Trimear preoccupied with the same old nonsense.

Over the years, I'd seen a few colleagues sat down for various transgressions, most of them specious. The truly gifted problem employees find a way to exercise just enough incompetence that it's stealthily subversive, and thus it inspires only heartburn among the bosses. It takes a consistently solid citizen like me to commit a suspension-worthy sin through accepted editorial means.

The fortunate ones aren't made to come back. They get pink-slipped, we end up having a glorious drunk in their front yard as a fuck you to the man, and they turn up a few months or years later in a far better place than Billings, Montana. Rick Westphal, truly the worst of the editors I'd had at the *Herald-Gleaner*, once shit-canned a reporter, Holly Hawkins, because she'd had the temerity to put in freedom-of-information requests on the property tax records of every elected official in Billings and had discovered that, lo and behold, a third of them were delinquent on their bills. She'd approached them all, asked why, gotten a bunch of worthless equivocations, and set about writing the story under the theory that, hey, you might want to know that the folks in charge of the public trust are themselves not trustworthy. The city attorney at the time, a fetid wasteland of human worthlessness named Calvin Tandy, walked into the newsroom, strode up to Holly's desk, and said, "Darling, that story will never see print." Ten minutes later, he was out of Westphal's office and Hawkins was in. The very definition of a raw deal, except for this: two years later, Hawkins won a Pulitzer in Omaha for an exposé on a buried sex scandal at a parochial school. Lucky for her that she wasn't good enough for the *Herald-Gleaner.*

Newspapers are funny places, man, and when I say *funny,* I mean it in every constellation. If one gets inside your skin, you keep showing up because you know that someday something extraordinary is going to go down, and there's no group of people funnier, more caustic, more bitter, more twisted than your coworkers, and you can't imagine experiencing it anywhere else. And in all the in-between times, when nothing of much import happens and the stories move across your eyes like gray static and you sell out your soul bit by bit, you show up because you have nothing better to do. And you're completely OK with that trade.

I walked in, and the downturned faces greeted me as if I'd been away at a dear family member's funeral. I got grim half smiles, the unspoken part being this: "It was a personnel matter and William Pennington didn't say anything, but you were gone and we know what happened, and you're back now and this must be so embarrassing for you."

I settled in. "Gene," I said.

"Hey, you're back." Trimear dropped some page dummies on their edge, squaring them off in his hand. "You ready?"

"Yeah, sure, you know. What's the plan?"

"Typical Monday night. Slow. Need you to fetch phones and take some scores."

"Sure."

"Need you to go out to Sidney on Wednesday."

"What for?" Trimear had just put me on a five-hundred-mile round trip to Montana's eastern edge and back. Driving straight into the sun on the way out, having it beat on my head on the way home. Endless asphalt ribbons. Not the duty I preferred.

"Eagles are gonna be really good this year, maybe the best in Class A. Need a story for the football section."

———

If you take on eastern Montana by way of Interstate 94—and you really should exhaust all other possibilities for your life before you do—you're likely to be taken in by the illusion that you're pressing on in a straight, unyielding line. With the exception of a few scrubby buttes and river-crossed badlands, the route is clear to the horizon.

That's the illusion. The fact is that the road unrolls north and east, in rough parallel to the flow of the Yellowstone River. Knowing this does little to stem the narcotic dullness of the drive, but I suppose it salves the soul a bit. There's more wonder nearby than finds its way to your optic nerve. Sure, you've still got to get where you're going—for me, on that particular Wednesday, it was a little boomtown on the Montana edge of the biggest domestic oil play going, 260 miles from the sun-kissed warmth of Lainie's bed—but at least you can be content that something's out there. Rattlesnakes and irrigation ditches and verdant fields and shattering solitude, but something. Something besides you and the road and the odd car passing you in an inexplicable hurry and the truckers opposite you headed for Billings and Bozeman and Missoula and, blessedly, Seattle.

I'd made two calls the night before. The first, to Sidney football coach Barry Brill, had told me that I'd need to thread the needle between two-a-day practices, and that's why I was on the road at five a.m. while my love snoozed back at her house. The second, to a cell phone number that Raj had given me earlier that day, told Hugo to expect me the next evening. We agreed to meet in Williston, just forty-five miles from where I was staying.

In Miles City, the midpoint of my drive, I'd veered off the highway for a couple of Egg McMuffins and a tanker-sized cup of coffee. Something was up with my appetite. There was no pretending that it wasn't so, not anymore, not as I fought every morning to get my jeans above the centerline and my protruding gut pushed hard at my shirt buttons. You could make the argument that I needed the weight; my doctor certainly had, ad nauseam, over the years. My inveterate smoking habit had made a hollow-chested freak out of me, but it had also served the more noble purpose of tamping down my appetite. I was swinging the other way now, headed for fat, happy, pink-lunged land.

Nearly eighty miles on, I swung off the interstate at Glendive and picked my way straight north, where the Yellowstone jogged toward its meet-up with the Missouri. The scoria-scarred badlands fell behind me, the river held me tight on the starboard side, and I made steady progress into a fertile valley ruled by sugar beets. I'd been born in Montana, raised here, never left for any extended amount of time, and this country always surprised me. It's the Montana nobody thinks of—no mountains, no deep, cold lakes, but still starkly beautiful, with horizons that stretch in all directions. It's a hard land shaped by hard people, and those austere families who made their stands here have reaped the bounty, first in agriculture and now in oil. The countryside crawled with land men, up to their necks in paperwork in the county courthouses as they researched mineral rights, and myriad were the modest farms that now sported telltale rows of holding tanks and the masts of oil rigs reaching for the sun. People here knew about booms and busts. They built their lives around them, either riding high or riding out. Now, with the technological changes that allowed rigs to tap into pockets of oil previously unreachable, by drilling sideways into the giving earth, some people said this wasn't just another boom but the fundamental reconfiguration of a region.

As the highway dumped me out into the wide arms of Sidney, Montana, I couldn't say that I disagreed with that assessment. On every corner, it seemed, a new motel took shape in wooden frames and Tyvek. Clumps of dried mud covered the road, the leavings of the big trucks that came through at all hours, all day. I'd read the alternating accounts, the joyous recitations of the money and people pouring in and the grim outlook for such basics as wastewater treatment and bridge maintenance. Jobs and cash multiplied and beckoned, and unknown faces appeared with greater frequency. Restaurants had no end of customers and no source of labor, what with the paychecks being greater in the patch. Coffers filled and crime flourished. At every turn, a trade-off.

I checked my watch. 9:37. I had a coach to find and a story to mold. I turned off the main road and plunged in.

37

In Williston, I found Hugo at a corner booth in a bar down on Riverside. He stood up and hugged me, then gave me a little faked uppercut to the melon. "You gotta keep your chin tucked, Mark."

He looked good. The same. He was outfitted in Carhartts and chambray, a cap pulled low on his head. He looked like most of the guys in the bar—hard-edged, rugged, the kind of guys who'd have grease in the wrinkles of their knuckles. It was only if you looked a little closer that you'd see the differences. Age had made bank on Hugo's face, leaving a road map of crags and gullies. Gray hairs threaded the black at his temples. The buddies who'd brought him to the bar—Hugo pointed them out at the blackjack table—were his son's age. Hugo carried every one of his years. Those guys had a hungrier look about them, a wilder look.

I sat down. "You doing OK?"

"Just been a few days, but yeah. It's fine."

"What have they got you doing?"

"Cleaning."

"You serious?"

"As a heart attack," he said. "That's the job. Keep the rig clean. Twenty-eight bucks an hour to scour with a scrub brush."

"Unbelievable."

He pointed at my eye. "That what Frank did?"

"Yep."

"Did it hurt when he hit you?"

"I don't remember."

I said it as Hugo took a draw on his beer, and he nearly spat it out laughing. "Frank's an old dude, but he's mean. You probably should have started with someone closer to your own size."

"He probably shouldn't have sassed my lady."

Hugo set the beer down. "You guys on the outs over this?"

"Me and Frank? I don't know. We've survived worse things."

It was another of those things I said as a tossed-off line, only to see it hit Hugo like a dart. I grimaced.

"I guess everybody's pretty disgusted with me," he said.

"I haven't talked to anybody but your son, Hugo, but I doubt it. You know how it is. People just want you to find something and stick with it. They want you to be happy, contented. Same thing they want for themselves."

"I know."

"So why this?"

He tipped the bottle again. "I don't know. It's good pay, and there's a lot of work. It got me out of Billings. I think that's probably good. There wasn't a lot for me there. But the big thing is Amber and that kid. I love them. I really do. I gotta show her I can be counted on."

"Sounds like that part and the bit about getting out of Billings are in conflict."

"Yeah, maybe."

"Did you tell her how you feel?"

"She won't talk to me."

At last, a harried server swung by the table. I ordered a Jack and Coke.

"Maybe she will," I said. "Maybe if you show her you're serious."

Hugo fixed me with a hard look, something meant to convince but also to intimidate, and it worked on both levels. "I am serious," he said.

———

We talked through dinner and beyond. I nursed my drink, not wanting to fall too deep into the bottle with a drive back to Sidney still in front of me. Hugo cut himself off at two beers and stuck to water, and that impressed me perhaps more than anything else.

Our twenty-plus-year history provided us with conversational shorthand. While we tended to go deep on current events and percolating dramas, our ventures into nostalgia skipped from subject to subject like a flat rock across a pond. And it was there, in the folds of memory, that I would always rediscover why I liked Hugo so damned much. If you shook loose the burdens of any given moment, or the frustrations of dealing with his idiosyncrasies, he was what he's always been: an engaging, interesting, fun guy.

I filled him in on life with Lainie, how I was getting to know her son. I'd been a little hesitant to get close to Tony, near as he was to Von's age. I don't know. It sounds irrational, but I worried a bit that letting him into my heart would somehow supplant my own son's hold on me. But then he welcomed me, and I saw how funny he and Lainie could be when they got together, completing each other's sentences, arguing over fine details, expansive with their love for each other. I told Hugo that I was defenseless against their charms.

"Reminds me of my mom," Hugo said.

"Yeah? She was funny?"

He ran a finger along the rim of his empty beer glass. "Not like a comedian. She had kind of a devilish sense of humor. Warped."

I kept my mouth closed, hoping he'd go on.

"This one time," he said, "her and Grammy were fighting about something, and Mom went into the yard—it's late fall, early winter, no snow on the ground, the grass is all brown and cracked—and she grabs a couple of handfuls of grass and comes back in clutching the side of her head.

"Grammy's all, 'What's wrong?' And Mom goes, 'I can't take it anymore,' and she throws the grass all over the house like she's pulled her hair out, and Grammy starts screaming."

"Holy crap!"

"I know," Hugo said. "The look on her face. Oh, man, it was so choice."

"What were they fighting about?"

He looked at me, blinking. "I don't know. What difference does it make?"

"I was just wondering."

"That's not the point, Westerly," he said in mock indignation. "The point is what Mom did. Are you looking to cause trouble?" He couldn't help it. A smile turned up the corners of his mouth.

I smiled and backpedaled. "No, no, of course not."

"You sure? Because I'll give you some trouble. I'll take you up to Knuckle Ridge." He held up a fist and shook it faux-menacingly at me.

He sputtered and then laughed, and so did I.

God, it was such a great night.

———

Just before ten, Hugo's buddies came around the table to collect him. Hugo brokered the introductions, and I shook hands with Jeff, who'd lost his ass at blackjack, and Sean, who'd taken down nearly $400 in winnings.

"I can take you back if you want to stick around," I told Hugo.

"Nah, we're in a man camp in Stanley. You'd be driving away from where you're headed. I'll be back home in a couple of weeks, and I'll see you then."

"It's really no trouble."

"Next time," he said.

I pulled him in for a hug. There was no reason to fake a journalistic distance anymore. That all seemed like it had happened to two other guys—younger guys, with more in front of them than we had now. I released him, and Hugo threw another mock punch, our eternal routine. I shook hands with his friends again, and then they were gone, out the door. The server came around with the tab, and I paid it and left.

Outside the bar, the air was restless, thick with late-summer humidity. The monster that Williston had become never slept. The city lit up the night. I'd noted the growth on my way in: the fresh roadways, the influx of chain restaurants, oil holding tanks, rail cars that went on forever, the smell of new money. In a parking lot full of tricked-out pickups, I found my forlorn little sedan, and I fired it up for the drive that would send me back into the stillness and the dark, into a land measured by Lewis and Clark, who had no way of imagining the frontiers they trod upon, how discovery would still shape this place two centuries later. Discovery and displacement. The Native Americans, then the white man, then the land men, and now and forever the almighty dollar. Opportunity is a matter of perspective, I suppose.

I hit a straightaway and sped up. An adequate bed and a minibar awaited me in Sidney, but all I wanted was to hit the rack and hasten the arrival of morning. Perhaps it's folly, at my age, to wish away any of the hours I'm given, but that night, in that place, all I could think about was getting home to Lainie. Hugo's declarations for Amber had touched me, and I found myself wishing hard that he could find a way to her, that he was truly serious about being a man for her. I hoped that he really felt about Amber the way I felt about my girl.

I'd been alive too long and had seen too much to believe in soul mates, as least in the way that romantic notion is packaged and sold in our culture. The idea that there's one girl for one guy, and all you have to do is suffer through all the many wrong ones until you find her or him, is just an endorsement of fairy tales. We need all kinds of people to get us through life. It's too hard without them. I sliced through the hot night in my car, and I thought of those who had sustained me. My parents. Marlene, even when things were bad. Von. Gene freaking Trimear, for God's sake.

And Lainie—sweet, sweet Lainie. She would be falling into bed in Billings now, curling up into the cotton sheets, and I was four hours away, and that just wasn't right.

I was going to have to marry that girl.

Excerpt from *Hugo Hunter: My Good Life and Bad Times*

I've given love five times in my life:

To my mother.

To Grammy.

To Seyna.

To Raj.

To cocaine.

I would give anything to have my mom and Grammy back. I would give anything to have done a better job as Seyna's husband. I would do anything for my son.

I would do more than that for cocaine.

Even now. Even today. Daily, I go to a meeting and admit to myself and others the power it holds over me. I talk about it because that drags my addiction into the light and makes it a real thing for me and those around me, and it forces us to deal with it. I don't want to be alone with it. I don't want to hide it. That's when it makes real trouble for me.

The drug had its hooks in me the first time I tried it. Love at first snort. All I knew was that I wanted more, immediately, and as much as I could get my hands on. It was euphoria—out of control, endless cartwheels, everything-is-electric euphoria.

I also knew I was in big, big trouble.

And I was. I am. I will forever be.

38

I made it back to Billings by noon Thursday, fueled by gasoline, coffee, and Swedish Fish. With a few necessary stops, I had the supplies I needed, and I was in Lainie's house by two. She had left me a note on the counter and some lasagna in the fridge, and I took measure of my time.

I could do this.

The first part was easy. I sat down with my laptop and did what I'd done thousands of times before, taking quotations and statistics and names and shaping a story out of them, wolfing down bites of lunch between flurries of keystrokes. It wasn't high art. It never had been, really, and I certainly held no illusions about that now. Expository paragraph, quote, expository paragraph, quote, lather, rinse, repeat. That's how you knock out a sports story. Gene Trimear wouldn't mind, and neither would the Sidney Eagles.

I had more important things to do.

Once the article headed off to Trimear's e-mail in-box, I checked the time again. 2:53. Next, I put a bottle of pinot grigio in an ice-filled salad bowl—I didn't have time for the finer presentation touches—and plucked rose petals free to spread through the house.

3:26.

I doffed my clothes and climbed into the shower. Scattered as I was, I gave silent thanks that I'd remembered not having underwear at Lainie's and had swung by my place to fetch a pair. Otherwise, I'd be stuck in the ones that had just traveled nearly three hundred sweaty miles or I'd be going commando: equally unappetizing possibilities.

Out of the shower, I looked at my face in Lainie's bathroom mirror, and I saw the valleys cut into it by the dribbling out of time. The thing is, I looked better, healthier, *happier* than I had in a long time. And I was. The cheeks that had been gaunt and drawn a year earlier were chubby and hale. I smiled, a big, goofy grin that didn't make me self-conscious in the least. I couldn't have erased it if I'd tried.

3:48.

For the first time in my life, I confronted a problem borne by a fat person. I couldn't get my damn cummerbund to stay where it belonged. I'd suck air in, pull it up, breathe out, and feel it slip toward my hips. And then I'd repeat the exercise.

Cuff links, too, presented what the kids called a first-world problem. I leaned into Lainie's dresser with my left arm, turned the palm up toward me, and tried to wrangle the works with my free right hand. Failing that, I got my teeth involved. Finally, I had the link in and switched arms and fought through the maneuver again.

Sweat beaded on my upper lip and my brow, and I could feel it pooling in the small of my back. Damn my bright idea of doing this on one of the hottest days of the year.

At last, I wriggled into my rented tux jacket, and the bedroom became a sauna. I took it off again and set it on the bed. It could wait till the last possible second.

4:23.

I sat on the couch and pushed the ring box to the center of the coffee table. The guy at Montague's said I had exquisite taste. That may be true—I rather liked the single stone in a simple platinum display—but I think he was just happy to get the credit account.

I pulled back the box and opened it, then shoved it back to the table's center.

I retrieved it, closed the box, stood and stuffed it into my right pocket, and sat down again.

Up once more, I carried it to the kitchen, opened the box again, and set it inside the refrigerator. I closed the door.

No. No. No.

I opened the door and removed the box, and I held it in my right hand as I consulted my watch.

4:34.

The hum of a motor, the squeal of turning wheels, and I dashed across the room in my high-sheen lace-up shoes to the bedroom, where I gathered the jacket. My right arm hung up in the sleeve as I tried to shimmy into it, and the ring tumbled from the box to the floor at my feet.

The slamming of a car door.

I knelt as gently and as quickly as I could and swept up the ring.

The sound of steps on the walk.

I ran a hand over my hair.

The key in the door.

I ran back to the front room and positioned myself on the lino-leum in front of the door.

4:35.

I smiled. I think I smiled. I'm pretty sure I smiled.

I pulled my cummerbund up.

A crack of sunlight in the darkened room, and then more than a crack . . .

———

I asked Marlene Morley to marry me on September 12, 1985. We'd driven down to Denver to see, God help us, Ratt in concert at McNichols Arena. In fairness to us, Ratt was just an accessory to our hair-metaled crime. We'd really gone down there to see Bon Jovi, the opening act that in just a couple of years would be the hottest thing going. I can't really defend our being there on artistic grounds, but I can say this: we were young, we were in love, and we liked loud music.

We'd taken midweek days off—Marlene from her nursing job at Deaconess, me from the Buttrey's on Thirteenth where I worked in the produce department until the *Herald-Gleaner* brought me aboard—and had headed for Colorado in my Datsun 720 pickup, which was making its final brave stand a year before that name would disappear and Nissans would multiply across the earth. When you're in love, you can conquer anything, even Wyoming, but we were no match for a blown water pump that left us stranded along northbound Interstate 25 on the return trip, in that great gaping maw between Cheyenne and Wheatland.

I could have sooner walked to the moon than to the next town. I wouldn't own a cell phone for nearly fifteen more years. Marlene and I sat on the tailgate, making halfhearted attempts at flagging down some help, and we talked. We had prospects, and we were well aware of them. My family liked her. Her family liked me. We were hot for each other. Neither of us could see into the future, but it didn't seem beyond our dreams to expect a house and some kids and a vacation to Disneyland or maybe Six Flags. We could hope for all of that.

"I want to marry you," I told her. I was twenty-two years old, full of certitude.

"I want you to," she said.

We sat there awhile longer and made moony eyes at each other, and we talked about our eagerness to get home to Billings and find a ring and tell our folks and let our friends shower us with their good wishes and envy. Before too long, a Wyoming Highway Patrol officer rolled up on us and asked what we needed. We asked for a tow truck, and he tipped his hat and put in the call.

Through everything that followed—every fight, every moment I knew I'd made a mistake, every moment I wished I could have spared Marlene the affliction of me, every year that marched on in emptiness, and, yes, every moment when things seemed like they might be OK—my feelings about that afternoon in Wyoming never changed.

It was one of the glorious days of my life.

———

Lainie stood before me, agape. Understandable. To see me there in her living room, midday, wearing a monkey suit, must have been like coming home and finding the US water polo team in the hot tub. A little hard to figure.

I held out the ring, unboxed, between trembling fingers.

"What have you done?" she said.

I cleared my throat. "I had this idea—"

"This isn't . . ."

I pulled the ring back, just a little. "Yeah."

"Oh, Mark." Her face had gone white first, then red. Vermillion. Her name.

"That's not—" I sputtered. I hadn't vaguely imagined this reaction.

"Oh, Mark, no . . ."

"No?" Shit. Oh, shit.

"I mean . . ." Her eyes went to water. "Shit," she said. Exactly.

I slumped.

"Lains, I . . . I . . ." I couldn't muster more than a stammer.

She reached for my hand. "Sit down."

———

The evening I stepped onto Bim Morley's porch and told him I'd like to marry his daughter, after first telling him that I'd already floated the proposition to her, he called me out on my procedural error.

"You should have come to see me first," he said, and my heart sank just a little, which must have been evident to him, because he quickly paved things over. "Don't get me wrong, son, we're glad to have you in the family, but I just pictured it a little differently. Forgive an old man for his illusions of chivalry."

And then he gave me the only piece of advice I ever got from him, and the advice I abandoned early and often.

"Put her first," he said. "She'll always believe in you if she knows she's first."

I can't account for why something like that sticks even when you're not listening. I think about those days now, and it's as if I was finishing a checklist: Ask her father, check. Get the ring, check. Find a reception venue, check. All the while, I was missing the things I really should have paid heed to.

I thought about all of that in the hotel room in Sidney, as the idea of marrying Lainie went from far-off prospect to immediate hunger. The excitement ran so thick and deep that I had to remind myself that I'd felt these things before and that it had all gone to hell. I talked to myself about lessons learned and wisdom gained, and how hard it had been.

I fell asleep vowing to remember this time.

———

Lainie sat me down on the couch next to her. She never let go of my hand. The tux jacket stretched uncomfortably across my shoulders. Such a fool I was.

"I love you," she said.

"I love you." I wasn't ready to look at her.

"I—" She squeezed my hand. "I'm surprised. It's not that I haven't thought about this. But I thought we'd talk about it, come to it gradually."

I said nothing. I hadn't stopped to think that seven months together wasn't enough.

She pressed me. "What are you thinking?"

I found patterns in the carpet. "I messed this up."

"Look at me."

I didn't.

"Look at me."

I did.

"You could never"—her free hand moved back and forth between us—"in a million years mess this up."

"Then why won't you marry me?"

"I'm not saying I won't. But—"

"What?"

"I've been married."

"So have I."

"It's only been two years since I lost him. He was supposed to be here forever, and he's not, and I get that, and I've moved on. It's just—"

"Tell me."

She sniffled and drew up her hand, the one that held mine, to wipe her nose. She didn't let go.

"I'm scared," she said.

"Of what?"

"I don't know."

"That doesn't help."

"I know."

I let go of her, and she grabbed me back. "Hold on," she said.

———

The night before I married Marlene, Joe Oldegaard, my best man and best friend since elementary school, walked me away from the party with my groomsmen at the 17 Club and suggested that we have a cigarette. The outside air that evening, heart of spring, still had a bite. We had to give each other hand cover to get blazed up.

"People will understand," he said.

"Understand what?"

"If you call it off. Yeah, it'll be inconvenient and embarrassing, but they'll get it."

I was dumbfounded. "Get the fuck out of here."

He shrugged. We finished our cigarettes in silence and went back inside.

Twenty-four hours later, I was married and holed up in the Stardust with Marlene, a long weekend in Vegas awaiting us before work and the drudgeries of marriage called us back home. I told her what Joe had said.

"Cass said the same thing to me," she said.

"Last night?"

"Yes."

"Do you think they planned it?"

"I don't know," she said. "They looked pretty chummy at the rehearsal dinner."

I stared into the ceiling. Marlene went rigid beside me.

"Why would they do that?" I said.

———

I left Lainie's and went home, to my bed. I pounded my pillow, as if some bedside violence would stop the motion inside my head and let me find sleep.

Lainie had asked me to stay. Begged me, really. I couldn't do it. By the time I left, I wasn't angry. I wasn't even hurt—at least not too much. Her reasons for caution, when she finally expressed them, made sense. Distance from her life with Delmar. Not wanting to one-up Tony and his fiancée, who were in the full flurry of planning their own nuptials. Time. Just more time.

I got it. I got it, but I couldn't stay. The downside of my elaborate proposal theater is I'd left no room for any answer other than yes. No would have been devastation. Let-me-think-about-it might well have turned me into a huckster, babbling anything to close the deal. She didn't say either of those things. She said, "I love you, and I'll always love you, and I'll always want you," and I kissed her forehead, her cheek, her lips. I had to go home, where I didn't want to be, and try to figure out why it wasn't yes.

After Dad was gone and before Mom slipped into the depths of the dementia that took her, I would sit at the little kitchen table in the house where I grew up, and I'd spend a few hours with her every Tuesday morning. Those hours made a slow reveal of the crevasses opening in my marriage. I told Mom one time that I didn't see how she and Dad had done it, how they'd managed to stay in tune all those years, and she laughed and said, "Mark, there were years at a time when we could barely stand each other." That surprised me. It shouldn't have. I'd come to know such years with Marlene. In any case, I don't think that dose of perspective helped me, because it gave rise to my most mulish impulses. It made me view my marriage as something to be conquered.

I got out of bed and paced the floor, wore a groove into the carpet between my room and the den. Each time I passed Von's door, I ran my finger along it.

I'd spent a lot of time with this subject, before Marlene found the gumption to go and long after, and all that thought had made a few things clear. I no longer hated Joe or Cass for what they'd done. The friendships hadn't survived their last-ditch efforts to save us from ourselves, but they'd made those decisions knowing the risks. They had accurately diagnosed our underlying trouble, and you can't hate someone for being right. I'd also come to be well in tune with the hesitations I felt before we said "I do," the many times I'd wanted to run and hadn't, and I could tell myself, categorically, that I felt none of that where Lainie was concerned. My delivery of the question had left me open to feelings of foolishness, but I'd get over that. I had to. My desire to ask again—and again, if I needed to—remained.

I returned to bed and crawled into the sheets. I lay my head down and sleep came for me, at last, in measures too heavy to resist. The blackness came on in full and I was gone, and it wasn't until after Lainie had let herself in with the key I'd given her and found me in my room and slid into the bed next to me and kissed my ear that I awoke again. Not with a start, but as if she had been there all along.

"Yes," she said.

Excerpt from *Hugo Hunter: My Good Life and Bad Times*

On the whole, I will never feel anything but gratitude for Frank Feeney and what he's done for me.

As for what he's done *to* me, that's a harder account to square.

I never knew my actual father, and so I'm not altogether certain how that relationship looks from the son's end of things. I also wasn't much of a father to Raj when he was young, so I'm deficient there, too. Frank was my father figure in the absence of anyone else willing to do the job, and I have considered whether that was expecting too much of him. Maybe it was. But that's where we are, and that's why his distancing himself from me hurts so much. I'm not saying he doesn't have a right to cut me out. I'm saying that I would hope a father, a real father, would never take that step. Frank did, and here we are, living in the same town, talking to the same people, but never seeing each other. It's hard. Damn right it's hard.

This is another area where my daily affirmations at my support group really help. I parse through the things I can control and the things I can't. Frank made his decision where I'm concerned. I can't change it for him. That duty lies with him.

39

I'd barely breached the door at Feeney's before I said, "I come in peace." Frank's plump face, wound up into a ready bark, did a slow unraveling.

"Have a seat," he said. The midday lunch crowd had come and gone and it was just the two of us. I tended to have impeccable timing when I wanted to see him alone.

I settled onto the stool in front of him. "How've you been?"

Frank shrugged. The smell of chili wafted across the bar, and my face must have betrayed my interest. "You hungry?" Frank said, pointing at the slow cooker.

"Yeah, I'll have some."

He dished it up—ground beef chili, no beans, the way God intended. I could have stood my spoon up in it.

"Did I do that?" Frank said. He pointed at the mark under my eye that, by now, was on its final, slow fade, a process that was taking its good sweet time.

"You have a good eye for your own handiwork," I said.

He laughed, quick and curt. "Well, I'm sorry. You might remember that you took a poke at me first. I was pretty much operating on instinct."

I socked away a couple of bites of chili before I responded.

"Well, you know, Frank, I'm trying to forget it happened. But you're right. Just the same, you disrespected my wife, so—"

"Your wife?"

I rummaged through my pocket and scared up the simple tungsten ring Lainie had slipped on my finger not forty-eight hours earlier, precisely two weeks after she'd said yes. I held it out to him, and he took it in for closer examination.

"Well, I'll be damned," Frank said. "Why aren't you wearing it?"

"We're kind of keeping it quiet. Her kid has a wedding coming up, and we didn't want to steal his thunder."

I held out my hand, and he dropped the ring into my palm.

"Well, Mark, I'm happy for you. Congratulations."

———

The night Lainie came to me in my bed, she and I talked about the implications of the yes she'd first avoided and then accepted. "I know I love you, and you want this," she'd said. "I want it, too." We didn't want a big wedding. We'd both done that. We wanted to keep things as intimate as possible, to the point where even the justice of the peace was a regrettable, though necessary, intrusion. And we dealt with the immediate baggage that comes with yes. We wanted it done as soon as possible. Before we could give a chance to no or maybe. Before we had to spend a minute longer with how things were now.

That had taken a bit longer than I'd have preferred, a couple of smoke breaks with Trimear to talk him into giving me three consecutive days off—one to get to Deadwood, a reasonable one-day drive from Billings; one for Lainie and me to approximate a honeymoon; one to get home.

Trimear can be such an intractable fuckhead. For a day he held me off, whinnying about the inherent unfairness of my request with football season upon us and our resources so thin. I held my tongue about his poor-mouthing and said, simply, "I really need this, Gene."

That first day, he turned me down flat. I said, "Fine. I'll quit." I'd threatened to quit any number of times over the years in various temper tantrums. What was one more?

"Don't be a sorehead," he said. "What do you need it for?"

"Does it matter?"

"It might."

The rat bastard. "OK, Gene, look. I'm getting married. I'm hoping to keep it quiet, you know, so don't blab about it, OK?"

"What's the problem? She got two heads or something?"

"Shut up."

He laughed. It was that irritating horse-wheeze, the one where the implication is that what amuses Gene Trimear should also amuse the target of his nonsense.

"Are you gonna do this for me?" I asked.

"I'll see what I can do."

A day after that, Trimear posted a fresh round of schedules. Two weeks out, there it was: a Friday-Saturday-Sunday stretch where my name didn't appear. I'd hoped for something sooner, but hope isn't something that often gets redeemed by the likes of Trimear. I thanked him, and the inchoate peckerwood actually approximated grace. "Good luck," he said.

————

At the bar, I filled Frank in on Hugo, or tried to. As it turned out, old forms retained their function. There wasn't anything I knew about Hugo's retreat to the oil patch that was news to Frank, nor did I bring new information about his stated intentions toward Frank's niece.

"He says he loves her," I said.

"I've heard."

"Don't believe him?"

Frank punched open the cash register and counted off some twenties, putting them in an envelope and dropping them into the floor safe. "It doesn't matter what I believe. We're at showtime, you know? What he says doesn't really matter, either."

I drained the last of my beer. "Yeah. I believe him. I want to believe him."

"That's what you do."

"What's that?"

"You want the happy story," Frank said. "I get it. You know? Everybody wants a happy ending. It doesn't always work out like that."

I started to speak, but he cut me off.

"Now, he's working. Great. But for how long? He says he loves Amber, but he's not here. This is a woman with a little boy. She needs somebody reliable, somebody here. He had a chance, and he blew it by being unreliable like he always is, and now he's not here. What's she supposed to think about that?"

"Yeah, but—"

"No 'yeah, but.' Seriously. What's she supposed to think?"

"Maybe she thinks he's trying."

Frank went to refill my glass, but I waved him off. He dropped it into the washtub. "She doesn't think that. You know why? Because he's always trying. So what?"

"I guess I just hope he's getting it right," I said.

Frank smiled—it was weary and a little sad, but a smile nonetheless.

"Of course," he said. "You want the happy ending."

40

I used to mark the seasons of my life by the activities of others. When Hugo was still fighting, I moved in rhythm with the arc of his bouts— the signing of the contracts, the ramping up and ramping down of training camp, the travel, the weigh-in, the anticipation, the collision in the ring. Other sports filled the in-between times. Football and soccer and volleyball in the fall, basketball and wrestling in the winter, golf and track in the spring, American Legion baseball in the summer. The years went by, the games began to blur, and the kids who played the games became indistinguishable from each other, but there I remained, notebook in hand, chronicling them all and then promptly forgetting them.

Lainie changed that. Changed me. As a professional obligation, I remained at my post, but I was gone from the moment. My thoughts stuck close to our plans, be it a quiet Thursday night at home or a night at the symphony, something I'd have never chosen on my own and an event so moving that I couldn't believe I'd ever denied myself. My circle closed. Most of the time, it was Lainie and me. Tony would come home every few weeks, but his girl, Jo, had his attention, same as his mother had mine. I'd have lunch with Hugo when he'd come back to town on break, but that was about it. I didn't see much of Frank. My thoughts elsewhere, I walked right past Squeaky and his wife one day at Albertsons, leaving him to chase me down in the ice cream aisle and say, "What the hell, man?"

I felt a little sheepish, sure, but what could I do? Things had changed, and never so much as that October night I came home to a full serving of my ignorance.

Here's a short list of the many things I didn't know:

I didn't know Lainie had missed a period. Truth be told, I never thought about the ten-year difference in our ages, so I hadn't given much thought to this part of her life still being in play.

I didn't know that she had taken a home pregnancy test ("My cycles are like Swiss watches, so I knew something was up") and that it had come up positive.

I didn't know that she'd waited an agonizing week after that before taking another test, just to be sure. That one was positive, too.

I didn't know the second test had gone down while we were in Las Vegas for Tony and Jo's wedding and I was foolishly trying to throw a net over my youth by dancing and drinking the nights away.

I didn't know that, while I was grinding through a shift at the *Herald-Gleaner*, Lainie was in her ob-gyn's office, coming to terms with being the mom of a grown twenty-one-year-old and the little cluster of cells multiplying inside her.

I didn't know she had spent hours crying. For her own happiness. For her own apprehensions. For fear of what I might say. For fear that I wouldn't want this.

I didn't know how to tell her how my heart was beating on my insides like a hammer of the gods.

I didn't know how to describe the emotions that came at me like a handful of thrown darts, paralyzing me.

I didn't know how to handle the telescoped thought of being a sixty-nine-year-old father at my child's high school graduation.

I didn't know how to put words to the fear that I would lose someone else.

I didn't know how to process the sudden, crashing, burning desire to believe in a just God.

I didn't know there could be such vast galaxies of gratitude.

Excerpt from *Hugo Hunter: My Good Life and Bad Times*

Sure, I have regrets. Who doesn't? I can fix so many of the things that I've done poorly. I can be a better father to my son. I can make amends for past behavior. I can fight the better fight against my addiction.

But I'll never be able to wind back the clock and get in the ring clean with Rhys Montrose. I'll never be able to go at Mozi Qwai with my full faculties. I'll never be able to tell my mom that I love her, or do one more chore for Grammy. I can't bring back the days that I've wasted, and I can't control how many I have left.

Those are all regrets, and they're mine. No use denying them.

But, look, I'm a fighter. A damn good one, even now, when it's not about boxing gloves and sequined trunks but about winning by attrition. Any fighter knows that regret that doesn't inform your future is wasted emotion. If you lose and dwell on the missed opportunity rather than the chances to come, you're finished. If you catalog your disappointments and relive those, instead of attacking the next moment, you've stopped living.

I never became the boxer I hoped to be, and I never will become that boxer. Too many years have piled up, and my skills are too far gone. Those chances are gone. Why fixate on them, when I have a much greater opportunity ahead of me: the chance to be a better man.

41

I sat in my car and took measure of the house. Two-level rambler, one up, one in the basement. Off-white with brown trim. Two-car garage. Front lawn that was getting more than the usual attention, even in late fall. Nice.

I'd gotten down here as quickly as I could, a four-hour morning drive south after a late shift the night before. Still inexplicably to me, I'd swung to the South Side and roused Hugo, home on his one-week break, and made him come with me. For the company, probably. For the emotional support, I imagine. Because he wouldn't let me back out of my stated intention, absolutely.

While Hugo snoozed in the passenger seat, I checked the address scrawled on the sheet of paper and matched it, again, to the number stenciled on the curb. Every now and then, I looked in the rearview mirror. Quiet times on Azalea Street.

I had planned everything out—everything except what, exactly, I'd do when I got here. I'd run the gauntlet on this one, the coming to terms with having to do it, talking it over with Lainie, making the request of Larry Largeman, waiting for him to give me the information, and then waiting again for my day off to roll around so I could do something with it. I hadn't wanted a full name or a current circumstance. Just an address.

The scene had been strange, comical with Largeman, as he alternated between the still-smitten ex-boyfriend of my wife and the down-in-the-dirt businessman he was.

"What do you want with your ex-wife?"

"None of your business."

"A little hanky-panky on the side?"

"Piss off."

"Relax," he said, slapping my shoulder. "I'm just joshing."

"So you can find her?"

"Does the ayatollah eat pork?"

"No, Largeman," I said. "He doesn't."

"Oh, crap. I always get that joke wrong."

"So can you?"

"Yeah."

"Good."

"Here's the deal," he said. "I'm doing this gratis."

"Why?"

"Because you're taking good care of her, like I told you to."

———

On the drive down, I'd told Hugo what I intended to do, but I'd kept the why to myself.

"Marlene, huh?" he'd said. "How long has it been?"

"She left the night you fought Qwai. Other than one time in court, that was it."

He gave me a quizzical look. "It happened that night?"

"Yeah."

"Did you ever tell me that?"

I glanced at him and then back to the road. "I don't know. You and I, we weren't exactly in a good place then." I gave him a knowing nod, and it clicked for him. The fight on the plane, the harsh words, the weeks of silence that ended just as abruptly when Hugo called me up and asked me to go have coffee, like we'd done a thousand times before.

"God, we're such fuckups," he said.

I snorted.

"What are you gonna say to her?" he asked.

"Pretty much that."

———

I'd just about decided that the best play was directness—just walk up and ring the doorbell—when Marlene emerged from the house. She wore Lycra pants, a knit jacket, and tennis shoes and had a duffel bag slung across her back. Large brown sunglasses framed her face. Her hair was pulled back in a ponytail, not the bob cut I'd last seen.

"Isn't that her?" Hugo said, startling me.

Her appearance had changed, no big surprise after nearly nine years, but her gait had not. I'd have known it anywhere, the big, nimble strides that carried her from the porch to the car almost faster than I could process that it was actually her.

"That's her."

I put the car in gear and waited for her to back down the driveway. I fell in behind her on CY Avenue, the spine of the Casper, Wyoming, grid system, running from the far west end of town, where Marlene's house was, to downtown, where she appeared to be headed. I hung two cars back, careful not to be seen even as I doubted that I would register with her.

After a few miles, Marlene made a right turn into a strip mall anchored by a Big Lots store. She cut across the largely empty parking lot to a storefront on the end, one of those ubiquitous gyms. She parked the car, got out, and loped inside.

I waited a few minutes, watching the second hand move around my watch three times before I stepped out of the car. Long enough for Marlene to put her stuff in a locker, grab a towel, start her routine. Long enough that she wouldn't collide with me at the front door if she'd inadvertently left something in the car.

"Stay here," I told Hugo. He gave me a salute and pulled his cap down on his head, slinking into the seat. I got out and walked toward the building.

The windows of the place were blacked out, all the better for the gym's patrons to sweat in peace and anonymity. I set myself down on a bench on the sidewalk. I waited, and I considered what to say.

———

I wasn't surprised when Largeman told me Marlene was in Casper. She'd grown up here, in a little bandbox of a house off Poison Spider Road. We'd come down a few times for Christmas, and Bim Morley had worn that ridiculous Rudolph sweater and handed out cups of eggnog like free-drink tickets in Vegas. She grew up loved and amid stability, and when love is gone and stability has eroded, maybe it's natural to go back to where you last had it. The thing was, the decision hadn't been immediate. For a year or two after we divorced, I'd hear from mutual friends that they'd seen her at the Albertsons downtown or in a Holiday store, and every time I felt the collision of regret for what had become of us, and happiness that Billings was just large enough to give us a decent statistical chance of not seeing each other again.

As more years went by, such reports dried up. I took it to mean that Marlene had moved on, and she obviously had, but it was more than that. Eventually, people forget that you ever were married, or they forget that it ever mattered to you, or they just don't care, because they're no longer mutual friends, or friends at all. They move on from you, and life—theirs and yours—simply goes on.

———

All of my deliberations were rendered moot when Marlene emerged and I said, almost involuntarily, "Hi, Marlene."

I don't know what I expected. Jumpiness, maybe. Fear. What I got was confusion.

She looked straight at me. "Mark?"

"Yeah."

"What are you doing here?"

"I—"

"You're fat."

That was enough to break the tension. I looked down at my belly, as if this were news to me, and then I looked up, and she was fumbling through an apology.

"I'm sorry," she said. "I didn't—"

"You didn't expect to see me."

"Yes, that's it."

"I'm the last person in the world you expected to see today."

"Yes. Or tomorrow. Or any other day."

I tried to gauge her manner. The delivery was matter-of-fact enough, and she hadn't gone rigid or shut down.

"I followed you," I said.

"I see."

"I'm sorry. I don't want to freak you out. Hugo's with me."

"Where?"

I pointed to the car. Hugo stared back at us. Marlene gave him a wave, and he smiled big and waved back.

"He's fat, too," she said.

"It happens. You want to say hello?"

She was way ahead of me, already walking to the car. Hugo rolled down the window, and Marlene leaned in and pecked him on the cheek, like it was no big deal, like Hugo Hunter, as relegated to her past as I was, just showed up every day for a visit. Funny that she seemed relaxed and I was so damned wobbly. I thought the only advantage I'd have was the knowledge this meeting would happen.

I took a moment to consider her. She'd fought off age better than I had. Some lines in the face. Inroads of gray in her hair. But she was trim. Healthy. She looked like a kick-ass suburban mom. I wondered if she was.

I walked up. "I need to talk to you. Can I buy you a cup of coffee, Marlene? I don't need long."

She smiled, and I wanted to cry. I needed that smile. I'd never noticed it after the first year or so, never appreciated it, never appreciated her. I needed it so much, and she gave it to me, and I couldn't tell her how much it meant to me.

"You and Hugo?" she said without prejudice. It had been Hugo and me for a long time now, and she knew she often got the bum end of that deal.

"Just me."

———

I followed Marlene to a café downtown, an honest-to-God carafe-on-the-table joint. I appreciated that. We found a booth in the corner. Hugo waited in the car.

"I've only got twenty minutes or so," she said. "I hope that's OK."

"That's great." I smiled at her, and just as I found the ring on her left finger, I could see that she was making the same discovery on mine.

"Congratulations to us both," I said, and Marlene flushed red, but with a smile.

"How long for you?" she asked.

"A couple of months. You?"

"Four years."

"Happy?" I asked.

"Yes."

"I'm glad."

I sipped my coffee. I was still trying to line up the words in my head before they came barreling out of my mouth.

"You drive down today?" she asked.

"Yeah."

"How was the weather?"

"Just cold. How's it been here?"

"No snow yet. Kind of strange. Wind, though. Wind all the time. That makes the snow bad, when it comes."

I smiled.

"What?" she said.

"We didn't come here to talk about the weather, did we?"

She shrugged. "We came to talk. The weather came up."

I nodded. "Yeah. There's something I need to tell you, OK?"

"OK."

"And I'm probably going to mess it up a few times, so just bear with me."

"OK, Mark."

I swallowed, and then I did it again. I set my hands on the table, clenched them together, and wrung them out.

"We're having a baby, my wife and I. Lainie. That's her name. My wife."

Marlene looked at me, waiting. I thought maybe I saw a little quiver in her chin, but that was it. She was otherwise a lake on a day without wind.

"I want you to know I think about him every day." I said this, and now she reached for a napkin to dab her eyes, and I tried not to see it happen so I could just keep going and not lose control. It was harder to say than I expected, and I expected it to be hell.

"He was so much like you, and that means he was the best part of us," I said. "I'm so sorry that I—"

"You didn't."

"I did. In a way, I did. That day, I did. I can't forget the things I said. I denied you the best effort I could give. That wasn't fair. I want you to know that I know it, and I'm sorry."

"I know."

I dropped my head. "I feel like I don't deserve what's happening now," I said. "The good things."

Marlene reached for my hand, and I looked up again.

"What's *deserve*?" she said. "Things happen for a reason, or for no reason at all. You can't go back and do them again. You can ask why you get another chance, but who'll give you an answer? Nobody."

"I'm scared," I said. I hadn't intended to admit such a thing, but it felt right to acknowledge it.

"Maybe that's a good thing," she said. "I never knew you to be scared before. Of anything. Maybe it means something now."

"Maybe that I'm not ready."

"Maybe," she said. "Or maybe that you finally are."

I bit my lip. Her grace was such a gift.

She let go of my hand. "I still read your stories sometimes," she said.

"You do?"

"Yeah. Hard habit to break." She smiled again, and I tried to remember to treasure it. "Mark, I want you to know something. I don't blame you for Von. I think I wanted to because I thought it would make me feel better about everything after, but I don't. It crushed us both. I know that."

"Yes." It was all I could do to hold it together.

"I just hoped you'd be OK. I couldn't stay, I couldn't help you with that, but I hoped that for you. For me, too."

"I did, too. For both of us."

I don't know what I wanted from the trip, except to satisfy an urge I had to see Marlene again. Closure? Sure. But what's that, really? I guess it's what I got that day in Casper.

Marlene looked out the window. Hugo had gotten out of the car and was now pacing the sidewalk, careful not to make eye contact.

"He watches over you," she said.

"He's a good friend."

She stood, and I stood to meet her. "Thank you for coming to see me, Mark. I'm glad you did. And I'm glad for your happiness. I really am."

"Thank you."

She paused in the doorway to put on her sunglasses, and then she headed for her car, waving to Hugo. The car door opened, and she folded herself into the seat. I watched through the café window as her eyes found me, and she smiled. I lifted a hand in a wave, and she responded in kind.

She backed out of the parking spot. I kept my hand up. She drove out of the frame, and that was it.

42

Lainie and I made it through Christmas without the wheels coming off our private enterprise. We had made a pact that we wouldn't tell friends and family members about Zygote Westerly until after the first trimester screen, which lay just beyond the new year. That would be just about the time Lainie would begin to show in a way that made circumspection a moot point anyway.

So it was that we cooked up a big holiday feast, stuffed the stockings, and listened as Tony and Jo told us about their impending happiness, the child who would be born four or five weeks after his or her uncle or aunt. Hugs and handshakes came out in public, and Lainie and I saved the maniacal giggles for later, when we were alone in bed. What a surprise we had in store for them, and what a twenty-first-century family we had shaping up.

Left to my own devices, I became intimately familiar with Google searches on terms like *amniocentesis*, and saw that our immediate life would be cast against an every-two-weeks measuring stick: the obstetrical history appointment, the obstetrical physical appointment, the chromosomal testing, the childbirth classes that we'd fit in on Tuesdays (my only option given the crappy split-day schedule

I was working at the *Herald-Gleaner*), quad screening, AFP testing, GTT, and the rest of the alphabet soup.

At twelve weeks, on a gloomy day that blew snow sideways in Billings, we got the pronouncement we were seeking. There's nothing easy about carrying a child to term; when you figure all of the things that have to happen just so, it's amazing we're as successful as we are at propagating the species. At Lainie's age, the caution, for her doctors and for us, ratcheted up considerably.

The ob-gyn gave us the news, in words I ended up using for the e-mail that announced the impending arrival to our friends: "Looks like the kid has done this before."

———

Before work, I carried a few celebratory cigars over to Feeney's. The pull of family and obligation had changed the spheres I operated in, but when it came to singular news I had to unload, Frank Feeney was as good a friend as I'd ever had, next to Hugo. I'd wanted to hate him after he punched me out, after he said what he did to Lainie, but I couldn't. Too much history. Too much knowledge. Too much.

"What's this?" he asked as I handed him a cigar.

"You can figure this one out," I said. "I know it. Think hard."

He gave me the finger. It was beautiful.

"I'm gonna be a daddy," I said.

"No shit?"

"One hundred percent shitless."

Frank came around from behind the bar and scooped me into a bear hug. My weight gain aside, the old boy could still throw me around like I was nothing. I really would have to think twice about taking a swing at him again.

"I gotta call Trevor," he said. "He'll get a kick out of this."

I pulled another cigar from my pocket and handed it to him. "For Squeaky. But hold on a second."

We settled into seats at the bar.

"Have you heard from Hugo?" I asked.

"Not since . . . well, you know."

"Really?"

"Yep."

"That was, what, four months ago?"

"I guess."

"I'll call Raj. Hugo's not answering the number I have for him." I'd tried that morning, and in the car on the way to the bar. Nothing. I had news for him, and some work clothes that Lainie had picked out for Christmas. I hadn't seen him since the trip to Casper. When we got back, time did what it tends to do. It dribbled away from us.

"I've seen the kid. Came in a few times with a girl he's been seeing."

"You ask him about Hugo?"

"No. Why would I?"

I was flummoxed. "Why wouldn't you?"

That irritated Frank. He stood up and retreated to his usual spot. "I haven't gone anywhere, you know? Somebody wants to say something to me, here I am. Like you, Mark. You found me. It ain't hard. And congratulations to you."

———

Raj didn't get back to me until deep into my shift at the *Herald-Gleaner*, when the phones were popping every couple of minutes with a coach calling in a basketball result. I had to make it quick.

"Where's your dad?" I asked.

"The patch, I guess. I don't know."

"When did you hear from him last?"

"A couple of weeks ago. Before Christmas. Said he was staying on to make some money. He sent me some cash."

"He sound OK?"

"What's with all the questions, Mark?"

I looked over the transom at Trimear, who was giving me angry eyes to indicate that I needed to dump this personal call and get back on the phones.

"Just wondering, is all," I said. "When you hear from him, let him know I've got some stuff for him. Have him call me, OK?"

"Yeah, OK."

"Thanks, kid." I hung up, then immediately picked up a ringing line.

"About time," Trimear said.

"*Herald-Gleaner* sports, this is Westerly," I said. Trimear kept staring me down, and I mouthed, "Sorry," then greeted the Twin Bridges basketball coach. "Great, Jim, how'd it go tonight?" Jim Cardwell downloaded the night's box score into my ear, and I punched it into the waiting form on my computer screen. Nearly thirty years of journalism, and this was my lot at the *Herald-Gleaner*.

Getting old sucks.

———

Between editions, Trimear asked me to step into the conference room. I had a feeling what the subject would be. Perspicacity, that's what it's called.

"Don't sit," he said. "This won't take long."

"OK."

"Phone's for business use only."

"I know. I—"

"It's in the employee handbook. You signed the form saying you read the handbook."

"You're right. I did. It won't happen again."

"It better not," he said.

"I assume you'll be taking this up with everybody, then? Hop calls the brewpub to order dinner every night. Landry talks to his girlfriend. I heard you talking to your kid tonight."

I looked at him. I didn't dare smile or make any overt acknowledgment of how I was killing him. I didn't need to. His neck was bobbing in hyperdrive.

"Just stay off the phone unless it's business," he said.

"You got it, Gene."

"And don't be a smart-ass."

"No, of course not."

He opened the door and sent me out, and then he rushed out the side door for his smoke break.

Excerpt from *Hugo Hunter: My Good Life and Bad Times*

By the measures of the sport, I am a failed boxer:

I'm a silver medalist. That means somebody finished better than I did.

I had two championship matches as a pro. I lost both, in different ways.

To the extent that I'm remembered at all, a certain narrative threads through this. It's one of incompletion. To the sportscasters and analysts, I had something lacking. I didn't want it bad enough. I couldn't control my impulses long enough. I wasn't good enough. Any way you slice it all up, it comes down to passion. I didn't have enough. That's the story.

On one hand, I can understand that line of argument. It's a breezy explanation for something that is otherwise inexplicable. But you know what? No contention makes me angrier than the one that suggests I lack heart.

I went from nothing in Billings, Montana, to the best amateur lightweight in the world. (Juan Domingo Ascencion and his gold medal will just have to accept that.) At my peak, as both a welter-weight and a junior middleweight, I was the second-best professional fighter in the world. Seven billion people on the planet, and only one of them was better at what I did than I was.

How do you suppose that happens? Well, let me tell you: it happened because I had passion for what I did. Nobody runs the kind of miles I did, chops wood, punches heavy bags, gets in the ring with sparring partners, eats the way I did, and turns himself into a wrecking machine because he's a dilettante. If I'd wanted to be average, I could have worked at an insurance agency or driven a truck. If you're a professional fighter, average can get you killed.

What I had was not a lack of passion. It was an abundance of human frailty. You want to tag me with that, go right ahead. Guilty.

But don't say I didn't have heart.

43

I thought for sure I'd died.

I kicked myself awake, and the moment was gone. I couldn't even catch a little tendril of it, just a vague memory of feeling like I was going to perish, and my arms and legs kicking straight up in the bed and my heart pounding and my breathing heavy and Lainie asleep next to me, as if nothing had happened. In a way, that was true. I was in our house, our bed. But I was rattled pretty deep.

I sat up and dropped my legs over the edge of the bed, and I tried to chase down the pieces of my dream, but it was no use. It was gone, a vision dispelled by my waking consciousness.

The house had been silent when I arrived home, with Lainie well off to dreamland, and I'd wound down by rearranging her office—my office, now that this was as much my home as hers. It seemed a foolish errand. We had a baby on the way, and the space would soon become a nursery, but the activity filled the hour between the end of work and the beginning of sleep.

My thoughts took root in a common lament, one that revisited me when I found myself at loose ends where Hugo was concerned. It was an unfair thought, not to mention an unreasonable one. It was a wish that Aurelia had found a way to live forever. The most maddening moments with Hugo had come in the void left by her passing. The addiction and the missed opportunities with Montrose and Qwai had left marks on us all, but Hugo's perpetual inability to sustain himself had emerged only in the years she'd been gone. Maybe it was too much to put on her, that she'd have somehow kept him locked in and on task. But that's where I was, and I knew it was the same for Frank. She had a way nobody else could manage with Hugo. I wouldn't say he feared her so much as he feared disappointing her. That hadn't been enough, of course. Disappointment made regular visitations, but when Aurelia was alive, the prospect of recovery seemed viable.

Hugo never had a meaningful fight after the loss to Qwai in 2005. Frank knew that was the last shot at a title, and he got out, bought his bar, became an ex-manager. Squeaky offered to keep going with Hugo—all he had was the South Side gym his daddy used to run— but Hugo didn't want that. In a real way, that night in Vegas severed everything for everybody. I never went on the road with Hugo again. Frank never saw another fight from the corner. Squeaky never worked with another world-class pro.

But Hugo wasn't done. He became his own manager, and he cut his own deals with the promoters who'd helped him make a name through the first ten years of his career. He hired mercenary corner men for the fights that followed. What he never figured out, or never seemed to acknowledge, is that he was on the wrong end of those deals. When Hugo was eighteen, nineteen years old, promoters served up opponents who would build his record. Not bums, necessarily—just decent fighters whose careers were on a downslope, who would look good under the *W* column on Hugo's ledger. After Qwai, Hugo was the fodder, the good but spent fighter with credibility that any ascendant boxer needs to beat as he builds his own reputation.

With this downgraded status came three losses, in succession, each distinctly devastating.

Hugo got fed first to Julius McGinley, the best of a bad lot of US Olympic team fighters from the 2004 Games. What McGinley lacked in grace and discipline he made up for with a hard head and the most vicious right hand you'll ever see. They fought in Reno, a doozy of a step down from a headlining Vegas show, and I listened in on a radio station's webcast from my office cube in Billings, thankful I wasn't having to witness it. Every time Hugo managed to get a punch off, McGinley would smother him on the ropes, then back off and unload that right hand. At some point, it no longer mattered whether the damned thing landed. McGinley used it to pound Hugo for five rounds, until the referee showed some mercy and called things off. Hugo came home to Billings and to Aurelia and climbed to that top-floor room, blacked out by blankets in the windows, and shut out the world.

He might still be up there if not for Aurelia, who pitched over dead in the front yard not three weeks later. Saddest thing I've ever been a part of that wasn't my own loss. Frank's the one who called me that morning from the mortuary, asking if I could come down and try to console Hugo. I didn't have the slightest idea what to say, given how much I was struggling in those months with what had happened to Von and to my marriage, but of course I went. Hugo and I sat together in the chapel and didn't say a word to each other. We'd already said them all, in better times and in better places.

I thought of that again there on the edge of the bed, as I listened to the nighttime symphony of my new wife's rising and falling breaths. I'd been slow to pick up on what family means, at least in the context of my own life, and reluctant to be expansive beyond the traditional definitions. But if Hugo wasn't my family, who was? We'd lived in each other's space and in each other's thoughts for two decades now. We'd conspired, we'd collided, and we'd kept the faith. At the lowest moment of his life, when Hugo was set to bury the person who loved him most, I sat with him. Not because he was alone in the world. Because he wasn't.

I couldn't separate that from what came next, four weeks later. Hugo went back to the ring, on a riverboat casino in Mississippi, and he fought a carnival freak show named Coconut Olson so he could pull together enough scratch to pay off Aurelia's funeral bill. The manufactured story with Olson is that he'd been found on a deserted atoll in the South Pacific, an apparently divinely conceived baby who had been rescued by US servicemen during a training exercise, brought to the States, and raised up right by a Minnesota man, who shot blank sperm, and his barren wife. The truth of the matter—that he was a truck driver born in Georgia who fought on the side—was much less dramatic. Whatever the case, Olson battered Hugo for eight rounds and won a unanimous decision, and back Hugo trudged to Billings, ready to call it a career.

I wanted that for him. We all did. We wanted him to be done, and to be OK with being done.

It never really works out that way, though, does it?

44

A month ago, mid-January, we came to the end and the beginning, Hugo and I.

I'd just seen Lainie to the car through the slush in the drive-way, her hand gripping my forearm as I guided her and our precious cargo through the treacherous bits.

"I'll shovel this stuff before you get back," I said. I stood there in my robe, my knees knocking together from the cold, and I kissed her.

"Get inside," she said.

"Soon as you're gone."

"You'll catch your death."

"No. Never."

"Don't give me promises you can't keep," she said, half joking and half admonishing. I held her steady as she dropped into the bucket seat.

"I'll wake you up when I get home," I said.

She kissed me again.

———

I was folding over my egg-white omelet—Lainie had finally reached the end of her tolerance of my weight gain and had put me on a regimen—when the cell phone went off. I checked it. Tony.

"Hey, bud. What's up?"

"Hey, Mark. Something's going on with your boy Hugo."

I pulled the frying pan off the fire. "What?"

"Not sure exactly. I heard some guys talking about it. Is he supposed to be fighting again?"

The anxiety rose up in me. "Hell no. He's supposed to be working a rig, same as you."

"He might be." Tony was trying to be cool, but I could hear the tremble in him. "The chatter I heard was that he's taking fights for money."

"Who said this?" I asked.

"Just a couple dudes in my camp. Said guys were ponying up for a crack at him."

"Where?"

"I don't know."

"He was up in Stanley, right?"

"Yeah, that's what I heard."

"How many people know about this?"

"A lot," he said. "Everybody in my camp, it sounds like. Not too many secrets out here."

My thoughts leaked out in about a dozen directions. "OK, Tony. You call me if you hear anything else."

"I will."

I ended the call, considered my options, and realized I'd run out of them. I'd ignored the line between objectivity and activism with Hugo for years. To do what needed to be done, I'd be obliterating it. I had to give myself some room to work. I called Lainie and told her what I intended to do, that I had some cushion to ride things out for a while. God bless her, she said, "Hugo's the priority. Do it."

I placed another call, this time to the office, and caught the Diploma off guard.

"Hey, Bill, it's Westerly. Listen, no other way to say it but this: I'm not coming in again. No, not ever. Can you have HR draw up the paperwork? I'll come in and sign it this week."

———

By quarter after nine, after repeated attempts to reach Hugo on his cell phone, I stood in Frank Feeney's living room and swallowed a double portion of his truculence.

"Sounds pretty thin to me," he said. "Guy says he's heard something, but he's not sure what or where."

"It's not just some guy, Frank. It's my goddamn stepson."

"Still."

"So you're not going?"

"No. I have things to do here."

I couldn't believe it. There'd been a time, years ago, when Frank had gone to Los Angeles on a flyer to get Hugo out of trouble. That took the better part of a month, everything on hold, everything uncertain. I was asking for a few hours just to go make sure Hugo was OK.

"You know what this means, right?" I said.

"Yeah."

"It's his head, Frank. His brain. He's had trauma. If he's fighting, he's in a lot of trouble."

Frank's eyes stayed on me, solid, resolute. "If he is, it's trouble he's brought on himself."

"What's with you, man? You sat there in the bar and told him you wanted him alive—"

"I do."

"—and you went on and on about football players. Jesus, man. Don't you know this is worse? Don't you care?"

"I've got stuff to do here."

"I wish I was as above it all as you," I said. "I wish I could just not give a shit."

He didn't say anything, and I didn't have anything left. I went out the door and headed for the car. I sat there for a couple of minutes, arguing with myself over whether to push this thing with Frank just a little further. I could see all the arguments, but I couldn't see the one that would make him say, *you know what, I'll go.* I backed out of the driveway and was just about to throw it into drive when Frank came jogging out, motioning for me to lower my window.

"What?"

"Meet Trevor at the McDonald's in Lockwood. He'll go. More use than me anyway."

45

We were about thirty miles east of Billings, making plodding progress in the snow, when a call came through. I motioned for Squeaky to turn off the radio, and then I answered.

"Heya, Bobby."

Olden's voice came back at me. "Mark. I heard you're leaving us. I don't know what's going on, but I hope it's a good thing for you."

"Thanks for that."

"So, listen, I've got kind of a weird question for you. Can I talk to you real quick?"

"Go ahead."

"Well, it's a little bit of bad news, I guess. You talked to Hugo lately?"

I covered the mouthpiece. *"Herald-Gleaner,"* I said to Squeaky.

"A couple of weeks ago, I think. Why?"

"You on the road?" Olden asked.

"Just heading home."

Squeaky looked at me, and I shook my head.

"What's going on, Bobby?" I said.

He cleared his throat. He wasn't sure what to do. "Been hearing stuff about some bare-knuckle fighting in the Bakken, that Hugo's involved in it. Gene wants me to go out there and check it out, but—"

"Shitty day to drive to North Dakota," I said.

"Yeah. I'm just wondering if you've heard anything."

"Gosh, no, Bobby. Shit. Bare-knuckle fighting?"

"That's what we're hearing."

"What is this, 1890? That's awful." I cringed. I was laying the dumb act on too thick.

"You wouldn't know where he is, would you?"

I tried to pull up my scant knowledge of western North Dakota. If I was going to do this thing—this thing being a lie the size of cannon ordnance—I needed to get the geography right.

"Last I talked to him, he was in New Town."

"New Town? Really? I'm hearing this is happening around Stanley."

"No, he started there, but he moved to a rig in New Town last I heard."

"OK, thanks, Mark. I'm glad I called. I really owe you one."

"Let me know what you find out, OK?"

"You bet," he said.

I ended the call. "Jesus."

"What the hell was all that?" Squeaky said.

I was worried, worried as all hell. Bobby was green, but he had real promise as a reporter, much more than I had at the same age. I hoped I'd sounded convincing.

"Mark?"

"That was the last of Hugo's dignity if we don't get to him first," I finally said. "We've got a forty-minute head start, and I maybe just bought us another forty, and the weather's getting worse, thank God."

Squeaky looked at me quizzically, and then the notion kicked in and he smiled.

"You want to go faster?" he said. He mashed down on the accelerator, and his big Ford pickup did a little shimmy, and we were out of there.

———

We turned hard north at Glendive. The Yellowstone, my guide just a few months earlier on my work trip to Sidney, stretched out, frozen, but we caught a break. The westerly storm blew through a narrow corridor along Interstate 94, and once we'd put about fifteen miles down toward Sidney and Fairview and the upper Dakota border, the snow stopped sliding across the windshield, visibility spread out, and Squeaky was able to put more horsepower on the case.

"What's this thing look like to you?" he said.

"What do you mean?"

"I mean, do you think we're gonna have to tangle with anybody to get him? Is he on drugs again?"

"Jesus, I hope not." I said it, but I could tell Squeaky didn't see much reason for optimism, and truth be told, neither did I. God, how I wished Hugo had answered his phone, just once.

"I'm just wondering what we're in for," he said.

"Well, it can't be very good, you know? I just want to find him and get him home. We can worry about the rest later."

"All right."

Squeaky has a dead giveaway for his own agitation. He starts cracking his knuckles.

"What?" I said.

"It pisses me off."

"What does?"

"This whole thing with Hugo. Man, that guy has had chances I'd have loved to get. He's a million times better than I ever was, and he has no discipline, no character. Pisses me off."

"So what I hear you saying is that you're pissed."

"Yeah. You making fun of me?"

"No."

"I'll turn right around."

"Squeaky—Trevor—I'm not. OK? I get that you're pissed. I get that he screwed up his chances. I'm just saying, I want to find him and get him home. We'll have plenty of time to wring everything out if we can just get him home."

"Yeah. Right. OK."

I chewed on the next bit for a good while, almost to Sidney before I got it right in my head and knew what I wanted to say. The shortness of the winter days cast a pall on the scene, a dour gray that settled over the valley. We still had a long haul in front of us, a little more than a hundred miles, but the rigs on the horizon marked this as the territory where we'd find him. A thickness, a fear, spread through my stomach.

"I'm not lying for him anymore," I said. "I'm not lying to him, either. I wish your dad had come. There's some stuff he needs to know."

"Tell me."

I gathered myself. Somehow, in my imagining of what I'd say, I hadn't pictured this scene or this particular confidante.

"London," I said.

"What about it?"

"He was doing coke in London. That story about tripping on the rug? Straight bullshit."

"So, what, he just—"

"Smashed his own arm to get out of the fight? Yeah."

Silence moved in. I understood. Squeaky was having to make sense of the nonsensical. I'd been there.

"How'd you find out?" he asked at last.

"I was there."

Squeaky looked at me, then looked at the road, then back again. Sidney's lit-up downtown slid past my window.

"Why'd you do it?" he asked at last. "Why didn't you say something?"

I swallowed a couple of times so I didn't break toward shrill in my answer. "You think I wanted to keep it to myself?" Squeaky started to speak, and I cut him off. We could talk about the meaning of rhetoric later. "You think it did me any good to know that? Shit, man, I did it because he was my friend, and because I'd lost all perspective on things."

Silence filled the cab again. We pushed on toward the state line.

"Dad thought he was using again when we fought Qwai," he said. "He thought the binge eating was just a cover-up. He was amazed when things came back clean."

"I don't know. Maybe," I said. I never built out the connections between what actually happened on that trip and what I suspected. It would be a lie to say the fight never crossed my mind. But I'd come to view the entire episode in the larger context of my grief over Von. I just didn't give a rat's ass what happened with Hugo. I shouldn't have been there at all.

"As long as we're squaring things up," Squeaky said, "I'll tell you what went down that night."

I gave him a cockeyed look.

"Before the fight, I mean," he said.

"OK, shoot."

Squeaky kept stealing sideways glances at me, an every-few-seconds assessment of my attitude. It was weird.

"You know how Dad was done with him after that fight? Retired?"

"Yeah."

"You ever wonder how he came up with the money for the bar? A full liquor license is expensive. Even then."

I knew what was coming before Squeaky said it, and I wanted to jam my fingers in my ears and rattle off "nanananananananananana" so my illusions weren't shattered. We'd all found ways to separate ourselves from any ethics we had where Hugo was concerned, but

Frank, knowing his guy would be depleted after the crash weight loss, had somebody lay a bet on Qwai and got a payoff at 2–1 odds. Whatever contempt and revulsion I felt—and it was plenty of both—Squeaky's revelation brought the totality of Frank's actions toward Hugo these past few years into sharper relief. Guilt, and the flailing defiance of it, brings out some mighty odd behavior. For all Frank's protestations about how Hugo played him, it now seemed to me that he had no high ground in that game.

"No wonder he didn't come," I said.

"Don't be too hard on him," Squeaky said. "He did a lot for Hugo. Maybe he thinks he can't give anything else."

"Yeah, he can."

"What?"

"The truth about what he did."

Squeaky considered that awhile and then, at last, said something that was beyond his pay grade in wisdom.

"On that deal, I think Dad would argue about where the truth of it is," he said. "That's what I think."

I wasn't going to argue that point, although I certainly could have my way with moral relativity. I was an expert. In any case, I needed Squeaky's help on this one, and bad-mouthing his old man wouldn't help matters.

"Turn left here," I said. We'd just whipped through Fairview and across the state line. Darkness was coming on in full now. The low line of trees on the horizon cut a darker outline against the sky, and long sheets of snow billowed across the postharvest landscape. Across the expanse in all directions, the flames from flaring gas wells waved against the deadening sky.

The road stretched out before us, laying down a path toward the biggest boomtown in the United States. Beyond that, I hoped, waited someone I'd come a long way to see.

I had this to make right, and a few other things, too. I could do that, for him and for me. I couldn't do it for anyone else.

Excerpt from *Hugo Hunter: My Good Life and Bad Times*

I envied the guys who got up and went to work, every day, same place, same job, year after year. I didn't see drudgery in that. To be fair, I didn't really have any perspective at all, but if I had to classify it, I'd say I saw honor in it. It was keeping the faith, with coworkers, with one's own set of skills, with an employer, with the family back home, if there was one.

Professional boxing wasn't anything like that. It wasn't an everyday kind of job. It was vast stretches of nothing to do except goof off, followed by a short, intense period of getting in shape, followed by a few minutes of work.

I was good at the getting in shape. I was good at the work. I was very, very bad at the nothingness in between.

I would have been better at punching a clock.

Here's the hell of that, though: by the time I figured this out, working at an average-Joe kind of job was almost—almost—beyond my reach. I'd spent years conditioning myself to do one thing, and the workaday life was something different entirely. Even if I could have risen to some of the jobs I tried, I don't know that the people I shared that work with could have accepted that in me. They wanted

Hugo Hunter, and I found it nearly impossible to explain to them just how much I didn't want to be that anymore.

Like so many things in my life, my breakthrough came when I had no other choices. When I emerged from drug treatment the last time—and it will be the last time—I knew two things:

First, what I've done since Coconut Olson beat me isn't working and has to change.

Second, I'm never going through that hell again.

Sometimes I look at the young man in the picture frames around my house. He's sixty pounds lighter than I am, his face drawn tight and his eyes like lasers. I look at him and I think:

Kid, you don't even know.

46

Even in full Bakken-boom bloom, Stanley, North Dakota, isn't much. A highway shoots through town on its way to other flatland destinations, there's a capillary system of town streets, and, if your timing is right, you'll get a good view of the Empire Builder as it moves along the rails between the West Coast and Chicago. Finding the man camp was simple enough. A cluster of single-wide trailers hugged the highway on the edge of town, smartly positioned across the road from an all-night convenience store.

Squeaky kept the truck idling as I got out to talk to a kid who'd decamped outside one of the trailers to kill off a Marlboro or two.

"Hey, bud," I said, "does Hugo live out here?"

"Who?" The roughneck turned his collar up against the cold.

"Hugo Hunter. He was working out here."

"I don't know who that is. What do you want with him, anyway?"

The second sentence contradicted the first. I tried another way in. I racked my weary thoughts, trying to remember the names.

"What about Sean?" I said.

"We got three Seans here."

"What about Jeff?"

"Just one of them."

I held out my arms, palms up, and gave the kid the look. Everybody knows the look. The I-ain't-got-all-day look. The I-need-this-buddy look. He nodded at the trailer across the gravel entry road.

"Thanks, bud."

I broke out in a jog, the snow and ice crunching under my feet, and threw a signal to Squeaky to park the truck and come with me.

———

Inside of two minutes, Squeaky and I knew our worst fears about this errand were in play. Jeff recognized me when he opened the door, and the color drained out of him in a way that reminded me of the time my old man made me chew a whole bag of Beech-Nut when he caught me rooting through his stash.

To his credit, Jeff let us in and was more forthcoming than the kid I'd encountered outside. He talked fast, nervous, but the bigger strokes were clear. Hugo hadn't been up to snuff out here in the patch—too old, at long last too slow, and too set in his ways to jump when told to, even for the kind of scratch these guys were pulling down. Loath to admit he'd failed again, Hugo had tried to linger on as a sort of camp mascot, a friend to any and all. It had been the thing he chafed against at Feeney's, sitting around and jawing about the past, and unlike a one-off dinner patron, the guys in the camp eventually grew tired of the stories. They wanted action, danger, something to stave off the boredom.

"One guy told Hugo he'd pay him a hundred bucks for a swing at him, just to see if he could hit him," Jeff said. "That's how it started."

"He did it?"

"Yeah."

"Was the guy able to hit him?" Squeaky asked.

Jeff shook his head. "No. Pissed him off. Other guys wanted to try, too."

"How many?" I said.

"Lots."

"And he let them?"

"Yeah. Drugs, money, whatever. They just gave it to him."

Squeaky kicked at the carpet. "Goddamnit!" Jeff got quiet. His eyes started moving around the room, looking for escape. I tried to take the pressure down a few notches.

"Did he get hurt?"

"Yeah."

"Bad?"

Jeff dropped his head. Kept it there awhile. No words. Nothing. And then, finally, "Yeah."

"Jeff," I said, and he looked up at me. "If you care about what happens to him, tell us where he is."

———

On our way to Williston, I called Raj and told him we were bringing his father home. I fought to deliver my message in matter-of-fact terms, mostly to keep Raj on an even keel so he could hear what I needed him to hear, but also to keep my own emotions at bay and to keep Squeaky's from spilling over any more than they already had. Goddamn Hugo. Here we went again.

"You know the rehab place behind the hospital—shit, I can't remember the name. Anyway, that's where he went before," I told Raj. "Go up there in the morning and tell them what happened. They'll be able to help get him in there."

"OK," Raj said.

"Are you scared, bud?" I swallowed hard.

"A little."

"Don't be. We'll get him."

I hung up.

"You gonna call your dad?" I asked Squeaky.

"Ain't nothing to say yet, is there? Nothing I want to say anyway."

"No, I guess not."

"You gonna call your wife?"

"Same answer."

———

We found Hugo where Jeff said he'd be, in a 1970s travel trailer parked behind the bar where I'd met him that summer night in Williston. A light in the front window burned. I didn't bother with a knock.

Hugo sat slumped in a camp chair, half in and half out of a pair of jeans, T-shirt caked in his blood, his face a circuit board of stitching that made Squeaky's handiwork look like a surgeon's. That beautiful face, crumbled. I choked back the rising bile.

I shook him. Nothing. I shook him again, and Hugo lurched out of sleep with a haymaker right, his forearm clubbing me against the head.

"Grab him!" I yelled.

Squeaky put his weight into it, smothering Hugo's wild where-am-I swings and tying up his arms.

"Hugo," he said. "It's Trevor. I'm here with Mark."

Hugo looked at Squeaky and then at me, and his eyes rolled back in his head.

"Unbelievable," Squeaky said. "Look at this shit."

"Let's just get him out of here."

We struggled with the might-as-well-be-dead weight of him, trying to get his clothes on. Once Squeaky had things under control, I made a quick inventory of the trailer. A space heater burned in the dining area, which was thick with pizza boxes and paper plates with barnacles of food dried on them. Broken caplets and their spilled contents littered the floor. I scooped a few into a plastic grocery bag, in case the medical folks wanted them. Scraps of paper caught in hardened pools of vomit.

"Jesus," Squeaky said.

"Well, we figured."

"Yeah, but Jesus."

I cupped Hugo under his arms and nodded at Squeaky to catch the legs.

"Let's go," I said.

47

We were brushing the eastern outskirts of Miles City, under a pitch-black sky and more than halfway home, when Hugo came to in the makeshift bed I'd fashioned in the crew cab of Squeaky's truck.

He sat up. "What're you guys doing here?"

"We were in the neighborhood," I said.

"My head."

"I imagine."

"I gotta lay back down."

I took off my seat belt and turned around in my seat. Hugo was covering his eyes with his hand. "We're taking you home," I said.

"I need a fix."

"Fuck you," Squeaky said.

Hugo didn't say anything, didn't react in any way I could see. And then his chin began quivering and his face wrenched up. I looked away.

"Mark?" The voice quavered and broke.

"Yeah, Hugo?"

"Nothing."

"OK."

I turned back around and watched as Miles City filled our view. Squeaky ground his teeth. I couldn't begrudge him the anger at Hugo, but Jesus. The timing couldn't be worse.

"Mark?"

I turned back around. "Yeah?"

"I'm sorry."

"I know you are."

"I can't stop fucking up."

"Yeah, you can."

"I'm sorry."

"I know."

I pulled out my phone. A little juice remained in it. "Hey, Hugo, Lainie wants to talk to you. You want me to call her for you?"

I interpreted the lack of a response as a yes. I dialed her up. I told her that we were bringing him in, that he was lucid, and that I'd be home in a few hours. Then I handed the phone over the seat.

What followed was mostly the squelched garble of my wife's voice at first, with a few more robust responses finally coming from Hugo, a yes here, a no there. Then "I know," and "Yes, please."

A few minutes later—it was the damnedest thing—I heard a voice coming through so clear and true that I had to turn around and see what was going on. There lay Hugo, asleep, an angel's face somewhere under the carnage, with my phone at his ear and my wife singing "Hush, Little Baby" to him across the miles.

48

It was three a.m. before we reached Billings, the final hundred-mile stretch driven by me. The chore couldn't have been done without Squeaky, there's no doubt about that, but every man has his limits. Squeaky's was Forsyth, Montana.

"Mark," he said, "I think I just saw a dinosaur running alongside the highway." He might have. I don't know. But I figured it best that I took the wheel anyway.

I didn't call Raj till Hugo was safely inside the emergency room with the doctors. *Codependency* was the kind of clinical mumbo jumbo word I was still several weeks from really learning, much less using in an actual sentence, but even so, I don't think that's what kept me from calling earlier. Maybe for the first time I interjected myself into one of Hugo's decisions for the clearest possible reason. His boy had no business seeing the version of Hugo that we brought into Billings Clinic that night.

When Raj did come around, however, I spared him no bad news. "He's cut up," I said. His midsection, mottled in purple and black and yellow, looked like somebody had been working him over with a pipe wrench, I told Raj. And the scatterings of opiates I found in the trailer suggested that a two-day patch job in the hospital wasn't going to near cut it.

"I'll go to the rehab place first thing in the morning," Raj said.

"It is morning, kid."

"Later, I mean."

Beyond that, words seemed an unnecessary expense. All we could do was wait. I dipped my head back and fell into adenoidal sleep, a lapsing of consciousness that could be undone any time a nurse or orderly walked by. A few times, I popped an eye open and caught Raj bagging his own z's. It was all good. He'd need his energy.

Squeaky had hightailed it out after the drop-off, back home to his wife and kids, and eventually to a confab with Frank. I left it with Squeaky to give the old man the score and let him decide what to do. A guy's gotta start somewhere with the right living, and I'd made the decision that my friendship, relationship, whatever you want to call it with Hugo was going to be based on honesty starting then. I'd seen enough of what the other side brings. I'd like to say it was a thunderclap moment of clarity, but now, with the benefit of hindsight, I think it's something I'd been working toward all that year.

"Are you Mr. Hunter's brother?"

The voice brought me out of my veneer of sleep. I looked up into the face of an ER nurse.

"This is his son." I pointed at Raj, asleep next to me.

She smiled at me, a suggestion that she was in on some kind of ruse. "He asked for his brother."

I clapped my knees and willed my body to stand. "I guess that's me, then." I pointed at Raj again. "What about him?"

"He asked to see you alone. If his son wakes up, I'll send him in."

———

Hugo lay on a gurney in a small operating room, waiting for transport to a suite upstairs. I sidled up to him and squeezed his hand, waking him.

"Mark."

Looking at him challenged every bit of constitution I had. The doctors' stitch-perfect patching had made my friend look like a shorter, more corpulent version of Frankenstein's monster.

"I'm here," I said.

"Mark, I'm so thirsty."

I scanned the room and found a Dixie cup dispenser. I filled a cup with water and brought it to Hugo. I helped ease his head up and poured the water into him. Down his smock, too.

He swallowed and gasped for breath.

"More," he said.

I repeated the maneuver, a bit more successfully this time.

"Thank you," he said.

I pulled up a chair and sat down. "Raj is here."

"Where?"

"Outside."

"Does he . . . did you . . . ?"

"He's got a pretty good grasp of the situation, yeah."

"Oh, no."

"He loves you. We all do."

Hugo's tears came again. I put my head down, grabbed his hand, and held on.

"Why?" he asked.

"Because we're hardheaded sonsabitches."

I waited for Hugo to fight off the sniffles.

"Listen, Hugo, he's going to be in here in a sec and I'm going to leave you alone," I said. "You guys have a lot to talk about, and the doctor wants to talk to me."

"OK."

"I'm your brother, you know."

"I know. That's what I told them."

"OK," I said. "But I need to tell you something first. It's something I should have told you a long time ago. It's not fair that I knew and you didn't, and I'm sorry, and we can talk a hundred million times after this if you want to work it out, or you want to scream at me, or whatever. OK? Whatever it takes."

Hugo didn't take his eyes off me, which I took as a good sign. A focused Hugo was better by far than the alternative.

"OK," he said.

"All right." I gripped his hand tighter. "I'm your brother. But you've got another brother, a real one, your own blood."

I gave it to him straight. He had two families. He had Raj and Lainie and me and Squeaky, and even Frank. Someday, he'd even have Frank again, I was sure of it. He also had someone he didn't know. It's better than nothing.

Tears brimmed in his eyes the deeper I got into it, and I struggled to hold my gaze on him and contain my own emotions. It's a hell of a thing to tell a grown man that everything he's taken for granted isn't as it seems. I could give him his people, but I couldn't give him directions on how to make his way to them. I couldn't take away the hurt that the father he never knew was in the ground, unable to validate him. If he still needed that, he'd have to find it somewhere else.

"Jesus," Hugo said.

"I know." God, how I knew. I knew the weight of the thing that I'd just put on him. I'd been carrying it for a long time. It was the right thing to do, but it wasn't without its toll.

"I don't know what to do," Hugo said. "About any of this."

"That's OK," I said. "You're not on the clock. It doesn't have to be decided now."

I reached for his forearm and grabbed hold, and Hugo—damn the pain, damn everything—seized hold of the back of my shirt, pulling himself into a sitting position and tumbling his head forward to my shoulder. For that one night, he buried his pain there.

49

Lainie found me asleep in the foyer just after eight and gave me an egg sandwich and some coffee to help knock the sluggishness out of me. She was dressed for work, her hair done up in a little ponytail. What a mess I must have looked in comparison.

"So?" she said.

"Cuts to the face, lacerated spleen, broken ribs, repeated concussions." I was making a laundry list that broke my wife down, and I pressed on in exhaustion, just wanting to get through it, same as I had with Raj. If I kept it to a simple list, maybe I could keep emotion in check for just a little while. "Broken ankle, broken wrist."

"Brain damage?" She knew about what the doctor had told him months earlier. Tears fell on her work clothes.

"They'll know more after the scan," I said. "Likely. Some, at least. Question is, will he be him on the other side of this? They couldn't tell me. They just don't know."

Lainie pulled me in, and I dropped my head atop her shoulder.

"A week or so here, and then rehab," I said, answering the remaining unasked question. "And after that—"

"We'll see what happens," Lainie said.

Yes. That was it precisely. You can have all the data points you want, you can make strategies all day long, and it doesn't matter.

For Hugo, the fix—however much of a fix there could be—would have to be an inside job.

Excerpt from the final chapter of
Hugo Hunter: My Good Life and Bad Times

The stories rarely end well for boxers.

For every Sugar Ray who has his money and his mental acuity long after he leaves the fight game, there's a dozen guys who die penniless in a room without heat, their brains so addled and their lives so scrambled that there's no saving them. This sport, it uses you up.

I know I'm a lot closer to those guys than I am to Sugar Ray, and I know that my future is full of unknowns.

How long before the physical toll starts to show in my personality, in my loss of memory, in my inability to function even on a simple scale?

How long can I keep staring down the devil of addiction?

What will I do if I fall all the way back down the hill I've worked so hard to climb?

I know the questions well. And the answers, it seems, are unknowable.

In the face of all this uncertainty, I try to stay focused on the things I can control. I go to work. I immerse myself in my studies. I lean on the friendships I have. I try to steel myself to reach out to the brother I have and don't know.

I bend my life toward hope. That there's some contribution I can make. That I'll continue to learn. That somebody might love me again.

My friend Mark Westerly and I have an old joke, something that dates back to when I was just a kid and he was a sportswriter who covered me. Whenever I see him, I tell him to keep his chin tucked. It's my way of saying that life will take a mighty rip at you and try to see how strong you can be. If you keep your chin tucked, it might ding you a bit, but it'll never hit you square.

All this time I've been saying it, and I never stopped to think that I was giving him only half the game plan.

Yeah, you've got to keep your chin tucked.

But you also have to keep punching.

50

The first time I saw Hugo Hunter in rehab was tonight, the kind of late-winter Tuesday that makes you think maybe spring is coming after all.

He'd put in his twenty-eight days of inpatient treatment and was moved to sober housing while he prepared himself to go home for good and try to find a way to move in rhythm with the world he was in now. Part of that world lies in his brain, and what the future might bring to it. Thanks to an emerging interest in the lives of those who've left blood sports behind, Hugo is going to get some top-notch care, once he's ready. A team at UCLA wants to scan his brain and see if he shows signs of chronic traumatic encephalopathy, the affliction being uncovered in former NFL players by the score. Closer to home, he's going to have the cost of his therapy picked up, too. He's consented to being studied. It's not exactly the mark he hoped to leave as a boxer, but it may be the biggest contribution he could make. Funny how things work out.

Tuesday is Family Night at the rehab center, a chance for loved ones to step inside the program and get an interior view.

We sat in plastic chairs arranged in a circle. Raj and I flanked Hugo, and Squeaky sat next to me. Lainie would have been there if not for Jo's baby shower, and even then she vacillated until I told her that we'd be well represented at Hugo's session and that life should go on as normal for us, that we had to take care of ourselves in addition to supporting Hugo. It wasn't the kind of thing I'd often been inclined to say—it sounded like counselor talk to me—but the truth is I'd been hitting some Al-Anon meetings for a few weeks. I'd had the time, and I'd begun to see the wisdom.

After we'd introduced ourselves, the whole I'm-so-and-so-and-I-or-my-loved-one-has-a-disease thing, the counselor, a freshly minted college grad, asked if anyone wanted to start.

Hugo, thin pink lines crossing his face from the recently excised stitches, raised his hand. For the first time, he told his story. All of it. The truth.

The cocaine started a few months before we got to London, and it carried on as long as the money did. When Hugo got clean, he got back on track—right up to the days before the Qwai fight, when nerves overtook him and he began gorging on food to keep from seeking out a fix.

"Every bad thing that happened was because of a choice I made," he said. The declaration bought Hugo a lot of goodwill from the other addicts in the room that night. They spoke directly to him, no punches pulled, and told him to keep owning his problem, that it was the only route to a lasting recovery. The night was his, but I got something out of it, too. I put my burden down.

———

After the session, I walked Hugo back to the house he shared with two other men trying to scramble back into the game. He hobbled on a cane, his right ankle in a cast. We lingered on the landing, just old friends catching up. It had been four weeks since I'd seen him. It felt like a hell of a lot longer than that.

"I'm proud of you," I said.

"Thanks, Mark." He smiled, but then it crumbled into a worrisome look. "Frank didn't come. He's mad at me, I guess."

"Not your problem."

"I wish he had, though."

"Maybe he just needs time. You did. Anyway, like I said—"

"Not my problem." He brightened. "Amber said she'd come next week."

"That's great." I clapped him on the arm. "That's really great, Hugo. Lainie and I will be there, too."

"What about you?" he asked.

"Same old. Getting ready for our arrival. I'm painting a nursery, hanging some wallpaper, that kind of stuff. Working part-time at Costco as a stocker. I have lots of time."

"You're going to be a great dad."

I probably smiled bigger than I wanted to. "I hope," I said.

"I'm sorry about your job," he said.

I waved him off. "Don't be."

I sure as hell wasn't sorry. Trimear found me in the hospital cafeteria the second day Hugo was in. He sat down opposite me, head bobbing in double time, and said, "You had to know we'd find out where he was eventually. You didn't have to lie to Bobby."

"I didn't much care. Nothing personal."

"You used to care. You were a damn good journalist once."

"I'm trying to be a better friend. Anyway, I didn't care about the job anymore, so I left. You ought to be glad about that."

"I'm not," he said.

"I can't help you, then."

He stood up and left, and I haven't heard from him since.

"So, listen," I said to Hugo, "you given any thought to what you're going to do once you're done here?"

Hugo's face lit up. "Yeah, actually. I'm going back to school. Get my GED, then try college."

"Really?"

"Yeah. It's what I want to do. These guys I've been talking to, they said the best thing I can do is keep my mind engaged. Seems like the place to do it. Raj said he'd help with the cost." Hugo may have been prone to squandering a fortune, but his son had gone to the bank with the money from nearly a decade earlier, the money Hugo didn't want to release. I stood amazed at how the past kept revisiting us in new forms.

"I think it's great, Hugo. Really great. Aurelia would be proud."

"Thanks, man."

I held him by the arm. I didn't want him to go.

"Hugo, have you given any thought to what I told you about? You know—"

"My brother," he finished. "Yeah. Sometimes, I don't think about anything else, and then I remind myself that this is my fight right now. This is all I have time for. There'll be time for other things later."

"Yeah."

"But I'm glad you told me," he said. "Truly."

I released my hold.

"Listen," he said. "I'd better get in."

He offered a handshake, and he should have known better than that. I grabbed him and pulled him into a hug. A bro hug. What brothers do.

I walked across the lawn toward the parking lot, through the brown weeds that had been choked out by winter. I checked my watch. Six o'clock. Lainie would be home soon, waiting for me and my report. I thought about grabbing some cheeseburgers, then discarded that notion. I was living for three now.

I opened the car door and slipped into the seat.

"Mark!"

Here came Hugo, easing his way down the hill, leaning into his cane.

I retracted the window and leaned out. "I forget something?" I asked.

"No, I did." He rested his arms in the window opening and sucked down a few breaths.

"What?"

"You remember that time I told you about how I wasn't self-aware? I'm working on it. One of my things is that I forget to inquire about other people."

"Don't worry about it."

"No, no. I'm asking. What about you, Mark? What are you going to do?"

"I've given it some thought."

"I bet you have." He had a smile like I was in on some kind of private joke.

"I've got a kid on the way. That's the main thing," I said. "But I've been thinking about your book idea. You still want to do that?"

"Hell, yes."

"Did you ever do the writing I asked you to do?"

That sheepish look again. "Some," he said. "It's at the house. I'd like to take another shot at it."

"Well, when you're ready, start writing down what you want to say. I've made some notes, dredged up some memories. I think it would be fun to help you write about that."

"The adventures we've had?" he said.

"Yeah, I guess so. The adventures you've had."

He stood up and offered a handshake. I accepted.

"I think you've gotta help me, Mark. Nobody else can keep me honest like you can. We've got to make sure it's the truth, OK? Stories are so much better when they're true."

With that, he turned away and started inching back up the hill. I watched as he moved away from me. Home, for now, lay just a few steps away. He was safe, for now. Beyond that, I could only hope. But that's the future for all of us, when you think about it. No guarantees. Just preparation and hope. It's all we have, and it has to be enough.

I backed the car out and made my way to Twenty-Seventh Street for the ride up the hill and along the backbone of the Rimrocks, here in the place that I'd always called my own. It seemed less familiar now, more imbued with possibility and discovery. For Hugo, everything was just getting started. For me, too. Damn. Who'd have guessed?

I crested the hill into dusk and turned right. The city twinkled below me, each light a sentry and a song. I gave it all a quick look, and then I got on with the business of getting home. I've found my happiness, and I know my friend is trying to find his.

I know this much, too: never again will we keep our hearts waiting.

THE END

ACKNOWLEDGMENTS

A lot goes into a book, more than I'll probably remember to mention here. I'm fortunate enough to have a family that supports my dreams, always, and a team that makes my ideas come alive on the page (be it print or electronic).

To my family, near and far, thank you. Much love to all.

My early readers pull no punches: Jim Thomsen, Jill Munson, Jill Rupert, Michele McCormack, Cheryl Schamp, Steve Prosinski, you have my undying thanks.

Mollie Glick, my agent, looks out for my interests with great cheer and a tough mind.

The folks at Lake Union Publishing have gone around a few blocks with me now: Terry Goodman, my editor, sees the potential in what I do and, more important, the areas where I can improve; Charlotte Herscher, my developmental editor, makes everything she touches better; the copy editors and designers and marketers bring great skill to their work; and, of course, the inimitable Jessica Poore and the author support team keep everything moving. I'm grateful for you all.

Finally, none of this would mean much without the readers waiting on the other end. The tweets, the e-mails, the Facebook posts, the reviews provide great sustenance in what is often a lonely venture. For anyone who's spent a few hours with my work, my gratitude knows no bounds. Thank you.

ABOUT THE AUTHOR

Craig Lancaster is the bestselling author of the novels *600 Hours of Edward, Edward Adrift*, and *The Summer Son*, as well as the short-story collection *Quantum Physics and the Art of Departure*. For twenty-five years he worked as a reporter and editor at newspapers all over the country. He now lives in Billings, Montana, and does freelance editing and design work in addition to his fiction writing. Visit him at www.Craig-Lancaster.com or follow @AuthorLancaster on Twitter.